Gentlemen

"Two parts adrenaline rush, one part medical thriller, this twisted story starts with a bang and rarely slows down. Full of offbeat characters, excruciatingly reckless twists, and sardonic humor, this fun ride shows great promise for a rising author." —*Library Journal* (starred review)

"This is delicious postmodern hard-boiled punk rock storytelling. Swierczynski's hit man character is as funny and fresh as he is fierce and quick. *The Blonde* is masterfully paced, wonderfully rendered, and devastatingly entertaining."
—Greg Rucka,
Eisner Award–winning author of *Queen & Country* and 2006 Barry Award–nominated thriller *Private Wars*

"[An] entertaining thriller . . . rapid-fire pacing, hard-boiled dialogue, and excellent local color." —*Publishers Weekly*

"Duane Swierczynski's new novel, *The Blonde*, is as lean as a starving model, mean as a snake, and fast as a jet. It's also one hell of a fine read. This guy has got to be the hottest new thing in crime fiction, and *The Blonde* is one of the best crime reads I've had in some time."
—Joe R. Lansdale, Edgar Award–winning author of *Sunset and Sawdust*

"Page-turning tension . . . a story so bizarre that it just might be true."
—*Kirkus Reviews*

"*The Blonde* had me at hello. Well, technically she had me at 'I poisoned your drink.' It's a hilarious nail-biter, a tour-de-force by a young writer who has already carved out this unique take on the crime genre so it's futile to compare it to anything else, or try to come up with those weird combinations, such as if X married Y while on Drug Z, their baby might come out looking like *The Blonde*. It is sui generis. It is perfect."
—Laura Lippman, bestselling author of *What the Dead Know*

"Another fast, funny, and action-packed outing from a writer who, fortunately for us, doesn't seem to know how to slow down." —*Booklist*

"I've rarely seen a review where the word adore was used. I adored this novel. The opening few pages are sheer brilliant—black as sin, [with] demented laugh-out-loud tension. Dialogue to sell your soul for and an array of characters as weird and wondrous as anything Hiassen ever conceived. This is new noir: neon lit with marvelous beautiful writing. And okay, I fess up . . . I fell in love with *The Blonde*. Jeez, I'd let her poison me any day." —Ken Bruen, Shamus Award–winning author of *Calibre* and *American Skin*

"Quite a ride. The prose is hard-boiled enough to crack walnuts and the action more precipitous than a bobsled run." —*The Philadelphia Inquirer*

"Insanely inventive. This inspired high-concept thriller rockets from climax to climax with an intensity that will leave you breathless. It's like the movie *Speed*—only with brains." —Charles Ardai, editor of the Hard Case Crime series

"*The Blonde* . . . rockets forward with inventive ferocity. [The] double helix of a plot uncoils in a rapid-fire series of time-coded moments that generate a relentless tension . . . brilliantly paced insanity."
—*The Houston Chronicle*

"I got whiplash from turning these pages so fast. The cleverest, wittiest, and most relentless novel I've read in a long, long time. A dazzling piece of work." —Ed Gorman, award-winning author of the Sam McCain mysteries

"Mr. Swierczynski knows how to streamline a story, keep the pace breakneck, sucking all the oxygen out of the room while he tells you this very gritty and nervy story about a pick-up gone wrong. Delicious dialogue, funny realizations, and one hell of a ride."
—Frank Bascombe, *Ain't It Cool News*

"*The Blonde* is a shot of pure noir adrenaline for the twenty-first century. It left me battered, bruised, bleeding, dazed, confused, and downright goofy. And all I did was read it! Think how the poor characters must feel. Duane Swierczynski writes the way Sam Peckinpah used to direct: with a mad passion to awaken the slumbering masses and energize them with his enthusiasm for the material at hand. *The Blonde* rocks!"

—Terrill Lee Lankford, author of *Earthquake Weather* and *Blonde Lightning*

"*The Blonde* will be the most madcap, mordantly funny, and completely mesmerizing novel you will read this year."

—*Mystery News*

"A frenzied, surreal, gore-splattered exploration into the dark side of humanity's psyche—from our self-absorbed dreams to our twisted obsessions and addictions. *The Blonde* is wild, fast, and breathtakingly bodacious—an absolute bombshell of a read."

—Paul Goat Allen, Barnes & Noble

"Swierczynski's lean writing is gritty and darkly comedic. *The Blonde* is riveting from the first page to the last."

—*Mystery Scene*

"Swierczynski's follow-up to *The Wheelman*—my favorite book of 2005—is a high-concept thriller that's a master class in succinct, imaginative, intelligent, suspenseful writing. The characters are fresh, the action is original, the pace is relentless, and the central premise is a doozy."

—Allan Guthrie, Edgar-nominated author of *Hard Man*

"Pure pulp-fiction popcorn, in all the best ways—simply one of the most ripsnorting reads of the year. Hook up with this blonde as soon as you can."

—Kevin Burton Smith,
January magazine's Best Crime Fiction of 2006 list

A *BookSense* Pick for December 2006
A Mystery Bookstore Top 10 of 2006 Employee Pick
A Mystery Bookstore November Crime Club Pick
A Mysterious Bookshop November Employee Pick
A *January* magazine Best Crime Fiction of 2006 Pick

Also by Duane Swierczynski

The Wheelman
Secret Dead Men
Damn Near Dead (editor)

THE BLONDE

Duane Swierczynski

ST. MARTIN'S MINOTAUR
NEW YORK

This is a work of fiction. All of the characters, organizations, and events portrayed in this novel are either products of the author's imagination or are used fictitiously.

THE BLONDE. Copyright © 2006 by Duane Swierczynski. All rights reserved. Printed in the United States of America. No part of this book may be used or reproduced in any manner whatsoever without written permission except in the case of brief quotations embodied in critical articles or reviews. For information, address St. Martin's Press, 175 Fifth Avenue, New York, N.Y. 10010.

www.minotaurbooks.com

Design by Kathryn Parise

LIBRARY OF CONGRESS CATALOGING-IN-PUBLICATION DATA

Swierczynski, Duane.
   The blonde / Duane Swierczynski.
      p. cm.
   ISBN-13: 978-0-312-37459-4
   ISBN-10: 0-312-37459-3
   1. Blondes—Fiction. 2. Poisoning—Fiction. 3. Assassins—Fiction.
   4. Murder for hire—Fiction. 5. Philadelphia (Pa.)—Fiction. I. Title.

PS3619.W53 B55 2006
813'.6—dc22

2006046214

First St. Martin's Minotaur Paperback Edition: November 2007

10 9 8 7 6 5 4 3 2 1

To Sunshine, the other redhead in my life

It was a blonde. A blonde to make a bishop kick a hole in a stained-glass window.

—RAYMOND CHANDLER

9:13 p.m.
Liberties Bar,
Philadelphia International Airport

"I poisoned your drink."

"Excuse me?"

"You heard me."

"Um, I don't think I did."

The blonde lifted her cosmopolitan. "Cheers."

But Jack didn't return the gesture. He kept a hand on his pint glass, which held the last two inches of the boilermaker he'd been nursing for the past fifteen minutes.

"Did you say you *poisoned* me?"

"Are you from Philadelphia?"

"What did you poison me with?"

"Can't you be gracious and answer a girl's question?"

Jack looked around the airport bar, which was done up like a Colonial-era public house, only with neon Coors Light signs. Instead of two more airline gates in the terminal, they'd put in a square bar, surrounded by small tables jammed up against one another. Sit at the bar and you were treated to the view of the backs of the neon signs—all black metal and tubing and dust—a dented metal ice bin, red plastic speed pourers stuck in the tops of Herradura, Absolut Citron, Dewar's, and a plastic cocktail napkin dispenser with the logo JACK & COKE: AMERICA'S COCKTAIL.

For commuters with a long layover, this was the only place to be. What, were you going to shop for plastic Liberty Bells and Rocky T-shirts all evening? The bar was packed.

But amazingly, no one else seemed to have heard her. Not the guy in the shark-colored suit standing next to the girl. Not the bartender, with a black vest and white sleeves rolled up to the elbow.

"You're kidding."

"About you being from Philadelphia?"

"About you poisoning me."

"That again? For the record, yes, I poisoned you. I squeezed a tasteless, odorless liquid into your beer while you were busy staring at a brunette with a shapely ass and low-hanging breasts. The one on her cell, running her fingers through her hair."

Jack considered this. "Okay. So where's the dropper?"

"Dropper?"

"The one you used to squeeze poison into my drink. You had to use something."

"Oh, I'll show you the dropper. But first you have to answer my question. Are you from Philadelphia?"

"What does it matter? You've just poisoned me, and I'm about to die in Philadelphia, so I guess, from this point on, I'll always be in Philadelphia."

"Not unless they ship your body home."

"I meant my ghost. My ghost will always be in Philadelphia."

"You believe in ghosts?"

Jack smiled despite himself. This was delightfully weird. He'd been delaying the inevitable—a cab ride through a strange city to a bland corporate hotel room to catch what little sleep he could before his dreaded morning appointment.

"Let's see the dropper."

The pretty blonde smiled in return. "Not until you answer my question."

What was the harm? Granted, this was perhaps the strangest pickup line he'd ever heard—if that's what this was. For all he knew, it was the opening bit of an elaborate con game that targeted weary business travelers in airport bars. But that was fine. Jack knew if this conversation led to him taking out his wallet or revealing his Social Security number, he'd stop it right there. No harm, no foul.

"No, I'm not from Philadelphia."

"Goody. I hate Philadelphia."

"You're from here, I take it?"

"I'm not from here, and yes, you can take it."

"That's harsh."

"What's there to like?"

"The Liberty Bell?"

"Funny you should mention that. I was reading about it in the airline magazine. They have this back page where they tell the story of some famous national monument every month. Or however often the magazine is published. Anyway, the Liberty Bell cracked the very first time it was rung."

"Back in 1776."

"*Wrong.* You should have read this story, my friend. Philly's been trading on a lie for, like, *years*. It wasn't rung in 1776. And worse yet, the bell? It was forged in England. You know, uh, the country we revolted against? Like, hello!"

"You've just ruined Philadelphia for me."

"Sweetheart, I haven't even started."

Jack smiled and finished the rest of the beer in his pint glass. There was no rush. He might as well order another—minus the whiskey. He'd already had two boilermakers, and it hadn't helped any. The drama of the past few months hung heavy in his mind. Might as well take it slow for a while, check out the people in the airport. The ones with a purpose in life. With a clear idea of where they were going, what they were doing.

The only thing waiting for Jack Eisley was a night in a bland hotel room and an appointment at eight o'clock in the morning. He was in no hurry to get to either.

The blonde was looking at his hand. At first, Jack thought she was looking at his wedding ring. Which he was still wearing, for some dumb reason. But then he saw that she was focused on the glass in his hand.

"You finished your drink," she said.

"You're very observant. Still working on yours?"

The girl smiled coyly. "Why? You offering to buy me a drink? Even after I poisoned yours?"

"It's the least I can do. What are you having? A martini?"

"Never you mind that. Though I think I should tell you what to expect. Symptomwise."

"From the undetectable liquid poison."

"Right."

"Go ahead."

"It works in stages. At first . . ." She glanced at a silver watch on her wrist. "Well, about an hour from now, you'll start to feel a knot in your stomach. Not too long after, I hope you'll be near a bathroom, because that's when the power vomiting starts."

"Sounds lovely."

"Think about your worst hangover ever. You know, where you're sitting on the cold tile of your bathroom floor, begging God to show mercy on your poor alcoholic soul? Telling him how you've seen the error of your ways, and you promise never, ever to touch the demon rum again? Well, that's a tenth of what you'll feel when *this* poison hits you. And in ten hours, you'll be dead."

Jack knew his mind was screwing with him—of course he knew—but damn if his stomach didn't tie itself into a little knot right at that moment. Ah, the power of suggestion. The power of suggestion of death.

Okay, this girl was fucking *psycho*. Last thing he needed was another one of those.

"Um, can I ask why you did this to me?"

"Sure, you can ask."

"But you won't tell."

"Maybe later."

"If I'm even alive."

"Good point."

If this was a con game, she had strange ideas about running it. The bit about the poison would be enough to scare away most people. Which is not the reaction con artists want from their marks. They kind of have to be around for a scam to work.

So what was her game? Or *was* this a pickup?

"Okay, you've poisoned me."

"You catch on quick."

"Do you have an antidote?"

"Sweet Jesus on the cross, I thought you'd never ask. Yes, I do have an antidote."

"Would you give me the antidote, if I asked nice?"

"Sure," she said. "But I can only give it to you somewhere quiet."

"Not here?"

"No."

"Where, then?"

"Your hotel room."

Yep, that sealed it. This was a con game—probably a bizarre variation of the old sweetheart scam. Take the woman to a hotel room, expect sex, get knocked on the head, wake up with your wallet gone, your kidney missing, your naked body in a tubful of stinky ice, whatever. Whichever way, you were fucked, all because you thought you were going to get a sloppy blow job in an airport hotel.

"That's a kind offer," he said, "but I think I'll take my chances with death."

Jack scooped up the loose bills on the bar—a ten, two singles. He reached down and grabbed his overnight bag, which had been resting between his feet.

"Good luck with that poison thing."

"Thanks, Jack."

After a second, it hit him.

"Wait. How did you know my name?"

The woman turned her back to him and started looking through her purse. She removed a plastic eyedropper and placed it on top of the bar. She then lifted her head and swiveled around to look at him.

"Weren't you leaving?"

"I said, how did you know my name?"

Her fingers played with the eyedropper, spinning it on the surface of the bar. He leaned in closer.

"You tell me or I'll bring airport security back here."

"I'll be gone by then. And even if they did catch me, it's my word against yours about the poison. I won't know what on earth they're talking about." She pursed her lips and raised her eyebrows. "Poison? An antidote?"

"We'll see." He turned to walk away.

"Oh, Jack?"

He stopped, turned around.

"Your name's on a tag attached to your bag."

He looked down at the carry-on in his hand.

"Paranoid much?"

He could feel it already—the knot forming in his stomach. It wasn't sickness. It was anger.

After leaving the airport bar, Jack followed the signs to baggage claim. He didn't have luggage to pick up—he made it a point to live out of one bag, no matter how many days he traveled. Lost luggage was too much a pain in the ass. But according to the airport's Web site, the taxi stands were to the left of baggage claim, and sure enough, they were. Cabs to Center City Philadelphia were a flat rate—$26.25, so said the Web site. He climbed into the back of the first available taxi and tried not to think too much about the strange girl in the bar.

Strike that.

The strange, *pretty* girl in the bar.

It was just as well he'd left her behind. Considering his morning appointment with his wife's divorce lawyer.

Poison me?

Sweetheart, I wish you had.

9:59 p.m.
Adler and Christian Streets, South Philly

One squeeze. One hell of a mess to clean up.

But that wouldn't be Mike Kowalski's problem. These days, it wasn't even up to the police. No, this pleasure would fall to one of the crime-scene cleanup outfits. For fifteen dollars an hour, they'd hose down the blood, mop up the bits of bone and tissue, return things to normal. Or back to normal as possible. In Philadelphia, crime-scene cleanup services were a booming industry. Thanks, in part, to guys like Kowalski.

And right now, he had his night-vision sights trained on a nice little head shot. Yeah, it'd be messy.

In fact, depending on how the bullet impacted and exploded, it could mean an extra couple of hours' pay for the crew that worked this part of South Philly.

Which would be the Dydak Brothers. Couple of nice, strapping, blond Polish guys based in Port Richmond. They'd been cleaning up a lot of Kowalski's scenes recently. Weird that they worked South Philly, traditionally an Italian stronghold, now full of mixed immigrants and twenty-something hipsters priced out of downtown.

But whatever. Kowalski liked seeing some of his own people get theirs. *Sto lat!*

He'd make this one a gusher. Just for the Dydaks.

See ya, cheeseball.

The guy whose head was covered by a professional assassin's sights had absolutely no fucking idea. He was eating a slice of white pizza—uh, yo, dumb-ass, it's the dough and cheese that make you fat, not the sauce—and sucking Orangina through a clear plastic straw.

Savor that last bite of white, my friend.

Steady now.

Index finger on the trigger.

Set angle to maximize blood splatter.

And . . .

And Kowalski's leg started humming.

There was only one person—one *organization*—who had the number to the ultrathin cell phone strapped to Kowalski's thigh. His handler, at CI-6. When they called, it usually meant that he should abort a particular sanction. He would feel the buzz and immediately stop what he was doing. Even if the blade was halfway through the seven layers of skin of some poor bastard's neck. Even if his finger had already started to apply pressure to the trigger.

But this sanction was personal. There was nothing to abort. Only *he* could abort it.

This was capital *V*—Vengeance.

Still, the buzz troubled him. Somebody at CI-6 was trying to reach him. Ignored, it could mean more hassle. More explaining to do, which was bad, since he was supposed to be on extended leave of absence. No operations, no sanctions, no nothing. The last thing an operative like Kowalski needed was to explain why he'd been systematically wiping out what remained of the South Philadelphia branch of the Cosa Nostra. That was seriously off-mission.

The Department of Homeland Security kind of frowned on the idea that their operatives—even supersecret ops, like Kowalski— would use their training and firepower to hunt down ordinary citizens on a mission of vegeance.

They might secretly applaud it, get off on the details, but approve? No way.

So okay, okay. Fuck it. *Abort.*

Your lucky day, cheeseball. I'll get back to you later. In the meantime, go for some sauce. Live it up.

Rifle down, glove off, roll over, pluck the cell phone from the thigh.

"Yeah."

The voice on the phone gave him another cell phone number. Kowalski pressed the button to end the call. Added six to every digit of the new cell phone number. Dialed the result. A male voice said, "You mean to say you've got a thirst even at this time in the morning?"

Kowalski said, "It's so hot and dry."

Wow. It'd been awhile since a relay used *Rhinoceros.* Kowalski had almost forgotten the reply.

The voice gave him another number, which Kowalski memorized—after adding a seven-digit PN (personal number, natch) to every digit. He packed up, stashed the gear in a nearby warehouse, then made his way down from the rooftop and walked six blocks before catching a cab. A $3.40 fare took him to the nearest convenience store, a 7-Eleven, where he purchased three prepaid calling cards in the amount of twenty dollars each. He wasn't sure how long the phone call would take.

Kowalski stepped outside the 7-Eleven and found a pay phone. He punched in the toll-free number on the back of the card, then dialed the number he'd memorized. By using a prepaid card and a pay phone, the call was untraceable, buried under a sea of discount calls being placed across the United States. Nobody had the technology to sort through all of that. Not even CI-6—a subdivision of Homeland Security they didn't discuss much on the evening news.

A female voice on the phone told him to fly to Houston. Kowalski immediately recognized the voice. It was *her*. His former handler. They hadn't worked together in months; they'd had an awkward falling-out. But it seemed they were to be paired up again. Ah, fate.

Kowalski thought he should say something friendly to break the ice, but she didn't give him the chance.

A university professor named Manchette had died earlier that morning, and Kowalski's employers needed to check something. She wanted Kowalski to bring back a biological sample.

"Some skin?"

"No."

"Blood?"

"No, no. We need the head."

"The whole thing?"

But of course. Pity was, Kowalski didn't know any crime-scene cleanup crews in Houston. It would be a new city for him. Shame it couldn't have been in Philadelphia. The Dydak Brothers would have had a field day with a head removal.

"We need something else."

"Anything for you," said Kowalski, but immediately he regretted it.

Keep things professional.

"We'd like you to pin down the location of a woman named Kelly White. Want me to spell it?"

"White as in the color?"

"Yes."

"What do I need to know about her?"

"She may have come in contact with Professor Manchette within the past forty-eight hours. We'd like to know if this is true."

Kowalski said fine, and thought about asking his handler to meet for dinner when he got back. Just to catch up. He wanted to say, Hey, it's not as if I'm tied down to any broad. Not anymore. Nope, not as of a few months ago.

And I'm not going to be a father, either.

But he let it drop.

Kowalski caught another cab and told the driver to take him to Philadelphia International Airport. The interior was blue vinyl. It smelled like someone had sliced a dozen oranges and then baked them to mask the aroma of sweat. A square red CHECK ENGINE was lit up on the dashboard.

"There is no flat fee," the driver said.

"What do you mean?"

"Only apply Center City. We are twelve block south. You must pay what's on meter."

"But South Philly is closer to the airport than Center City. Hence, it should be cheaper."

"No flat fee."

Kowalski considered asking the driver to take him to Dydak Brothers turf and then shoving him up against a wall and blasting his head off—that'd be a nice little cleanup job for the Polish boys. Bet you didn't know you were messing with the South Philly Slayer, did ya pal? Too much to risk, though. Kowalski had to return to this city soon enough, and he didn't need additional complications. The press was already writing stories about a psycho with a rifle hunting down gangsters. He had to finish this before he was caught and had to cash in too many favors.

"You know what? I'm not worried about the flat fee. Let's go."

10:35 p.m.
*Sheraton Hotel,
Rittenhouse Square East, Room 702*

After he finished power vomiting in the bathroom, Jack was finally willing to admit that okay, yeah, maybe it *was* poison.

At first, he didn't want to believe it; had to be nerves. His mind playing tricks. Obsessing over his trip to Philadelphia.

And his morning appointment with Donovan Platt.

Jack had done some checking up on Platt. A local mag had voted him the city's "most feared divorce attorney" and noted that he'd "hacked off more testicles than the Holy Roman Empire." Nice. There was a little black-and-white photo on-line: The fiftyish bastard had black beady eyes and a beard of burnished steel. Jack was going to have to face the real thing at 8:00 A.M.

That was enough to make someone vomit, wasn't it?

But his second attack was even more brutal than the first, and Jack started to realize that this wasn't simple nerves. This was a full-on assault.

The third trip to the bowl was the worst yet.

Could he have any food left in his stomach? That greasy spinach and cheese airline stromboli had been the first thing to go. He wasn't sure what was worse—the agony of vomiting or the fact that he recognized his in-flight meal in the toilet. The second time was mostly liquid. And now, the third . . . yes, now there were globs of tiny blood floating in the water. His stomach was tearing itself apart.

This was *fucked*.

Jack slapped cold water all over his face, then looked at his watch: 10:36 P.M. He'd left the airport bar around 9:30. He'd vomited for the first time about forty minutes ago. If that girl was to be believed, the poison was working according to schedule.

And in ten hours, you'll be dead.

The smart thing would be to call the police. But even if he did, what would he say? A strange girl in an airport bar had given him poison, and then he'd said, "Hey, okay, thanks, catch you later"? Why hadn't he called the police right then? Because she was too pretty to be taken seriously?

Come on now. *Think.*

Maybe tip off the police with a vague description—he was bad at height and weight, and come to think of it, he couldn't even remember the girl's eye color. Most he could say was that her chest was huge. Yeah, that would narrow it down.

Clearly, he needed to go back to the airport, find her himself. Make her tell him what she'd dropped in his boilermaker. Get help. Swear never to drink in an airport bar again.

Or maybe he needed to go to a hospital. Have his stomach—ugh—pumped. Let the professionals figure out what was wrong. Move on.

Unless the poison was already coursing through his veins. How long would it take for the doctors to pin it down? He could die in a plastic waiting room chair long before a nurse so much as stuck a thermometer in his mouth. Besides, he needed more than a cure. He needed to find this girl, figure out why she'd done this to him. Maybe she was doing this to other people, too.

Which is why you should call the police, Jack.

Enough of this. Get in a cab, get back down to the airport, and find the girl. Now. Leave your bag here. Take your wallet and cell phone. Go.

Wait.

It was 10:38 P.M. He was due for another vomiting session in five minutes.

How was he going to survive a cab ride? The trip from the airport to the Rittenhouse Square Sheraton took at least twenty minutes. What, was he going to have the driver pull over halfway to the airport?

Figure it out, then. Leave *now*. Before you lose your chance to find her.

And you never see your daughter again.

He was suddenly struck with the desire to stay in his room and call home. Hear her voice. But even though it was only a little after 9:30 back home, Callie would have already been in bed for an hour and a half.

No. He had to find the blonde.

Jack took the elevator down to the lobby and found a cab waiting outside the front doors. Philadelphia was dead this time of night. He'd heard the old joke about the city rolling up the sidewalks at night, and sadly, it was true. Granted, it was a Thursday, but this was the heart of the fifth-largest city in the United States. Shouldn't there be more people out pissing their lives away in restaurants or bars?

"The airport, as fast as you can."

"Time's your flight?"

"I don't have one. It's just important that I get there. . . ."

"Well, you are going to arrivals or departures?"

Which one?

Jack thought about it, then said, "Arrivals." Because he had arrived, and could retrace his steps back to the airport bar that way.

"Terminal?"

"Huh?"

"Which terminal? They're serious about security. I can't go wandering around the—"

"Which one is Continental?" That was the airline Jack had flown in on.

"That'd be C. Anybody tell you about the flat rate?"

Next the guy was going to tell Jack to buckle his seat belt, maybe even hop out of the car to make sure it clicked into the buckle correctly.

"I'm kind of in a hurry."

Wordlessly, the driver took off up Eighteenth Street, passing Rittenhouse Square and Market Street, then JFK Boulevard, then a construction site. He had never visited Philadelphia before, but he'd studied a map of Center City. His hotel was three blocks from the Sofitel, where he was supposed to be meeting Donovan Platt. He wondered if he was going to make it. Maybe he'd, *ha ha ha*, be dead.

If he *had* been poisoned.

Within a few minutes they were back on I-95, headed south. Past the same row houses, shrouded in darkness, then two newish-looking sports arenas, then an industrial wasteland of refineries and—

Oh no. Not again.

"Excuse me. I need you to pull over."

"I thought you were in a hurry."

"*Please.*"

The desperation in his voice must have done it. Without another word, the driver pulled across two lanes and came to a gradual halt on the shoulder. Jack fumbled with the passenger door on the left—no chance to slide across to the other side—and barely kicked open the door before he started spewing.

There was a little more blood this time.

10:46 p.m.
*I-95 South,
Near the Girard Point Bridge*

Kowalski was treated to the sight of a man hanging out of a Yellow Cab, heaving his guts out onto the blacktop of I-95.

Fucking drunk. Couldn't the guy've had the courtesy to pick the other door? You know, the one facing the scenic refineries of southwest Philly? Now he was going to have that image in his mind all night long. I mean, c'mon. It's a Thursday night, pal. Everybody's working for the weekend.

Kowalski had been able to reserve a seat on a 1:00 A.M. flight to Houston. With luck, he'd make it to the gate and through security checks in time. Get to Houston by 3:00 A.M. Check for his envelope at the Shuttle Texas courtesy counter. Inside the envelope would be the address of the morgue. There wasn't time to rent a car; he'd catch another cab. That was all he'd worked out so far. On the plane, he'd come up with three or four ways to slip inside the morgue, get what he needed, get out, and get to the drop-off point.

The head. They wanted Professor Manchette's entire head.

Which, hey, whatever, not his problem. But it presented a set of logistical challenges. Like walking out of the morgue with a human head. Kowalski would need a gym bag and a hacksaw, at the very least.

The bag could be found at the airport. Scope a busy baggage-claim station—there were a bunch at George Bush Intercontinental—cherry-pick one from the steel conveyor. Someone raises a fuss? Apologize, claim to have one just like it. Then look for another one. Black, or navy blue. Two most common colors. Nobody thinks about buying distinctive luggage until they're standing there by a baggage-claim queue, wishing they'd had the foresight to buy pink neon Samsonite.

Yeah, and that lasts until they leave baggage claim, and forget all about it. Nobody really wants to walk around toting a fucking Day-Glo bag.

Hacksaw? Morgue probably had a box full of 'em. Plastic bags, too, to line the gym bag.

The best operations supplied their own tools.

Kowalski would be walking in with little more than his clothes and cell phone. The clothes could be easily ditched and burned.

And his cell phone was equipped with a nifty little self-destruct sequence—his father's Social Security number, which meant that someday it would finally be put to good use—that could double as a getaway diversion. And what were the authorities going to do with a crazy naked man who was caught trying to saw the head off a dead college professor?

Not much.

By the time his fingerprints were entered into CODIS, his organization could already be working on paperwork for his immediate release. Some debriefing, maybe a reprimand, but nothing too busy. Then he could get back to Philadelphia. Resume his mission of personal vengeance by next Thursday at the latest.

And that was the *worst*-case scenario.

Government jobs. Absolutely the greatest.

Kowalski's taxi pulled up to Terminal C. The fare was $42.30. So much for the flat rate. He removed his travel wallet from the inside of his suit jacket—this would be stuffed in a storage locker when he arrived in Houston. He peeled off two twenties and a five and told the driver to keep the change. Nothing too generous, nothing too miserly. No reason for the cabdriver to remember him.

He walked through the revolving doors to the Continental terminal, walked up to the E-ticket check-in. Slid in his credit card, which was under a name that matched the Texas driver's license in his travel wallet.

Baggage? the computer asked.

Kowalski punched 0.

Might be different on the way back. If he couldn't make the drop-off, maybe he'd be carting Manchette's head back to Philadelphia. Hang on to it for a few days. Show it the Liberty Bell.

Ha ha ho ho hewwwwww.

Katie would have thought that was funny.

His ticket printed.

Halfway up the escalator to the Continental gate, Kowalski's thigh started buzzing. He grabbed the phone, flipped it open.

"Yeah."

Kowalski was given a phone number. He added six to every digit. Walked to a pay phone located down the hall from the gate. Dialed the new number, using the second of his prepaid cards. This was why he purchased them in threes.

"Don't leave. We believe the subject is in Philadelphia."

"The professor? Is it all of him, or was his head spotted rolling down the tarmac?"

His handler ignored him.

"A credit card believed to be carried by Kelly White was used at the airport lounge one hour ago."

"I'm at the airport now."

"This was an hour ago, but she still may be in the lounge. Please check."

"Can you give me a description?"

"I sent a photo to your phone. She *has* changed her appearance since entering the country one week ago."

"Nothing surgical?"

"No."

"Then I'll know her."

Kowalski was already retrieving new mail. The subject line: "Happy Birthday!"

"Got it?"

"Yeah." Kowalski looked at the image on the screen. "You know who she looks like? That actress... Ah hell, I just saw the movie...."

"Reply to that number with a text message. 'So glad you remembered,' if you've located her. If not, 'Better late than never.'"

Kowalski hung up the phone. This was good. If he didn't have to leave the city to take care of this new operation, he wouldn't waste travel time getting back to his own project.

So where do pretty girls go when they're wandering the airport at midnight?

10:49 p.m.

"I'm just glad you didn't get it all over the interior."

Jack could only moan in reply.

The cab continued down I-95, toward the airport, but he was in no condition to admire the view. The knot in his stomach was bad. Real bad. That last set of heaves apparently had awakened some primordial part of his brain—the one that monitored likelihood of death. This part triggered bodily reactions designed to forestall death: increased body temperature, a surge of adrenaline, the sweats. It was as if his body had finally gotten the memo: *Yes, it has come to our attention that we have been poisoned. Your body is now taking appropriate countermeasures to rid itself of poison. Best of luck, chaps, and now, once more, into the breach!*

He wasn't going to leave it to his body.

He was going to find the blonde and force her to give him the antidote.

"Most guys don't have the courtesy. But if you don't mind me saying, I don't think I should be taking you to the airport. I think you need an emergency room."

"No," Jack whispered. "The airport."

"If you're sure."

The way he figured it, he had another ten minutes before the next attack. Fortunately, they were close to the airport. He'd have about seven, eight minutes to race back through the gate, hit the airport lounge, and pray like hell that she was still—

Fuck. How was he supposed to get into the airport bar *behind* the main gate? Only ticketed passengers were allowed through. Once you left, you weren't allowed back in without another ticket.

His return ticket was back in his luggage, in the hotel room. Theresa had ordered them through a discount travel Web site; they'd been printed and mailed to his new apartment. It was the only small spark of kindness he'd seen in her in months. Since everything slipped off the rails. Since she'd hired Donovan fucking Platt. Friend of Theresa's mother. They went way back.

Fat lot of good the return ticket was doing him now. How was he going to get into the airport?

"Okay. That's twenty-six-twenty-five. Flat rate."

He reached for his wallet, pulled out a twenty, a five, and two ones. He held them through the gap in the Plexiglas partition.

"Oh," the driver said, looking at the bills.

What did the guy want? A five? There probably should be a law: guy going through a divorce, no need to pay tips. Not in a cab, restaurant, or strip club. If a man's about to be bled dry, cut him a break on the loose change. One brother to another.

Jack walked into the arrivals terminal. To buy a ticket, he needed to be in departures. There had to be another way. Jack checked his watch. Two till midnight. It had been over two hours since he'd left her at the bar. Chances were, she'd gotten lucky with some other poor idiot.

Wait a second.

Jack approached the Continental customer service kiosk. "Hi. I need to page someone."

"Sorry, we don't do that. If you'd like to contact a representative of the airport's security—"

"It's *really* important."

"We *really* don't do that."

Jack knew there was probably some clever way of convincing

this agent—a modelish-looking guy with the name tag BRYON—that it was of utmost importance that this person be paged. That, in fact, it was a matter of national security, or something. Happened in movies all the time. But Jack couldn't think of anything clever. He was feeling that knot in his stomach again, and his head pounded. His skin felt hot. He was out of charm. Out of goodwill.

Jack walked away, heading in the general direction of baggage claim. Farther up were the rest rooms. He was sure he'd be needing the men's room again in . . . oh, six minutes. Then beyond that, the taxi stand. He should hit an ATM machine, take out another forty dollars, catch a ride back to the hotel. Warn the driver in advance: Halfway through this trip, I'll probably have to lean out of the cab and puke blood. And then return to the room and call Theresa and tell her what had happened and maybe—

"See! There he is! Jack!"

It was a girl's voice. His girl from the bar.

The blonde.

Jack turned around. She was standing there with a paunchy middle-aged guy who had a black MEMBERS ONLY jacket draped around one shoulder. A green backpack was slung over the other.

The blonde ran up to him and wrapped her arms around his neck. She whispered, "Go along with this or you'll die."

Members Only stuck his hand out. "Damn pleased to meet you, Jack. Your sister Kelly is quite a character."

Kelly—was that really her name?—kept her arms locked around Jack.

"Name's Ed Hunter. I do tax law. Kelly tells me you're a newspaperman."

Kelly pressed her cool palm to his forehead. "You feel hot, baby."

"I am," he said in reply to both. He was both feverish and a newspaperman. But how did his blonde—Kelly—know that? He'd said nothing in the bar that would have tipped her off. He'd been careful. Tell someone you're a journalist in a bar, and then everybody and their grandmother has a story idea. No thanks.

"So you guys ready to enjoy the best martinis you've ever had in your life?" Ed asked, draping an arm around Kelly.

"Ed wants to take us to a place called Rouge," the blonde explained.

"That's French for *red*. Owner went bankrupt, lost his entire restaurant empire, but he's kept this one open. Best martinis you'll ever have."

"You look like you could use a drink, Jack," she said.

"Sure." He was too stunned to say much else. The trio—thank God, not wrapped up in a bear hug anymore—walked out the sliding doors to the cabstand. Kelly kept her hand on his arm, as if she was afraid he'd slip away. No chance of that. Not until he received his antidote.

If there was an antidote.

If there was a poison.

Ed led the way.

"This one's on me. Besides, it's a flat rate. Twenty-six-twenty-five takes you from the airport to anywhere in Center City. That's what we call our downtown, by the way."

Again with the flat rate. What, was it printed on the side of the Liberty Bell? *Happen to be traveling by cab to the airport? Well, friend, Philadelphia has a helluva a deal for you.*

Kelly opened the back door before the driver even had a chance to pop out of his seat. "You first, Jack. Slide over."

Jack did as he was told. Sliding over to the opposite door wasn't a problem, either. The knot was tightening, and if he was going to throw up again, he wanted to do it in the privacy of the opposite side of the cab. Kelly might have poisoned him, but Jack was still too proud to vomit blood on her. And there was Ed to consider.

Through the open door, Jack saw Kelly pivot to face Ed. What was going on? He ducked his head to look out the window.

Oh.

Oh Christ, they were French-kissing.

That's French for red.

It went on for a while. He could hear an audible slurp now and again. The driver looked at Jack, who could only shrug his shoulders. Hey, search me, buddy, he wanted to say. Guess my sister's a ho.

The knot in his stomach tightened.

11:13 p.m.
Philadelphia International Airport

Good thing Philly International was a one taxi stand kind of joint; Kowalski didn't have to bounce around a bunch of them. There were only two options: Kelly White was here or she'd left. The bartender in the Terminal C bar remembered a girl fitting her description leaving around 11:30. She left with a man, middle-aged, in a black jacket. Bartender assumed he'd picked her up. "They were real clingy," she said. Chances were, they were still around.

Okay, so two likely options. They're somewhere else in the terminal, or they're going to catch a cab. Headed somewhere else to get friendly.

Once Kowalski checked the terminal a few times to his satisfaction, he decided to flush them out.

He approached a Continental manager, flashed a card identifying himself as an agent of Homeland Security—which was sorta true, only not official. Kowalski's organization, CI-6, was buried in a blur of funding, obscured by a purposefully murky organizational chart. Even Kowalski didn't know whom his boss reported to, if anybody. For all he knew, his boss ran the world.

But the card looked legit enough. Even had the new embossed foil with the holographic flying eagles.

One minute later, Kowalski heard the page he'd requested:

Passenger Kelly White, please report to the Continental customer service kiosk. Passenger Kelly White, report to the Continental customer service kiosk.

No way White would go to the kiosk. If she did, the manager was prepared to detain her and page Kowalski. Most likely, she'd shoot for the exits. One set of sliding doors led to the taxi stand. The other led onto the long-term parking lot. Since White wasn't from Philly and, according to his handler, had only landed recently, a car seemed unlikely. The cab was going to be it.

Sure enough, there she was. Kowalski saw Kelly and that middle-aged guy in a black jacket. They were embracing in front of an open cab door. And inside . . . oh, another guy in the backseat. Kowalski fixed his eyes on the orange box of an alternative newsweekly across the street, then headed forward as if to retrieve a copy. Meanwhile, he reached into his jacket pocket and sent a text message—"So glad you remembered"—as he memorized the cab's license plate. The next step was up to his handler.

Kelly and the unidentified male were still going at it. Kowalski wondered, idly, what the deal with the guy in the cab was. He couldn't see the man's face. Had Kelly proposed some kind of three-way scenario?

Not that it mattered. He didn't know why the female subject was wanted. That was the way it was with CI-6. No need to dig up a motive. Just simple, clear objectives. Which made his job quantifiable, if not exactly satisfying.

Which was why he was so eager to return to his current project in Philadelphia. This time, it was personal. He knew the reasons—

most of them anyway. He knew the net effect of every action. He had a singular purpose, and it was extremely satisfying when he completed each task he'd designed to achieve that purpose.

Vengeance of Katie.

Katie was a girl he'd met a year ago; she became pregnant with their child. Unfortunately, Katie's brother was a professional criminal who had embroiled himself with the Philadelphia branch of the Cosa Nostra. After too many double crosses to count, the mob took their payment out on Katie . . . and, by default, their unborn child.

They killed her.

They smeared her with peanut butter so that rats would destroy the body after they'd dumped her.

Kowalski had been out of town. When he arrived in Philadelphia, he drove straight to the morgue. He identified her naked, chewed, clawed, lacerated body, under the murky pretense of Homeland Security. He read the reports. Once he pieced it together, Kowalski decided to take out the mob, down to the man. He wasn't in a rush. No need to get sloppy. He'd simply pick away at every cheeseball until there were none left. Simple, clear objectives. But *with a motive*. Which was incredibly satisfying.

Except when he thought about Katie, or what their child—might have been a son—would have looked like. Sounded like. Smelled like.

This bothered Kowalski, because he was not the kind of man to think about children.

The cell phone in his pocket vibrated. There could be no subterfuge now. Things were moving fast. The organization was reacting, planning.

He pressed the cell phone to his ear and reached down with his free hand to take a copy of the newspaper. The cover story was about beer—apparently, there was a festival in town this week.

"You have her."

"Looking at her now," Kowalski said.

"Who is she with?"

"Two men, one middle-aged, another one inside a waiting cab. I can't see the second guy."

"Okay."

"She just finished playing tonsil hockey with the middle-aged male."

"They were kissing?"

"Oh yeah."

"Hold please."

Kowalski watched the pair finally break the embrace. About goddamned time. It was wrong to flaunt that kind of thing in front of a widower, wasn't it?

But wait. What is this?

Her pale hand on his chest. A shocked look on the guy's thick face. The girl pushing him away, stepping backward and sliding herself into the cab, slamming the door the shut. The guy pounding on the roof. Looking really pissed. The engine revving.

"We've got a situation here," Kowalski said.

"What's happening?"

"Kelly White and the second male leaving by car. First guy left behind. He's standing on the sidewalk. Need some direction here, sugar."

"Stand by."

But of course. The cab bucked backward for a moment, then lurched forward. In the meantime, the middle-aged guy was reaching for the door, as if that would do any good. Give it up, buddy. She's got bigger and better things to do. Namely, the guy sitting next to her.

"You have the cab's license number?"

"What you think these are, walnuts?"

She didn't laugh at the in joke. One lazy Sunday morning together, flipping channels, finding *Sesame Street*. A Cookie Monster skit. Ernie asking a stupid-ass question. Cookie getting indignant, pointing to his googly eyes. *What you think these are, walnuts?*

"Send a text message, encrypted. Then follow male subject number one."

"Not Kelly White."

"Correct. Stick to subject number one as closely as possible."

There was no point in asking why. Could be one of a thousand possibilities. Girl passing guy drugs, a document, a serum, a weapon. Girl no longer in the game; guy the subject now. That's what mattered. Now it was time to follow the new guy. Kowalski thought about Professor Manchette. Will I have to decapitate *this* guy in a couple of hours?

Ah, the job.

11:24 p.m.
I-95 North, Near the Girard Point Bridge

"Driver, take us to the nearest police precinct. Immediately."

Kelly rolled her eyes and eased back into the dark blue vinyl seat. She folded her arms.

"They are not called precincts here," the driver said. "They are districts."

"What?"

The driver had curly, thinning black hair. He spoke carefully and clearly. "I do not know the local districts. I operate mainly in the Northeast. I only brought someone down here to catch a late flight. I am working my way back up to the Northeast; that is all."

"Sir, ignore my husband. Jackie boy had too many Jamesons on the plane."

"You're not my wife, and I'm completely sober. I don't care if they're districts or what, but I need a police officer. *Now.*"

Jack knew this was his safest bet. He hadn't gone to the police before because he thought the blonde had been joking. But he'd vomited enough to know otherwise. The proof was splattered all the hell over I-95. In fact, they could drive past it, and he could point it out to the police. *See that! The contents of my stomach! There's more of that fucking spinach stromboli!* Even if they didn't believe him at first, they'd hold both of them—he'd make sure of that—until they could pump his stomach (whatever was left of it) or take some blood. Or whatever. Somehow, they'd be able to prove she'd slipped him something. If it took all night, so be it. His 8:00 A.M. appointment with Donovan "the Testicle Hunter" Platt would have to be rescheduled. No great loss there.

"Watch him, sir. Any minute now, he'll ask you to pull over so he can vomit."

"Don't listen to her."

"Please do not vomit in my cab."

"I told you before. Don't listen to her!"

Then he felt fingers on his chin. Soft, warm. They turned his face to the left. Kelly looked at him.

"You only have eight hours left. I can stonewall *anyone* for eight hours."

"But if I die, they'll know I was telling the truth."

"And I'm sure that will be a great comfort to you."

The blonde had a point.

"Tell him where we're staying. This night doesn't have to be difficult. You just *made* it difficult."

The driver, meanwhile, looked uneasy. He kept stealing glances through the rearview mirror. Worrying about the blue vinyl seats, no doubt. Guess people in the Northeast didn't puke much.

Oh hell. Jack felt his stomach wrench itself into a knot again. That was the stress talking. Christ, this was unbelievable. Was he actually going to invite a strange woman back to his hotel room? Tonight, of all nights? But he didn't seem to have a choice.

"Fine. The Sheraton on Rittenhouse Square."

Kelly eased back into the seat again and smirked. "Swank."

"That is on the way to the Northeast," the driver said happily. Not that anyone was asking.

The knot in Jack's stomach tightened. Severely. He doubled over, as if his midsection were a giant hinge. He couldn't help it. His head ended up near Kelly's lap.

Then she did something strange. She gently eased his head down into her lap and started gently stroking his scalp. "Relax, Jack."

Her fingers felt surprisingly good. They distracted him from the twisting knife in the middle of his lower intestines.

The cab continued up I-95, toward Center City.

11:25 p.m.
Long-Term Parking, Section D, Aisle 22

The guy lived way out in the Northeast. In Somerton, which was near the edge of the county line. Beyond that, Bucks County, the affluent suburbs populated by Philadelphians, and by New Yorkers who *really* wanted to get away from the city without having to live in New Jersey. Kowalski couldn't blame them. Much as he disliked Philadelphia, he simply loathed Jersey. Everything was industrial, suburban, or a faded shore town. What was the point of that?

After watching the dumbstruck expression on his subject's face for a few minutes—What the hell happened? Was I really dumped curbside?—Kowalski had followed him to a shuttle bus waiting area. Strange. The man had seemed to be ready to jump in a cab with Kelly White. Where was he headed now? Kowalski trailed him onto a shuttle bus and knew the answer: long-term parking.

Guy had a car here after all. It was a new Subaru Tribeca—dusky gray exterior, black leather interior, with a built-in booster car seat meant for a child about sixty to ninety pounds. Magazines littered the floor of the backseat. Kowalski saw a *Men's Health*, an *Economist*. Kowalski knew this because he'd slipped inside of it when the man was distracted by a small rock he'd winged at the hood. Enough to chip paint, and cause the man to fuss over it for a minute or two, curse. But not enough to notice his new passenger.

Sure, he could have stolen a long-term car, followed the man wherever he was going. But Kowalski always tried to keep things are simple as possible, with as few tools as possible. Steal a car, you have to dispose of a car. There's a trail. Forensic evidence. And, of course, the subject to worry about. Why bother? Hiding in the back, Kowalski was able to sink himself into a slightly lower level of consciousness to recharge his batteries. He'd found that fifteen to twenty minutes of downtime left him feeling more refreshed than eight hours in a warm bed. Which was good. He had a feeling this was going to be a long night.

The subject pulled the Tribeca into a two-car garage at the top of a steep hill. The guy stepped out, stretched, glanced at the hood, cursed, grabbed his overnight bag from the passenger seat, and walked through the door that connected to the house. He was immediately greeted by a dog—a golden retriever. Kowalski waited until the lights went out. He used a box cutter he found to jimmy open the connecting door; the set of house keys, predictably, was hooked on a plastic holder affixed by a magnet to the side of a refrigerator. No sign of the dog, which meant he must be upstairs asleep with his master. Still, he didn't linger. He slipped back to the garage, turned the ignition key enough for the electrical systems to pop on. The Tribeca came with a built-in GPS navigation unit. That's how he learned where he was in Philadelphia. Somerton. Edison Avenue, to be precise. The Philadelphia International Airport lay just beyond the southwestern extreme of the city; this was in the northeastern extreme. The subject couldn't live any farther from the airport and still be within the city limits if he tried. Kowalski turned the car off and waited.

He was very much looking forward to finishing his work, both business and personal, and leaving this city.

Kowalski decided when this was over he'd rent a house near Houston, close to the Gulf. He'd make sure it had a back porch. And an electrical outlet for a blender. Pick up a charcoal grill, then fish and vegetables for breakfast, lunch, and dinner. Blend fruit smoothies, catch up on his reading. Get some sun. Enjoy some clean living to get the toxins of the past few months out of his blood. The rage especially. Then figure out the next step.

That next step might be wandering down to the Gulf and eating a bullet. But at least he'd make that decision with a clear mind.

Kowalski sat and tumbled recent events around in his head and felt the rage spike in his blood. He was almost grateful when someone in the house—a woman—started screaming.

11:54 p.m.
Sheraton Hotel,
Rittenhouse Square East, Room 702

"Nice digs, Jack," Kelly said. "Not sure about the two different levels, though. Makes it look like the beds are in a pit or something. Hey, you okay?"

Jack wanted a bed, in a pit or not. There were two, thank God. Just let me stumble down the stairs, choose the closest, and collapse onto it. He had the chills, bad. A pounding head. He couldn't see straight, either. Maybe if he was lucky, he'd die soon and it would be over. At least he wouldn't have to go through with his morning meeting with Donovan Platt. If he was dead, it wouldn't matter.

But Kelly held his arm tightly as he tried to make his way to the bed.

"Take it easy, boyo."

"I need to lie down."

"Let me help you. It'll all be over soon."

Whatever, Jack thought. His stomach was clenched too tightly to care. It was tough enough faking it while walking past the front desk—Kelly had warned him about drawing any more attention to himself than he had to. Again, whatever. His stomach was long emptied, but that didn't mean it didn't stop trying.

"Lie back and relax." She squeezed his left hand reassuringly. "The worst will be over soon. The poison will settle into your blood and your stomach will stop trying to get rid of it."

"Don't kill me. I've got a family. A little girl."

God, if Theresa and Callie could see him now. In a hotel room, holding hands with a strange woman. Never mind what it actually was. It was all about how it looked. On top of everything else that had happened over the past few months.

I can't stand that when you're here, you're not really here, Theresa had said. *Don't you want to read to your daughter? Or are you still too busy thinking about work?*

"Shhhhh. It won't be so bad. You seem like the kind of guy who knows how to show a lady a good time in a hotel room. Am I right or am I right? A real lady-killer."

Jack closed his eyes, and drifted away a bit. Yeah, lady-killer, that was him. He tuned back in when he heard her rooting through his overnight bag with her free hand—the one not holding his hand. The bag he'd placed on the floor next to the bed.

"What are you doing?"

He pulled his hand free of hers.

"I thought you'd be a boxer briefs kind of guy. Can't quite commit to the idea of boxers, can't go commando, can't do tighty-whiteys. An excellent compromise all around. But what's this? All black and gray? Where's your imagination, Jackie boy? No reds or purples? Not even a safe, conservative blue?"

Jack closed his eyes.

Maybe when he opened his eyes, this would all be gone.

One way or the other.

I was in love with a beautiful blonde once. She drove me to drink. That's the one thing I'm indebted to her for.
—W.C. FIELDS

12:10 a.m.
Edison Avenue, Somerton

Kowalski made his way into the house and pinpointed the source of the screams. Upstairs. Female. Older woman. Sobbing and wailing between the screams, like a car alarm cycling through its various sounds.

There wasn't much time now. Even though this was a single house, there were still two houses in shouting range, and in such a quiet neighborhood as this, they would not go unnoticed.

The living room was up the hallway and to the left. Kowalski checked the walls: framed photos of his subject, a woman, presumably his wife, and two females, presumably daughters. They looked old enough to be at least college age. They might not be home. The fact that there was only one voice screaming led him to believe this. Otherwise, he was going to have a royal mess on his hands.

Upstairs, a door slammed shut.

The staircase was situated in the middle of the house. Kowalski bounded up them, and saw one source of light: through the cracks in the bathroom door. A woman leaning against the doorway, clutching the doorknob as if for support. She had stopped screaming and stared into space instead, her face ashen.

"Ma'am, I'm here to help." Kowalski showed her his palms.

The woman's eyes focused and she let out a sharp shriek, then slid off the door, collapsing to the carpet.

"Relax, ma'am. I'm with the police."

He knelt down next to her.

"How did you know? I just found him. How did you know to come?"

Quick, Kowalski. Remember, you're not wearing a uniform. Nor do you have a badge or gun.

"Plainclothes. I was driving home from a late shift when I heard screaming coming from your house. Your garage door was open; I thought you had an intruder. Is there someone in your bathroom?

"My h-husband. Ed. Oh God. Ed."

"Is Ed okay?" Always use first names. Puts people at ease.

"No . . . no he's *not*. . . ."

"What's wrong? Does he need an ambulance?"

The woman showed him her fingers. Even in the dark hallway, Kowalski could tell they were slick with blood.

"Stay here."

Kowalski stood up and opened the bathroom door. There were four oversized bulbs mounted above the medicine cabinet, and they bathed the room in an ultraharsh white light. Someone really liked their light in here.

But that made it all the worse. There was no hiding Ed, who was sitting on the toilet, fully clothed.

Or his blood, which was *everywhere*.

It was as if someone had reached inside his skull, grabbed his brain, and squeezed—hard. The blood ran down his cheeks, from his eyes. The sides of his neck. His chin. His shirt. His hands. Whatever his hands had touched.

Ed was real dead.

Kowalski reached for his cell phone.

12:15 a.m.
Sheraton, Room 702

Jack jolted. Sat up. He must have dozed off for a few moments.

"Morning, sunshine."

He nodded dully, somewhat startled by the peace he felt. It was like the euphoric calm after violent vomiting. Your body realizes that it isn't about to die and then releases soothing endorphins into the bloodstream. It was as if his body had crawled up from the inner circles of Hell, and was surprised to have survived the trip.

Of course, his body had been fooled. The poison was still running through his veins.

"You look a little better. I didn't like seeing you in pain."

"Maybe you shouldn't have fucking poisoned me."

"So bitter."

"Seriously. Why *me*?"

"There's something about your face that makes people trust you. I'll bet you're always the guy people are stopping to ask for directions."

Jack looked at least a few years younger than his true age. He didn't follow fads in hairstyle or dress, which kind of lent him a clueless, midwestern timelessness. He looked like a Boy Scout or an altar boy who'd somehow managed to make it to adulthood without being molested. People *did* seem to trust him.

"It was the same with me," the blonde said. "I saw you and knew I could trust you. And once I tell you why, I think you'll understand. Maybe even forgive me."

Kelly opened her mouth, then slowly closed it again. She swept some of the hair from her forehead, looked around the room.

"I have one last favor to ask first. Please bear with me."

"Sure. Whatever. You poisoned me, you call the shots."

"I need to use the bathroom. Badly."

"Try the room with the white seat."

"Very funny, Jack. But I need you in there with me."

"Look, I promise I won't leave. At the very least, I have to find out why you've poisoned me. And frankly, I may decide to keep you here for the police."

"It's not that. I can't go alone."

"What, are you scared? I told you: I'll be right here."

"You *have* to be in there with me."

"You're seriously insane, aren't you?"

"Jack, you've only known me a few hours. But by now, you should know I mean what I say."

I poisoned your drink. Definitely true.

Go along with this or you'll die. Most likely true.

I need to use the bathroom. . . . I can't go alone.

Okay, give her the benefit of the doubt.

"Don't worry," she said. "It's only number one. I think I'd die if it was the other. You should see what I've gone through to do that."

Jack didn't know what she was talking about; didn't really care. He wanted answers. So fine, she needed to pee with him in the room, here we go. Very least, it'd be something amusing to share with Donovan Platt first thing in the morning: *Don, my man, I had this blonde in my hotel room. And she wanted me to watch her pee. Wild, huh?*

Kelly helped him up from the bed—he realized he still felt a little shaky, dizzy—and he shuffled after her into the bathroom. Typical hotel setup: bathtub with shower, vanity, towels washed so hard that you could practically smell the bleach in the air. Jack sat on the edge of the tub and watched Kelly unhook her belt, then unbutton her jeans. She started to unzip, then stopped.

"You don't have to look."

Now he was being accused of being a perv.

"Sorry."

Jack turned his head away, stared at a white square tile on the opposite wall. The sealant around it was a little sloppy. He heard the rustle of jeans slipping down over a pair of legs, followed by what he presumed was a pair of panties. This would make for another excellent image for the wife. Jack, alone in a hotel bathroom with a blonde who had her pants around her ankles. But honey, he'd argue. I was facing a tile wall the whole time. I don't even know if she's a natural blonde.

She started to go, making for an incredibly awkward silence. The water hitting water sounded as loud as the Hoover Dam.

"So . . . is this, like, a nervous disorder?"

"Nothing like that. You said you had a family. Aren't you ever in the bathroom at the same time as your wife?"

"Not if we can help it." Not since she filed for divorce. "We're private people."

"I thought men were a little more open than that. I used to date a guy who loved to take care of business with the door wide open. He'd stroll around my flat naked. No shame whatsoever. Then again, he did have something to be proud of. I suspect he was part exhibitionist."

"Well, that's not me."

Now that he thought about it, the only girl he'd ever watched in the bathroom was his daughter, Callie. But that had been when she was toilet training. And that he'd stopped about a year ago, when she was three. "I need privacy, Daddy," she told him one day. Made him laugh and broke his heart at the same time.

Kelly finished. He heard her rip some toilet paper from the roll, then flush. As she stood to pull up her pants, Jack found himself turning back to face her.

He told himself he thought she was done, already covered, but the moment the thought entered his brain, he knew it was a lie. Because he wanted to see. Because he was a guy.

Men were visual creatures, endlessly fascinated by the random body parts of women they didn't even find particularly attractive. In his case, even a woman who had poisoned him. He couldn't *not* look.

"Hey."

Jack caught a fleeting glimpse: Kelly's pale white skin, with a perfectly trimmed triangle of red hair, shaved close. Definitely not a natural blonde. Then it was gone, hidden by the pink stripes of a pair of bikini briefs.

"I'm sorry. Thought you were done."

"Right." Kelly smirked. "Though I suppose I owe you at least a look, don't I? After all I've put you through?"

"You don't owe me anything."

"I owe you an explanation. But are you ready to hear it?"

12:18 a.m.
Edison Avenue

"Explain it to me best you can."

Kowalski was on his cell. He'd convinced Ed's wife—Claudia, her name was—to return to her bedroom for a moment while he called for backup. He, of course, was doing no such thing, and Claudia would know within a minute something hinky was going on. The clock, as always, was ticking.

Welcome to my life.

Then he'd headed back to the bathroom. Christ. The Dydak Brothers would have come in their pants, all this blood. This was at least a six- or seven-hour detail.

Next, he'd hit the phone. Called his handler on the last number he'd memorized. Asked her what to do.

"Explain it to me best you can," she'd said.

Kowalski stepped inside the bathroom, closed the door—he didn't want Claudia hearing this stuff—and quickly described the injuries. It was all from the neck up. No visible gunshot wounds or lacerations. All of the blood seemed to have spurted out through the eyes, nose, ears, and mouth. Like the man's brain were a blood orange and some invisible force had reached in and squeezed tight in one spasmodic jerk.

"Hold, please."

Claudia started sobbing again. He could hear her through the wall. Damn it, this wasn't going to last long. Hopefully, the brain boys up in CI-6 were moving fast. Telling his handler how to respond. What to do next.

"We're going to need the subject's head," his handler said. "Seal it and await pickup instructions. I'll call you on this phone."

That's what Kowalski thought. Fuck. With the wife next door, this was going to be complicated. Then another thought occurred to him. One subject, kissing another, the new subject dead within an hour. Bioweapon? Supervirus? Ebola?

"Should I quarantine the house? The subject's wife is here."

I'm here.

"No need. But do not let any of the subject's blood to come in contact with any open wounds or scrapes or mucous membranes. Treat it like AIDS. Clear? We also need you to clean the house."

Kowalski didn't need clarification on that one. "Clean" didn't mean Windex and rags.

Claudia was still crying.

Now this joker in the bathroom might or might not have gotten what he deserved. It's never good karma to kiss a strange woman in an airport when you've got a wife at home. But the wife was innocent, as far as he knew.

Claudia, grieving like anyone would.

Anyone normal.

Push it away, Kowalski. Look for tools at hand; obsess over this shit later. It's what you're good at, remember? Push *everything* away.

He opened the medicine cabinet. He found what he needed in

three seconds. His eyes checked the label. Yeah, it was the kind he needed. The kind that wouldn't snap halfway through. Claudia came back to see what was taking so long, why there weren't a thousand flashing lights and sirens outside her house because her husband, Christ in heaven, her husband's brain had exploded inside his skull, and the entire fucking world should be racing to the scene to help, to figure out what went wrong. That's what Kowalski would expect her to be thinking anyway.

"What are you doing in there?"

He grabbed the plastic box of dental floss, flicked the top open. *The best operations supplied their own tools.*

"There's something you need to see, Mrs. Hunter."

12:25 a.m.
Sheraton, Room 702

They sat on the couch in the upper level of the room, three steps up from the bedroom pit. It was a soft couch, decorated in a bland pattern of light tans and browns. Look at it too long and you'd fall asleep. That was the point, in a hotel like this. Spend most of your time unconscious. Then pay us and head back home. Jack sat on one end, while Kelly sat on the other. She removed her shoes and put her bare feet up on the couch, mere inches away from Jack.

"Okay, let's get to it. First, I have to tell you why I selected you."

"So this wasn't random."

"Hardly. Had you picked out on the plane from Houston. I was sitting two rows behind. I can't blame you for not noticing me. You walked to the bathroom in the rear of the place only once, but the plane was rocking a bit. You fought hard to keep your balance. Remember?"

It was true. Jack damn near sprayed his own pants in the rest room, with all the turbulence.

"I heard you talking to the guy in the next seat. He was a lawyer, and you told him you were a journalist. Were you telling the truth?"

"Yeah, I'm a reporter. I work for a weekly newspaper in Chicago. You know, if this is about a story pitch, you could have explained this to me. We could have set up interviews on tape, on the record. I *could* have helped you, whatever kind of trouble you're in. Why did you do all of this?"

"Because without you, I'd be dead."

"Oh."

Jack paused.

"What does that *mean*?"

"I mean that literally. If I don't have someone within ten feet of me at all times, I'll die."

12:28 a.m.
Basement, Edison Avenue

Tool time. Kowalski found oversized Glad freezer bags in a kitchen drawer; the Hunters liked to freeze large slabs of meat. Inside their 20.3-cubic-foot Frigidaire freezer chest, he founds whole chickens, legs of lamb, pork chops, flank steaks, you name it. They probably belonged to a warehouse shoppers' club. Kowalski wondered if Katie would have tried to talk him into something like that—something that went against his longtime ethos of spare, frugal living. Then again, with a baby on the way, it would have been different. Hard to scrounge a diaper at the last minute. You needed stacks of those on hand. Or so he'd heard.

Stop that shit. Get the head, get out.

The freezer bags were the perfect size for a human head.

Down in the basement, Kowalski had his pick of gym bags in a cedar closet. He chose the blandest and sturdiest: a small Adidas Diablo duffel with an easy-access U-shaped opening at the top.

In a cabinet beneath a worktable, Kowalski found a cheap but usable hacksaw. The blade looked like it had never been used.

He'd hoped for a power tool of some sort, but nothing doing. Ed wasn't into home repair, obviously.

Kowalski's arm was going to be sore later. He just knew it.

As for destroying the house—and what a shame; it was a nice house, with hardwood floors and a kidney bean–shaped pool out back, complete with hot tub, surrounded by pine trees—that was easy enough. It was a stand-alone, so no neighbors to worry about. The explosion could be devastating, and it would stay limited to these grounds.

He'd use his favorite: the timed-spark gas-line burst. Enough accelerant spread around here and there, the structure would be obliterated within minutes. As would most forensics. Not that it mattered; nothing here could be tied to Kowalski. He was an investigatory dead end. A ghost.

As Kowalski walked upstairs, he thought about Claudia Hunter and how she'd fought her own death. She'd so desperately wanted to live. And for a strange moment, Kowalski found himself weak. Did Katie fight like this, at the very end? he wondered.

He looked at framed photos of Ed and Claudia. She was the strong one, no doubt about it. Ed looked vaguely uncomfortable in every shot, as if he were thinking, Do I really have to be here for this? And Claudia was kicking him in the shins, telling him, You not only have to be here, you have to fucking look like you're enjoying it.

Ed, kissing a stranger at the airport, hoping for a quickie instead of working shit out at home with his wife.

Kowalski carried the Adidas duffel, Glad freezer bag, and hacksaw into the bathroom. It was time to see how thick Ed Hunter's spine was.

The skin and muscle were easy. Sawing through the neck bone was a real effort. With every push and pull of the hacksaw, Kowalski found himself silently repeating a sentence, one syllable at a time. *Can't [push] be [pull] lieve [push] I [pull] do [push] this [pull] for [push] a [pull] live [push] ing. . . .*

12:32 a.m.
Sheraton, Room 702

"Ready, Jack? Don't make me repeat myself."

"Go ahead."

"I have an experimental tracking device in my blood. Not one device; thousands of them. Nanomachines. You familiar with the term? Microscopic, undetectable by the human eye. I'm simplifying when I say that they're in my blood. They're in every fluid system in my body—my saliva, my tears, my lymph nodes."

Jack blinked. He looked at Kelly, then at the nightstand across the room.

"Mind if I write this down?"

"I was hoping you would."

There was a Sheraton pen and a scratch pad on the nightstand. He picked them up and took them back to the couch. He wrote "nanomachines." Just in case this *was* leading somewhere.

Or if he should need evidence for the prosecution.

"Okay, so you've got these tiny machines inside of you."

"Is this you being a reporter?"

"Yeah."

"Well, stop. Let me tell it."

Jack put down the pen and paper. "Keep in mind I only have seven hours to live."

Kelly tightened her lips for a moment, then continued. "The machines are tracking devices. They constantly feed information to a satellite: body temperature, heart rate, global position. And that information is relayed to a tracking station."

"Sounds very Big Brother."

"That's one way of looking at it. But think about the possibilities of tracking criminals or terrorists. Another is—wait, you said you have children?"

"A daughter."

"What's her name?"

"I'm not sure I want to tell you." Jack looked at the clock on the nightstand. It was 11:30 back in Gurnee. Callie was no doubt asleep, clinging to her pink bear, which was also a miniblanket. The thing looked like a mutant tree sloth, but she'd had it since birth and refused to part with it.

"Don't be a baby. How old is she?"

"Callie's four."

"Well, imagine, God forbid, if some sick bastard grabbed Callie from a shopping mall one day. You'd have no way of finding her, unless the kidnapper was stupid enough to walk past a surveillance camera."

The very thought of it formed a cold, dark knot in Jack's stomach.

"With this system, it would take a second to pinpoint Callie's position, and the police would be able to recover her minutes later. Abductions would become a thing of the past."

Jack thought about this. "Unless the kidnappers got smart and learned how to turn these nanomachines off."

"Not possible. There are too many of them. Self-replicating, using blood waste as raw material. All the benefits of a virus, none of the weaknesses. Except if they leave the body. With nothing to feed on, they die. But once inside, there's no getting rid of them."

"You seem proud of these things."

"I worked in the lab that created them. That's my job. Was my job, back in Ireland."

"You don't have the accent. Though you did slip and say 'flat' a short while ago."

"I'm trying to blend in, boyo," she said in a thick brogue. "But now you're here. And now it's only you and me and the Mary—you know what I call these things?"

"No, what?"

"The Mary Kates. You know . . . those blond twins? The Olsens? They're just like these little things. They're everywhere."

So Kelly here has tiny machines named after a pair of barely legal blondes running around in her blood. Right.

"There's one more special feature, and this impressed the shite out of everyone. The Mary Kates, you see, can not only track your location; they can tell us if there's someone in the room with you. The abduction angle again. It's meant to help rescuers pounce on the kidnappers, not the victim."

"So right now, these Mary Kates know I'm here with you."

"Yes. They detect you're less than ten feet away from me. They're picking up your brain waves and heartbeat. Very sensitive, these girls."

"Fucking creepy."

"Not as creepy as what I'm about to tell you. Remember?"

"What?"

"If the Mary Kates detect that I'm alone, they'll travel to my brain and make it explode."

12:42 a.m.
Edison Avenue

The bag was not as heavy as he'd thought. The average human head was about six pounds—two for the skull, a quarter for the skin, and three for the brain, and spare change for water and fat and such. But this Adidas bag definitely felt lighter than six pounds.

Maybe it was all the blood and brains that had spurted out.

Nice, huh?

Kowalski wondered how far he'd have to travel with it. A plane was out of the question. Homeland Security would x-ray his $19.95 bag and see Ed's goofy mug staring back up at them. Most likely, CI-6 would dispatch someone local to recover it, analyze, do whatever they wanted with it. That's DHS, folks. Keeping America Safe, One Decapitated Head at a Time.

He placed the bag on the floor of the backseat, propping it up on one side with a box of Kleenex and on the other with a hardback copy of a fitness book called *The Lean Body Promise*. Weight loss wasn't going to be a concern for Ed anymore. He'd already lost about six pounds today.

Ah fuck it. Katie would have laughed.

After double-checking his exit route on the Tribeca's GPS system, he opened the garage doors and drove down the driveway to the street. He pulled Ed's cell phone out of his pocket—he'd found it in Ed's bag. Then he dialed the Hunter's home number, helpfully written in pen on the kitchen wall phone. The home line was wired to his jerry-rigged gas-main detonator. Simplest thing in the world. One phone call, one massive basement explosion.

Kowalski pressed the Send button, appreciated the white-hot

blast that blew out the first-floor windows and sent a booming echo rolling through the neighborhood.

Then he saw Claudia Hunter dive through a second-floor window, tuck and roll down the grassy hill on the side of the house, struggle to her feet, then take off behind her neighbor's house. She was gone before all of the beads of glass showered the lawn below.

Holy crap.

That was impressive.

Kowalski knew he'd gone easy when he was strangling her with the dental floss. But her pulse had been shallow; she'd been checking out. Apparently, she had other plans.

Kowalski popped out of the car, thought about it, then grabbed the Adidas bag from the backseat. No telling how long it would take him to run Claudia down. He wasn't about to leave his objective behind to be recovered by some dumb car thief.

Up the driveway, behind the house, down the hill, Ed's head bounced around in the bag.

Hey, buddy. It's your wife.

Claudia was a fast runner, even in bare feet and a summer nightie.

After a few backyards, Kowalski paused to stash the bag in a child's tree house. The structure was fairly complex, with two separate entrances and stained, smooth pieces that were too perfect to have been assembled by hand. The bag was slowing him down, and he didn't want to damage the contents too much. Or leave it back in the car, where a curious cop might spot it.

Kowalski checked the ground for a weapon, saw what he wanted, picked it up, and raced after Claudia.

Goddamn she was fast.

12:46 a.m.
Sheraton, Room 702

"So if I walk across the room, and you stay here on this couch, you'll die."

"In about ten seconds. Give or take a second."

"You're kidding me."

"I'd say try it, but I'd rather you not. It really hurts."

"Why is it ten feet? I mean, why not nine, or eleven? Is it ten feet exactly?"

"You know, it's a bit hard to make careful scientific measurements when it feels like your brain is going to explode inside of your skull. But based on available evidence, I'd say yeah, this microscopic noose around my neck stretches to damn near exactly ten feet."

Jack considered this.

"Hang on. You obviously don't work in a lab all by yourself. Can't your colleagues help you out? Fix this fatal error in the program? I don't know . . . give you a blood transfusion?"

"They're all dead. It's why I left Ireland."

Kelly looked at him, her eyes pleading with him to shut the fuck up and listen. Saying, This is going to be a difficult speech, so I'd prefer it if you stopped asking questions and let me tell it my own way.

At least that's what Jack read her in eyes. He was familiar with that look. Theresa had mastered it long ago.

"I've always known that my line of work is dangerously competitive," she said. "We're not officially part of the government, but we're not independent, either. We sign confidentiality agreements like you wouldn't believe. And we're required to attend exhaustive seminars on lab security. But all of that doesn't mean fuck on a bike when five thugs with Kevlar suits and Rambo knives storm into your lab one morning and start slitting your coworkers' throats.

"These guys, whoever the fuck they were, wanted the Mary Kates, and all of our project research. They left two of us alive to gather it up—yours truly and my boss. He managed to trigger a self-destruct sequence on our servers, but they got wise to it, stopped it, and they cut off a hand for being uncooperative. I'm not sure if he's alive or dead."

"And you?"

"I jumped through a window and ran."

"Then how—"

"How did I get the Mary Kates in my blood? Lab accident. The time we were ambushed, each of us already had a fair amount of the little buggers in our systems. It's one of the things we were, um, trying to perfect."

"So the fatal error was introduced, and the satellite was still fixed on you."

"Exactly."

"And you haven't been alone since then?"

"Grand, isn't it?"

She rested her hand on his forearm. Her skin was soft and warm.

"Let me get this out before we go any further: You don't have to believe me. In fact, I think you'd be crazy if you did. There's a box full of printouts and a USB memory stick full of research that will corroborate my story. It's in San Diego, in case anything happens to me."

She paused. "Are you listening?"

Jack had been staring down, processing it all. "I am."

"Thank God. I'd hate to think you were zoning out while I was telling you vital information that might be useful in the event of my premature death."

"I was just—"

"Never mind. If I buy the dirt farm, go to the Westin Horton

Plaza, downtown near the Gaslamp Quarter. At the front desk, ask for a package for Mary Kate."

"Should I write this down?"

"No way, boyo. Memorize it."

Jack scratched down the initials anyway: MK, WHP, SD.

"Okay, I got it. Mary Kate, Westin Horton Plaza, San Diego. But wait. . . . Can't you try to locate your boss? Isn't there a chance he's alive?"

"Even if he were, that would be difficult. I don't know his name. He referred to himself as 'the Operator,' and nothing more. He was obsessed with security. But now all that's fucked, isn't it?"

12:51 a.m.
Behind the Edison Avenue House

There she was. Running along the banks of a rock-strewn creek that flowed behind the properties. You got yourself a smart woman, Ed. Instead of racing out into an empty street, where she could be easily picked off, she decided to follow a central path away from the danger, most likely planning to emerge when the danger had passed.

Sorry, Mrs. Hunter, Kowalski thought. This danger has a job to finish.

Pumping hard, Kowalski closed the distance. His fingertips caressed the smooth stone he had picked up back at the tree house. Dense little sucker.

"Claudia!"

Always better to use the first name. Increases the likelihood that someone will respond to you.

She didn't turn, but she slowed for a second, and in that instant a tiny bit of hope seemed to drain from her body. That was all Kowalski needed. He hurled the stone at her head; direct strike. Claudia's knee buckled and she tripped forward into the creek.

Kowalski didn't slow down. He needed to confirm death—failing that, induce death—then recover the head and get the hell out of there. Behind him, in what was not quite the distance, the Hunter home burned like a three-story stone bonfire.

Claudia still had a little fight left in her. She was lying faceup in the shallow creek, despite the fact that Kowalski had seen her fall face-first. She'd had enough energy left to flip over. He admired that. Face your attacker, rather than hide from the inevitable. Kowalski could imagine her calling up her last reserves of strength just so she could spit on him as he approached.

He felt for a pulse; it was fading rapidly. She was on her way out.

He thought about leaving her as is. Investigators could surmise that she'd fallen and banged her head while fleeing from a burning house. . . .

Okay, yeah, that was crap. Her neck needed to be professionally snapped.

Before he did that, though, Kowalski surprised himself by thinking about leaning over and kissing her forehead.

He didn't of course.

Instead, he placed his left palm on her chin, and his right hand around the back of her neck. Then twisted . . .

Why would he think things like that?

. . . hard.

Now, back to the tree house. Back to Ed's head. Back to his handler, back to his mission of vengeance before wrestling with the inevitable, crippling grief of losing Katie and their baby. . . .

Kowalski reached up again, felt around. Got a splinter, but nothing else.

The gym bag?

Gone.

12:52 a.m.
Sheraton, Room 702

"Will you stop?"

As she spoke, Kelly had kept inching closer to him, and Jack tried to keep some personal space. It was starting to freak him out.

"What?"

"Look, I swear I won't walk away. You sit on your end of the couch, and I'll sit on mine. I've had a long fucking day, and it's only getting longer. I need to process this stuff."

"Then go, Jack, go. Process away." She leaned back and closed her eyes. She seemed upset.

Great. He was feeling guilty about a woman who had tried to kill him. No, even better—was *still in the process* of killing him. The poison was still running through his veins.

Kelly opened her eyes. "Look, forget everything I told you. You can believe me; you can think I'm crazy. You can write a story about this, or you can go off and never think about this again. I ask one thing of you: a night's sleep. I'm begging you. Just lie next to me in bed until morning; then I'll give you the antidote and you'll never have to see me again."

Jack looked at her. She did look exhausted. Exactly like he felt.

"What if I take the antidote from your bag when you're sleeping? How do you know I'll stay?"

"You haven't tried taking it so far, Jackie boy. You're not that kind of guy."

"You're so sure of that?"

"Besides, it's a bit tricky. I dosed you with luminous toxin. Nasty stuff if not treated correctly. I need to step-dose you out of it. You find the antidote, by some small miracle, you have to know how to take it."

"Luminous *what?*"

"I'm a scientist, Jack. I've got access to all kinds of disturbing chemicals."

"Okay, say I get your bag and take it to a doctor. Tell them what you told me. That you gave me luminous tox—"

"*Toxin.*"

"Toxin. Right. Luminous toxin. You're not the only scientist who knows how to deal with that stuff."

"Whatever you say. But if you try to leave this room while I'm sleeping, at least linger in the hall for a few seconds so you can listen to me die."

Jack looked at the digital clock next to the bed: 12:54 A.M. He had his appointment to keep in less than eight hours.

"I just need sleep. *Please.* Let me sleep."

So did he. And for the first time all evening, Kelly sounded somewhat rational. Maybe she'd calmed down a bit by talking this stuff through. An idea formed in his Jack's mind. He found himself saying, "Okay."

Kelly leaned over and kissed him on the cheek. Instinctively, he turned his face toward her, then caught himself at the last minute. Jesus. For a moment there, he'd thought it was Theresa. He'd almost kissed her on the lips.

But even if Jack hadn't stopped himself, her recoil would have done the trick. She pushed herself away like he'd given her an electric shock.

"You don't want to kiss me."

"I wasn't going to."

The thought was the furthest thing from his mind for a number of reasons—not the least of which being he usually didn't kiss people who had tried to kill him. But now that she had stressed it . . . of course, now it was all he could think about. Kissing her.

"Trust me, Jack. It's a very bad idea. Remember the Mary Kates?"

"I wasn't going to kiss you."

"Just imagine I'd got a cold. A very bad cold. That's how these damned things work anyway."

"Okay," Jack said, staring at her lips. Her natural, full, soft lips.

She turned her face away, then lowered her head onto his shoulder.

"You don't know how long I've been waiting for someone to believe me. Someone who didn't think I was crazy. If I weren't infected with killer nanomachines, I've give you a blow job out of gratitude."

Jack didn't know what to say to that. He settled for "Um, thanks."

Her body started shaking, as if she had started crying.

No, it wasn't tears. She was laughing.

"What?"

"I'm glad I didn't have to resort to plan B. You would *really* have gotten the wrong idea."

"Plan B?"

"Handcuffs."

12:55 a.m.
Behind the Edison Avenue House

Not good, not good. Kowalski could see the flashing cherries of the fire trucks filling the night sky. Wouldn't be long before police started searching the immediate area, looking for survivors. Wouldn't be long before the neighbors would pop their lights on, look out their front doors, wondering what the hell was going on at one o'clock in the morning.

And the tree house was empty.

His bag was gone.

Not a soul in the immediate vicinity. Bag wasn't there long enough for someone to have "accidentally" discovered it. What, was he away three minutes? Four, tops? What the hell happened? Did Ed's decapitated head sprout green hairy spider legs and go for a stroll?

Lights were flicking on in houses spread across the hills. Then, out of the corner of his eye, Kowalski noticed the opposite: a light flicking *off*.

It all came together within seconds.

He *so* didn't have time for this.

Within thirty seconds, Kowalski was in the living room, staring at the guy who was staring at the stolen Adidas bag on his dining table. In the dim light, he looked like a young workaholic college professor, staying up late to do grades and putter away at a novel in spare moments. He had that bedhead look, even though he was still dressed in jeans and a button-down shirt a shade too tight for his age. The guy was so entranced by the bag—maybe he was thinking, Forget this novel stuff; I may have a bag full of stolen loot here. And that made sense. Who else would stash a bag in a tree house but a criminal? The prof, however, was in for a little surprise. Kowalski considered waiting until the guy opened it before speaking up. There you go, buddy. Put *that* in your novel. But the whole killing innocent bystanders thing was beginning to disturb him. He didn't need another dead body on his conscience.

Not tonight.

"Ahem."

The guy jolted, then froze. Only his eyes moved.

"Yeah, right over here, see?" Kowalski waved.

The prof nodded slowly.

"That bag does not belong to you. It does not contain cash or jewelry, or anything else you might consider valuable. Take a few steps back, let me take my bag, and I'll be gone. No harm, no foul."

"How do I know this is yours?"

"Because I say it is. And you should always believe a man with a semiautomatic pointed at your stomach."

Kowalski had no such thing pointed anywhere.

The man's voice cracked: "I want my cut."

"Of what?"

"What's in this bag. You can spare a little. Consider it a holding tax. I know how you armed robbers operate."

"You don't need anything in that bag."

"And *you* don't have a gun. No chance you'd be caught with the money *and* a piece. That's another twenty, mandatory. You ditched the gun the moment you left the job."

The guy was a stubborn fucker. Definitely a college professor, thinking he could throw his intellect around like a sledgehammer. Always thinking he was too clever to get caught. He must have been sipping a cappuccino, up late, thinking amazing thoughts, and then watched Kowalski stash the bag in the tree house.

"You're not worried about your children? Because once I kill you, they're next."

"What makes you think I have children?"

"Right before they die, I'll tell them Daddy let this happen."

"Oh, the tree house, right? That was here when I bought the house. I don't have kids, asshole. Just like you don't have a gun."

Kowalski had been perfectly content to take the bag by force and leave this guy alive. That's what he'd thought about as he broke the lock on this guy's back door: Let him live. Because the body count was already high—hell, he'd just walked away from a dying woman in a shallow creek. No need to toss another body onto the pyre.

This, though, demanded a response.

"Go ahead. Take what you want out of the bag, and let me get out of here. I can hear the sirens."

The professor smiled, then unfastened the bag. He looked down into it. His jaw dropped.

Kowalski closed the distance and slapped the man across his nose with an open palm. Better than a fist—less likely to break your own hand that way. The prof was stunned, but he threw a wild right roundhouse punch, which Kowalski deflected by snapping it to the side with the flat of his hand. Without losing momentum, he grabbed the professor's wrist and yanked him forward, giving Kowalski a clear shot at the kidneys and base of the spine. He pounded his fist down repeatedly until the man was paralyzed on the carpet and sobbing.

"You're probably a sociology professor, aren't you? All that talk about mandatory sentencing."

The guy squirmed, and moaned. Kowalski patted his pants pockets until he found what he was looking for.

"Tell me something. What's mandatory sentence for dental floss?"

1:45 a.m.
Sheraton, Room 702

Kelly was asleep. Jack could tell by her breathing, which had settled into a slow, comfortable rhythm.

Thank Christ.

Nanomachines? The Operator? The Olsen twins? A killer satellite? Proof in San Diego? Luminous toxin? Deflecting a kiss one moment, offering a blow job the next? What kind of con game was this?

But deep down, Jack knew this wasn't a con. More likely, this woman was simply stone nuts. Some kind of research scientist who had lost her mind, or stayed up one too many nights with a complex equation.

Boiiiiiing! Spring loose! Let's go out and kidnap a man nursing a boilermaker in an airport bar! A sad substitute for a lost social life.

Jack slowly rolled off the bed and made his way to the other side, where she had stashed her bag. It was one of those vinyl messenger bags you see strapped to twenty-something hipsters. He opened the flap, and yep, she wasn't kidding. Handcuffs. He gently placed them on the carpet, trying to avoid the sound of metal jangling.

They weren't authentic police handcuffs. Unless some city departments had started purchasing restraints from a store called the Pleasure Chest. The name was featured on a purple stamp on the base of one of the cuffs. Hot-cha.

Still, they seemed solid enough. Sex games were no fun unless there was that element of realism.

Enough to cuff her to the bed while he called the police.

Let them arrive, and she can tell them all about the Operator and Mary Kate and Bob Saget and whoever else is in the Full Nut-House in her mind. They could force her to surrender the antidote.... In fact, wait a fucking sec. It was probably right here, in her bag.

As quietly as he could, Jack fished around in her bag, but he found only three items of interest, poisonwise. A bottle of CVS-brand contact lens rewetting drops. Clear liquid inside. Could she have used this to store the antidote? There was also a plastic tube with a Tylenol Extra Strength label on it. He twisted it open. It was full of round white tablets. He shook one out—they were stamped OP 706. No idea. So maybe they were it. Finally, there was a sheet of foil-wrapped Imodium tablets. Or at least they looked like Imodium. Could be anything.

Was it one of these three? Did she even have it on her? Well, the police would be able to make her talk.

Jack picked up the handcuffs and crept closer to Kelly. She was the kind of woman who slept with her arms over her head, which was perfect. He placed one of the cuffs around her wrist and gently snapped it into place.

Her eyes opened. She breathed sharply. Then she screamed, "*No!*"

Jack hooked the other cuff around the bedpost. *Snap it, snap it, c'mon, snap it.* . . . Kelly yanked her hand away. The cuff clanged against brass, then slid free. Then she smashed her forehead into Jack's nose. His face went numb. His eyes closed defensively. It was like someone had pushed him under chlorinated water before he had a chance to hold his nose. Burning liquid, up his nose and down his throat.

Then he felt a blow to his chest, and he fell backward to the carpet.

Kelly was astride him in seconds. Her thighs squeezed his rib cage, which was amazingly painful.

"I don't want to hurt you," she said. Jack coughed; the burning in his nose intensified. "But you almost killed me. You have to understand that."

She squeezed his chest again, and Jack felt the cool metal over his wrist. Then a click.

"I thought you *believed me.*"

1:50 a.m.
Little Pete's Restaurant, Seventeenth Street

The all-night diner was called Little Pete's. It lived up to its name. It was a tiny rectangular wedge on the first floor of a seven-story garage complex. Just enough room for a row of six booths, a breakfast counter, a compact cashier's station, and a stainless-steel kitchen in back. It was a greasy spoon as imagined by

Fisher-Price. But it was the only thing open this time of night in this part of town. And that's where his handler had told him to go.

Good news was, the night was almost over for him. Sure, it'd had its bumps, but four hours of work wasn't too hideous. He could get some sleep and resume his personal mission the next evening.

Kowalski had called his handler once he was safely away from the scene of his most recent crimes. One headless burned guy (not his fault!) in a burned-out shell of a house, one dead woman in a shallow creek, one strangled asshole in his own living room. He'd taken the asshole's Audi—an awfully nice car for a young college professor. Maybe the guy—Robert Lankford, according to his ID—had had a sideline going. Stay up all night, hoping that armed robbers would wander by his backyard. Take a cut of the loot, buy some flashy wheels to impress the barely dressed undergrad criminal justice majors.

His handler'd had a rare bit of good news for him: "No need to travel. We're sending someone to recover the bag from you."

She'd given him the address of a diner two blocks from Rittenhouse Square.

And here he was, Ed's head stashed between his feet on the floor, plate of bacon, bowl of cottage cheese, bowl of mixed fruit, and a cup of chocolate skim milk on the table before him. Usually, he waited until after an assignment, but the running and killing and planning had left him ravenous. An infusion of protein would help.

He'd wanted to talk to his handler.

Maybe say, We should talk.

Or: I need to explain a few things to you.

Or even the classic: This is not what it looks like.

But how could it not?

Let's say you're her.

A handler in an ultrasecretive government agency. Your boyfriend—also your number-one field agent—disappears on a long-term op, only to emerge with a pregnant fiancée. How's it supposed to look?

Never mind that the fiancée is dead. That doesn't help things at all. Not in your eyes.

Her eyes.

Kowalski couldn't even bring himself to think of his handler by name. Her lovely name.

They'd worked together for years, anonymous to each other, the passion growing. By the time they'd broken down together in Warsaw, in that violent thunderstorm, and she revealed her true first name, it was like bearing her naked body to him for the first time. It was the most intimate thing about her.

And now that he thought about it, *that* was supremely fucked up.

He used his butter knife to slice a strip of bacon in half. Surprisingly good bacon—not many globules of fat, not too burned.

Want some, Ed?

He could put the bag on the table, unzip it, unhinge Ed's jaw and give him a little taste. Least he could do, after all he'd been through. Kowalski decided he'd been a little harsh previously. What was Ed's crime? Flirting with a pretty blonde on a plane ride to Philadelphia?

Meanwhile, Kowalski had a stack of mafiosi bodies piling up this summer—an Italian holocaust. And *he* was the guy enjoying the bacon.

The worst thing was, he'd lost count of how many goombahs he'd snipered since ID'ing Katie's body at the morgue. The local paper had it somewhere around thirteen, according to the last news brief he'd read. Speculation was that it was intermob warfare, a bunch of bargain-basement capos capping one another over worthless bits of turf left behind by the Russian mob. And he'd only read *that* brief because they had printed the anonymous tip he'd phoned in: "Yeah, somebody's out there. He's pissed. And he's a good shot, too. They call him Mr. K."

The reporter ran with that, verbatim. They didn't check a damn thing. It was amazing. The media would print anything.

But Ed, I did it for a reason. I wanted them to know why they were dying. That I was coming after them. All of them.

You understand, right, Ed?

1:55 a.m.
Sheraton, Room 702

She pressed a corner of a blanket to his nose. "Keep your head back and the bleeding will stop."

"I'm bleeding? Oh, fuck, you made me bleed!"

"Shhhh, you big baby. It'll be fine. I didn't break anything. If I had, you'd know."

"Fuck."

There were three sharp knocks at the door.

"Oh, fuck," Kelly said.

A muffled voice through the door: "Hey, sorry to bother. I'm one of your neighbors from across the hall, and I thought I heard something. Everything okay in there?"

"We're great!"

"Somebody *help me*!"

Kelly squeezed tighter, and the fresh agony in Jack's ribs took his breath away. She clamped her free hand—the one that wasn't handcuffed—over his lips and pressed down hard. Her eyes were daggers.

"My husband's kidding. We're doing a little *rough play*. You understand, right?"

"Are you okay, miss? Look, how about you open the door and let me know."

"I appreciate your concern, but I can assure you, we're completely fine. Go back to bed."

"Open up for a second. Let me see you."

"With all due respect, sir, we paid quite a lot of money for privacy in this hotel. Didn't we, dear?"

Jack considered this. Yeah, *he* had paid quite a bit for this room. Donovan Platt had offered. Wanted to pick up the plane fare, too. But Jack had refused. If he was going to be castrated, he was going to pay his own way.

Kelly removed her hand from Jack's mouth and reached back to cup it around his testicles. Pressure was immediately applied.

"*Tell him.*"

Jack nodded.

Then he threw himself to one side. Kelly's legs slipped off his chest. But not the hand clenching his balls. Despite the handcuffs, this seemed to be Kelly's true lifeline; weakening her grip would mean a fall into the abyss. She squeezed *hard*. Jack tried to curl up into a defensive fetal position, but the pain was too intense. He couldn't move. Or speak. It looked like they were engaged in an S-M version of Twister.

"Come on, miss, just open this door for a minute? I'd feel a lot better, and we can all get back to sleep."

"Sir, don't take this the wrong way . . ."

Kelly finally let go of Jack's testicles. He again tried to curl into a ball, but she remounted his chest before he had a chance. She pointed an accusatory finger at him and moved it back and forth.

". . . but why don't you fuck off and leave the consenting adults alone?"

Jack found that he couldn't breathe, both from the agony in his groin and the pressure on his chest. So in that instant, he decided to suspend one of the rules of chivalry hard-wired into his brain since he was a child.

He punched her in the stomach as hard as he could.

So hard, she was lifted up above his body for a brief moment and was thrown backward, clear away from him. If she hadn't been handcuffed to him, she might have been thrown halfway across the hotel room. Instead, the links between the cuffs snapped tight, and Kelly dropped to the floor.

Jack flipped himself over and used his free hand to claw at the carpet, dragging himself forward, and his captor along with him, toward the door. He could hear her gasping for air, but that wasn't his problem. The events of the past few moments had convinced him of one thing: her insanity. Her fucking wild stories, her kidnapping, her threats, her steel grip on his balls . . . Who the fuck does stuff like that but a crazy woman?

"Have it your way. I'm going back to my room and calling security. You can explain it to them."

"Sweet Jesus Hallelujah. At long last."

The fight wasn't out of Kelly, though. She recovered from the stomach punch enough to pounce on Jack's back. He heard her coming, though, and rolled at the same time she made impact. A flip later, Jack was on top.

On top of a pretty blonde, to whom he was handcuffed, in a fancy hotel room in a strange city.

Oh, would this make quite an image for the wife.

And while he was here, why not complete the image?

And prove to this woman that she was, in fact, fucking certifiable.

"Hey."

She was breathing hard; her bottom lip trembled. Jack cupped his free hand around the back of her neck and drew her close and pressed his lips to hers. He forced his tongue inside her mouth, just like she'd done with that middle-aged guy at the airport.

She probably thought he'd forgotten about that.

Mary Kates, my ass.

If she were *that* contagious with these things, that kiss would have killed that guy.

She fought, but he gripped her neck tightly and didn't stop until she clamped her teeth around his tongue.

Jack yelled and broke the embrace, then rolled off her. He chose the wrong side. Her handcuffed arm yanked over him. On the floor, they looked like two mimes who had made violent love and were hugging an invisible pillow.

"Jack. You don't know what you've done. You really don't."

She was twenty-one, a blonde, a Chicago Polack with too good a face and figure to be in something like this.
——NEWTON THORNBURG

1:56 a.m.
Little Pete's

Kowalski's cell rang. Someone dictated a number to him, and he scribbled the number on a Little Pete's napkin. Added his PN, used his prepaid calling card, hit a pay phone, reached his handler. She spoke fast and furious. Things were moving.

So much for chitchat.

Anyway: Based on preliminary evidence from Professor Manchette's head—CI-6 thought it was best to have someone closer expedite the removal, the handler explained; like Kowalski fucking minded?—it was top priority to locate Kelly White and take her into custody.

"I'm on it."

He'd planned ahead for this. He had the license plate sequence of the cab she'd taken from Philly International; he knew the cab company. A quick call, a bit of "Homeland Security" strong-arm stuff, and he'd have their drop-off location. That wasn't a worry. What worried Kowalski was the bag between his feet.

"Hey—what about the, um, other head?"

"Store it somewhere safe for now."

He wanted to ask his handler, Like where? Ask Little Pete if I can stick it in his deep freezer for a while? Right next to the hamburger patties and pork chops? Kowalski knew he was better off taking it with him. His experience with the tree house in Somerton had spooked him. The bag seemed to be in too much demand. The only risk was a cop stopping him, asking to see what was in the bag. But if it came to that, and Kowalski was unable to incapacitate the cop, he knew he had a safety net out there. It might mean some jail time, but not forever. Homeland Security had an infinite number of Get Out of Jail Free cards.

"Where's your guy? The one who's supposed to pick it up?"

"He's unavailable."

"Mad scientists usually busy at two in the morning?"

A pause.

"Discretion would serve you well."

"Oh, I'm discreet. How could I not be? I don't know a thing. Except that I'm the guy who's stuck holding the bag. And I meant that literally as well as metaphorically."

Another pause.

"Is that all?"

"I guess so. Unless you're want to wish me luck."

"Good-bye."

"Bye . . ." he said, then silently mouthed her name. He felt dirty saying it.

1:57 a.m.
Security Office, Sheraton Hotel

When the phone rang, Charlie Vincent jolted. He had nodded off with a book in his lap. It was a small paperback sampler of Japanese *manga* his kid had given him, published by some company called Tokyopop. Charlie had been giving him money for these things for a few weeks now, and during weekend visits he'd steal glances at some of the art. Looked like Asian porn stuff he'd seen on the Skinternet, but his kid reassured him they were just stories—mystery, sci-fi, romance, comedy, fantasy, action. He gave Charlie the sampler to check out, and Charlie was confused as shit until his kid told him they were meant to be read back to front. Like that made any fucking sense. Charlie wondered if his kid was going to tell his mother about it, give her a good laugh.

Charlie put the book on his desk, picked up the phone. It was the front desk.

"We got a call about a domestic dispute in seven oh two. From the neighbor across the hall. Can you check it out?"

"Christ. What's the name?"

"Jack Eisley. Like the Eisley brothers, I guess."

Charlie paused, then decided he had to ask. "Is the guy black?"

"Does that matter?" asked the desk clerk, who was also black.

"C'mon. You know what I mean."

"I'm looking. . . . Here's his license. Nah, he's a white dude from Illinois."

"Okay. I'll be right up."

"One thing you should know."

"What's that?"

"I think we got a case of woman-on-man violence. Guy upstairs said it sounded like it was the dude who was getting beaten."

Now that's something different, he thought. "Okay, I'll be gentle."

Charlie hung up the phone and wondered if he was suddenly living in a backward world. Comic books you read in the opposite direction, women smacking around guys. What was next? His ex-wife being nice to him?

1:58 a.m.

Jack and Kelly lay on their backs on the carpet, joined at their wrists by Pleasure Chest handcuffs. Jack's tongue was throbbing; Kelly was crying softly. Once again, Jack found himself in the strange position of feeling guilty about how he was treating his captor. Never mind that she'd head butted him in the face, cracked a rib, squeezed his chest, and bit his tongue nearly in half. He felt awful about kissing her. As if he'd tried to date-rape her.

"I don't know why you're crying."

"You didn't believe me. You lied, and listened to me like you believed me. But if you believed me, you wouldn't have done that."

Jack sat up and looked at her. Kelly moved her free hand up and placed it on his chest, almost as if she were expecting another kiss.

"Don't worry—I'm not trying that again. There's no need for a restraining order."

She stared at him, through him. Her eyes were rimmed with tears, and her face was racked with exhaustion. Her lips trembled slightly.

"Wait. You're worried I've poisoned *you* in return. When I kissed you. That's it, right?"

"No," she said softly.

"What is it?"

"You *still* don't believe me. You were my last hope. I can't keep running anymore. I'm so tired of running, talking, plotting . . . every second of every single fookin' minute of the day. . . ." Kelly's Irish accent was returning. "Don't you know what I've done to you?"

"What are you taking about?"

"The Mary Kates are inside you! Right now! Multiplying! I killed all of the others to make a point. But you were supposed to be the one who would vindicate me, who would explain it all." She touched his cheek. "Now we're both dead."

But Jack didn't seem to hear.

"Killed all of what *others*?"

2:03 a.m.
Back to the Sheraton

What do you know. Call the newspapers, alert TV and radio: Ol' Kowalski catches a break. Old City Cab gave him the drop-off point, and it was the Rittenhouse Sheraton, literally around the corner, and up one block on Locust. Too good to be fucking true. That, or Philly was one absurdly small town. As he walked, he got an idea. He dialed his handler.

"I'm about to be extremely impressed."

"Not yet. Can you cross-reference passengers on all flights to Philadelphia this evening and the occupants of the Sheraton?"

"Hold on."

"Then eliminate everyone except white men traveling alone who checked in after—"

"Already ahead of you. Hold on."

Kowalski walked up Locust. Nice block, which ended at the edge of Rittenhouse Square itself. One side of the street was taken up by the Sheraton, but the other side retained some of its nineteenth-century charm. And hey, look. The Curtis Institute of Music. If he wasn't mistaken, that was where they'd shot *Trading Places* with Eddie Murphy and Dan Aykroyd. As a teenager, it had been one of his favorite comedies. Today, he would explain that he'd been fascinated by the film because of its smart examination of class warfare and the mutability of identity. But as kid, he liked it because you got to see Jamie Lee Curtis's tits.

His handler returned.

"John Joseph Eisley, goes by 'Jack.' He's in room seven oh two."

God, what did we do before the Patriot Act? By the time he'd pressed the button to end the call, Kowalski was already through the front doors and making his way to the reception desk.

"Hey, buddy. Hang on to this for me, will ya? I've got a guy upstairs who needs to be on the radio over in Bala Cynwyd in . . . oh, Christ on a cracker, an hour or so. I might need two hands to drag him out of bed."

The clerk nodded without making much eye contact. He stashed the gym bag behind the front desk.

"Back in five for that. Along with a very sleepy real estate expert. Man, the people they drag on this show at this hour. Who's up listening, right?"

Kowalski caught a pair of elevator doors closing, stuck his hand in there. But the occupant of the car had already pressed a button; the doors opened.

"Much obliged."

"No prob."

A hotel security officer wearing a black rectangular name tag with VINCENT in white letters.

"What floor?"

2:05 a.m.
Sheraton, Room 702

Kelly started crying again, and all Jack could do was reach over and hold her, and hope she didn't reward the gesture with another shot to his ribs. She rested her head on his chest. Jack rubbed her back with his free hand while trying to shift his position a little. His left arm was beginning to get that pins and needles feeling.

"I've killed many men."

Jack wondered what you were supposed to say to something like that. Ah, c'mon, buck up. How many is "many"? Couldn't be that bad, now could it?

"So I'm not the first person you've poisoned with luminous toxin."

"No, Jack. That's not what I'm talking about. You still don't believe me."

"Then what *are* you talking about?"

She grasped both of his forearms and squeezed.

"Listen to me. I am infected with an experimental tracking device. If I am alone for more than ten seconds, I will die. This was no accident. This was done to me. By my boss. The Operator. Our lab wasn't raided. It wasn't sabotage. He *did* this to me."

"I thought you said—"

"The past thirteen days," she said, ignoring him, "I've been traveling all over the world, first in Ireland, then here. Kissing strange men, sometimes fucking them. Anything it takes to avoid being alone. But I'm also sending a message to the Operator. I want him to know that I'm still alive, and that I'm going to do everything in my power to bring him down, even if I have to leave a trail of bodies behind me. Because eventually, someone will listen. Someone will come for me. Someone important. Someone who knows the Operator, and who will know how to destroy him. I thought you would help. But you won't be able to. You'll be joining the dead, all because you kissed me. No, not because of that. Because you kissed me and you didn't believe me. Do you believe me now, Jack?"

Later, Jack would look back on this moment and realize that this was the moment his nightmare truly started. Not the moment he was infected.

The moment he started to *believe*.

2:08 a.m.
Sheraton, Seventh Floor

Kowalski was mildly annoyed when he learned that he and Mr. Vincent, security chief here, were headed to the same floor—seven. Yet another hurdle. Chances were, this guy would be headed down the same stretch of hallway, and to be thorough, Kowalski was going to have to incapacitate this guy. Was this never going to end? This endless parade of victims? It was as if God had looked down and said, Oh, I get it, Kowalski—you like mowing down people left and right. Well, let me give you a few more to deal with. Hope you can keep up!

The car reached seven. Ever the gentleman, Kowalski extended his arm, but Mr. Vincent here wasn't having that.

"You first, sir."

Great. Kowalski stepped off the elevator and read the floor key posted on the wall. The room he wanted was to the left.

Mr. Vincent asked, "Can I help you?"

"Just getting my bearings, thanks."

He was hoping the security chief would shrug his shoulders and go off and do whatever the hell he'd come up here to do. Maybe there wasn't enough diet Coke in the vending area. Maybe the snack machine was out of butterscotch Krimpets.

"What room you looking for?"

This bastard was persistent.

"It's right down here. Man, I really should have stopped at three apple martinis, you know? But they're so damned good. My boss is going to hand me my ass in the morning. He's down there right now, sleeping like a good boy. Not me."

Mr. Vincent chuckled and nodded, but he didn't budge. "You can probably squeeze in a few winks before dawn."

"Like that'll help. I need a big glass of water and a fistful of aspirin."

Another polite chuckle. "After you, boss. Here at the Sheraton, the guests come first."

Kowalski had no choice but to walk toward 702. He faked a bit of drunken swagger to sell the apple martini line, but he had a feeling that wouldn't be necessary. It was going to come down to incapacitation. Get this bozo out of the hall and out of his way for at least ten minutes. He visualized Mr. Vincent in his head. Tall and stocky, with close-clipped hair that screamed *ex-military*. Creeping up on forty, but not there yet. Possibly a Gulf War vet. An easy smile, but cold eyes. Probably a lot smarter than he ever let on. A simple slap and kidney punch wasn't going to work on this guy. The rooms ticked down to the left and right: 708, 707, 706.

Kowalski threw an elbow backward. It caught Mr. Vincent in the nose. He followed up with a roundhouse punch to the side of Mr. Vincent's head, which, if it had been delivered correctly, would blind him for a few seconds. Then Kowalski went for the balls, which made the security chief fold in half and drop to his knees right outside room 705. Now it was time for a little creative asphyxiation. It was a move he'd learned in Bosnia, for when there wasn't time (or need) to hold a boot to a man's face and slice open his throat. A minor strangulation that would rob the subject of air long enough to make your escape without killing him.

And killing this guy was the last thing he wanted to do. He was getting *way* off-mission tonight. Claudia Hunter's sweet, shocked, strangled face still haunted him. It was all so gratuitous. A man had to draw the line somewhere.

Mr. Vincent, however, still had a little fight left in him. He threw out a punch that caught Kowalski off guard—and pummeled his stomach. The air gushed out of him. He staggered back and bumped up against the wall. He felt his knees weaken. That had been one brilliant shot. Totally unexpected. Superb. A follow-up landed on the side of Kowalski's knee. There was that military training. Mr. Vincent here was trying to bust his kneecap from the side, where there was little natural protection. It almost worked, too. As he stumbled, Kowalski threw a fist at Mr. Vincent's neck—one that should rob him of air for a few seconds. He heard the man gasp. Kowalski hit the carpet but then popped up quickly, intending to deliver a roundhouse kick to the head. But Mr. Vincent was already on him, tackling him, hurtling him forward.

Room 704, 703 . . .

2:10 a.m.
Sheraton, Room 702

The door burst open. Two men, one in a navy blue blazer, the other in an expensive-looking black suit, came tumbling in from the hall. The guy in the expensive suit hit the carpet face-first, while the beefy man in the blazer sat on his back, like he was riding a horse.

Jack tried to stand up, but the handcuffs pulled him back down to the carpet. He looked at Kelly, but her mouth was hanging open, too. Who were these guys? Did they burst into this room by accident? Or was this hotel security coming to check up on them in some strange roundabout way? The beefy guy in the blazer looked like he was winning the argument, whatever the hell it might be. He was pummeling away at the back of the other guy's head like he was trying to tenderize a slab of roast chuck.

But the guy in the expensive suit had a trick up his sleeve. He pounded his fists behind him, catching Mr. Blazer on the sides of his ribs. His mouth made a perfect O shape, one that tightened as the guy on the floor delivered a wild kick that struck him on the back of his head. Mr. Blazer's eyes fluttered.

Jack had no idea whom to cheer for. Mr. Blazer seemed like a safe bet. Then again, he admired the spirit of the guy on the floor. That had been one hell of a kick—part John Woo, part breakdance move.

Within seconds, the tables had completely turned. Mr. Expensive Suit had Mr. Blazer in some kind of painful-looking headlock—not exactly the kind you see on Saturday-morning wrestling shows. Mr. Expensive Suit kicked the hotel door shut with his heel, and for the first time, he looked at Jack and Kelly.

"Good evening, kids."

Mr. Blazer's eyes were shut, but he was awake and struggling madly, as if he knew what was happening to him. Consciousness being stolen from him one oxygen-deprived brain cell at a time. His lips trembled.

"Hope I didn't interrupt anything important."

Kelly stood up, and Jack had enough sense to stand up alongside her.

"I see you two have been busy," Mr. Expensive Suit said, glancing down at the handcuffs. "Look, I won't take too much of your time. Just got a question for you. Which one of you bitches is Kelly White?"

This *was* about her.

"Who are you?"

"Does it matter, Kelly?"

"Who the fuck *sent* you?"

Jack said, "Let go of him."

"Ah, don't worry about Mr. Vincent here—though that's mighty sweet of you. I'm cutting off his air long enough to knock him out, but nothing serious. He'll be right as rain."

This apparently was no comfort to Mr. Vincent, whose body bucked, fingers clawing wildly at his captor's forearms.

Jack wanted to do something to help the poor bastard, but Kelly was two steps ahead of him. She screamed and threw a fist at Mr. Expensive Suit's face. Jack felt the handcuffs drag him forward. Oh shit.

Mr. Expensive Suit blocked Kelly's punch but not her kick, which, unfortunately, caught Mr. Vincent in the leg. No reaction. Kelly threw another punch. It connected. Mr. Expensive Suit let Mr. Vincent fall to the floor, then returned an open-palm slap to the side of Kelly's head. It dazed her. The handcuffs yanked at Jack's wrist. Mr. Expensive Suit slapped her again, and Jack heard her shriek, "*No.*" Whatever this was, this guy was playing for the wrong team. Fuck it. Jack kicked outside and wide, around Kelly, aiming for testicles. At the same time, Kelly slammed her fist, the flat of her hand like the business end of a hammer, into Mr. Expensive Suit's left eye.

Mr. Expensive Suit was ahead of both of them. He twisted to avoid the groin kick. He ducked so that Kelly's jackhammer blow merely bounced off the top of his head.

And then he chopped his own hand into the chain links of the handcuffs. Powerfully. Cleanly. The chain hit carpet. Jack and Kelly tumbled to the ground after it.

He slapped Kelly again, as if to wake her up, then grabbed her by the throat. Squeezed. Then he slipped his forearm around Jack's neck.

"Nighty night," Kowalski whispered in his ear.

2:25 a.m.

Lordy lordy, thought Kowalski. I've got two unconscious guys on the floor of a hotel room. A broken door. A semiconscious woman gagged and handcuffed to a chair. Hey now—add an oversized tube of K-Y jelly, a car battery, and some jumper cables, we could call this a Saturday night.

But back to business.

The two unconscious guys. First: Charles Lee Vincent, hard-ass hotel security chief. A worthy adversary. A lot more worthy than Kowalski would have guessed. Hell, his stomach still trembled a bit. But Mr. Vincent would be out for another twenty minutes or so. And by that time, Kowalski would be a bitter memory.

Second: the mysterious John "Jack" Eisley. Another one of Kelly White's intended victims, no doubt. Was he infected? Who knew. Better to assume he was until he had instructions from his handler. Kowalski hoped this wasn't another decapitation job. The gym bag was only so big, and he doubted poor Ed would like sharing his personal space with a stranger. Especially some dope in a black T-shirt and khakis who'd driven away with his pretty little blonde.

Which brought Kowalski to the woman of the hour. The blonde herself. Back at the airport, she'd seemed like just another blonde-from-the-bottle blonde. Crackin' bust, pretty eyes, not much upstairs. He still couldn't think of the actress she reminded him of. But it was somebody he'd seen recently.

Up close, though, Kowalski could see that her eyes were fierce. Hunter's eyes. Oh yes, he thought, She's seen some things. It would be unkind to call them beady; they were simply focused to a high level of attention. The way she was looking at him now, even though she was clearly beyond exhaustion.

Kowalski dialed the number for his handler, all the while keeping Kelly in his sights. She was secured to the chair with her own handcuffs. The keys were in her bag. "Pleasure Chest, eh?" he'd said, but she'd just stared at him. His handler answered.

"Okay, now you can be impressed."

"She's alive?"

"And pissed."

"That doesn't matter. Take her by car and drive towards D.C. When you reach Silver Spring, call for directions."

"That will put me near you by four-thirty or so. Up for an early breakfast? Nothing fancy. Some coffee and eggs. Wait. I just had breakfast an hour ago. Maybe we could order some lunch-type food. A hamburger and potato salad."

"Listen, because this is important. You need to keep her within ten feet of you at all times, but do not allow her to get too close. Also, avoid any fluid contact—kissing, biting, maybe even scratching. And she'll probably try."

"Come on, N—" he began, then caught himself. He'd almost said her name. "What is this, sorority initiation night?"

"Just follow my instructions."

"This is such bullshit. This is you and me, remember?"

"There is no you and me. There's you and your employers. Follow my instructions."

"Your instructions suck."

Kowalski thumbed the cell off and realized how childish he'd sounded. Whatever. Maybe he'd get more answers out of Ms. White. She was looking more awake by the second. Probing him with her pretty, green, beady eyes.

"What?" he asked.

"Yeah, you're him. I was wondering how long it would take you to show up."

"You knew I was coming for you."

"Hoping for it. For almost a week now. I'm surprised it took him this long."

"Who?"

Kelly snorted air.

This was what Kowalski hated the most about his job. Sometimes, he felt like the ultimate insider, the man with his finger on the pulse. History's triggerman, no footnote necessary. Other times, he felt like an anonymous guy in some felt-lined cubicle, pushing staples into pieces of paper typed in a foreign language. They could be documents vital to national security. Or they could be invoices for turkey clubs.

This felt like one of those turkey club moments. Complete with toothpick and olive.

"Fine, you're not going to tell me, doesn't matter."

"How long have you been working for him?"

"Ever since I quit flippin' burgers at Wendy's. I couldn't take it anymore. All of those square patties. They freaked me out."

Kowalski walked behind her, sizing up the situation. No biting, no scratching, avoid fluid contact. Easy thing to do, if she were unconscious.

"You're just like him. Oh so funny. Is that part of the training they give boys like you? A little stand-up to lighten the mood before killing somebody?"

He liked her. She was quick.

"Okay, look, the easy thing would be to knock you out. Tie you up, nothing kinky, stick you in the backseat under a blanket, and off we go. That's probably not something you want to happen. Am I right?"

"The tying up part sounded fun."

"Of course. But then I'd have to find a way to drag your unconscious body out of the hotel, and at . . . what? Two-thirty in the morning? That's a pain in the ass. So here's my idea: We walk out together, holding hands. We get into a car."

"What kind of car?"

"I don't know. Haven't stolen it yet."

"Nice."

"We get into a car, and I take you to where you need to be."

"What if I resist?"

"Then I tie you up, like, really tight."

"Still sounds like fun."

No matter what, Kowalski was going to knock her out, tie her up, and dump her in the backseat. But it would be easier to walk out of here together, find a car, and take care out of business outside the hotel. It was early in the morning, but sooner or later, somebody downstairs would be calling for this security guy here. They might already have. Kowalski had taken the batteries out of Mr. Vincent's walkie-talkie, as well as the cell phone clipped to his belt. The batteries went into the tank of the toilet.

Kowalski looked at Kelly's hand. They were mannish hands—strong wrists, slightly stubby fingers. Working-class hands.

He studied the middle finger of her left hand in particular.

"Let's get ready to go."

2:30 a.m.
CI-6 Headquarters (Undisclosed Location)

The call was placed, buried, then reburied beneath a sea of thousands of other phone calls being made across the United States at any given second. It was hidden, even from DHS. She knew better than to make it from her office, an anonymous flat two-story stuccoed box with emergency staircases made of concrete. The building had been around since the 1950s; kids in the neighborhood grew up without even wondering what went on in there. She went down the street, into an apartment building, and then downstairs to a laundry room in the basement. A pay phone she knew about. She used a prepaid calling card.

God, if anyone else in CI-6 knew what she'd been doing for the past six weeks . . .

"We have her."

"I'm getting on a plane now. Where am I going?"

"D.C."
"Where is she right now?"
"On her way."
"Not in a fucking plane . . . don't tell me she's in a plane."
"I said, We have her. She'll be here in a matter of hours."
"Yeah yeah."
"After all this, I get attitude? Do you know how much—"
"I know how much, dear."
"I wonder."
Silence.
"Where are you?"
"Close enough to be there in a few hours."
"Then I'll see you soon."
"When you see that slut," the Operator said, "tell her I'm coming for her."

2:45 a.m.
Sheraton Elevators, Right Bank, North Side

Kowalski and Kelly held hands. He was still in the same outfit he'd worn all day: Dolce & Gabbana suit and dress shirt, Ferragamo shoes; she had slipped into a pair of Citizens of Humanity jeans, Pumas, and a white tank. It didn't look like a date. It looked like the aftermath of a date. As if they'd met at Bar Noir, walked down the street for a hookup at the hotel, and now were headed back downstairs for the courtesy cab hail for her. Their eyes were puffy enough for that.

The doors closed. Kowalski tightened his grip on her hand. Specifically, her middle finger.

He'd taken her hand back in the room, even before he opened the cuffs, and warned her, "I can snap your middle finger in a such a hideously painful way, you'll instantly lose consciousness. I'd prefer not to have to carry you out of here, but it's easy enough to explain. My girlfriend here sure loves her apple martinis!"

Kowalski had pulled back her finger, just as his own mentor had taught him in the early days of his CI-6 training. It required two simple actions, carried out at the same time.

"Feel that?"

She'd turned to him, God love her, and asked, "Can you do the same thing with a nipple?"

Kowalski had applied more pressure to let her know he was serious. She'd grunted. Her jaw had snapped shut instantly. She'd teared up. Kelly had gotten the point. But inside, he'd smiled. She was *good*.

The car began to descend, then stopped one floor below. Six. Great.

The doors opened, and a guy in black running shorts, ankle-cut socks, and T-shirt emblazoned with the words TWO-WAY SPLIT stepped into the car. He was startled to discover he had company. He was holding an ice bucket. He pressed the button for five.

"Machine's broken on my floor."

"See, hon? Philly's not a dead town. Everybody's up partying."

Kelly said nothing. She looked at the guy in the shorts with those piercing eyes, as if passing along a telepathic message.

The guy, probably self-conscious about locking eyes with someone else's woman, broke the transmission.

The doors closed.

"I need some ice for my Diet Coke. Packed my own, but it's warm. Need to chill it for first thing tomorrow."

"Diet Coke for breakfast?"

"Can't take coffee. Too much caffeine. Makes me jittery."

"Do what I do. Cut it with bourbon."

Kowalski looked at Kelly and gave her the slightest squeeze on her hand.

"Right, hon?"

She was still staring at the Diet Coke guy.

The elevator car stopped at five. The doors opened. He nodded at both of them and stepped out of the car, ice bucket in hand. The car continued its descent. Kelly looked up at Kowalski.

"I don't want to die."

"I didn't say anything about dying. If death had been on the menu, it would have already been ordered."

The car reached the ground floor.

"You don't understand."

The doors opened. She leaned closer to him.

"I don't want to die. But if I *have* to . . ."

Kowalski felt Kelly's hand slip away from his. He snatched at her, but she'd already stepped back, grabbed the rail of the elevator car with both hands, and rabbit-kicked him. The blow knocked the wind out of him. He was airborne. Kowalski spun in midair, flinging his hands out behind himself to break his fall, at which he half-succeeded. The palm of his left hand caught the carpeted ground cleanly, but his right wrist twisted awkwardly. By the time he'd staggered to his feet, the pain in his wrist was sharp and real, the doors were already closing, and she was saying, "Tell the Operator *I fucking won.*"

2:48 and 30 seconds
Sheraton, Room 702

Jack Eisley rolled over to drape his arm around Theresa, like he did every morning to see if she was awake yet. But his hand dropped straight down to the mattress. Funny—the mattress was rock-hard.

His eyes popped open. Short-term memories rushed back: drinks, blonde, cab ride, hotel room, Mary Kates, San Diego . . .

You'll be joining the dead, all because you kissed me. No, not because of that. Because you kissed me and you didn't believe me. Do you believe me now, Jack?

"You okay, buddy?"

Jack rolled over to the other side. His neck and head were throbbing.

Oh, man . . .

It was the hotel security guy, on his knees next to Jack. This guy was just waking up, too. The black name tag pinned to the man's uniform read VINCENT. Was that a first name or a last?

"Look, stay right here. I'm going to get us some help."

Jack nodded, but he heard faint alarm bells go off somewhere. In the hotel? No. It was more a tingling sensation. A high-pitched tone, like an audio test from grade school. Tones, cycling higher and higher, clunky headphones pasted over your ears, school nurse asking you to raise your hand if . . . No.

Wait.

. . . 35 seconds

Kelly White—which wasn't her real name, at least not the one her parents had given her—knew she was going to die.

It would take only eight seconds, and the throbbing of the veins in her head would grow worse, the Mary Kates rushing north to expand and destroy all they encountered, and then the gushing . . .

And then it would be over.

She knew it would happen sooner or later. At least she had been able to choose it.

The elevator car continued its ascent.

But in the passing of one second to the next, her brain ignored the invading swarm of nanomachines, and a series of synapses fired. An idea.

. . . 36 seconds

There was screaming in Jack Eisley's head, and he'd never felt it before, but now he could . . . the blood in his veins. On *fire*. And the throbbing in his head growing stronger with every heartbeat, and the screaming whine in his brain growing louder.

Jack shook his head, pounded his fists on the carpet.

Listen to me. I am infected with an experimental tracking device. If I am alone for more than ten seconds, I will die.

Christ, she wasn't kidding.

This is real.

This is real.

This is real.

. . . 37 seconds

Guy with the ice bucket for his Diet Coke. Up on five.

She jabbed forward with her index finger.

Collapsed to her knees.

Found the button for five.

Screamed.

Pounded the floor of the ascending elevator car.

Button five was lighted; the digital readout above the doors ticked upward in concert with the seconds.

She screamed louder, as if it would give the Mary Kates pause. It didn't.

. . . 38 seconds

Jack Eisley pounded furiously at the carpet with the wild idea that he could pound right through the floor and fall into the next floor, and the weight of his body and the chunk of floor would cause that floor to collapse, and then another and another and another, until he was in the lobby, surrounded by people, and the Mary Kates would know that and stop the screaming and throbbing in his head. . . .

It was his only chance.

Jack pounded and pounded and pounded. . . .

. . . 39 seconds

On the fifth floor, the elevator doors opened, and Kelly White was screaming, she knew she was, but she couldn't hear sound anymore, and all she could do was fall forward, and she collided with skin and plastic and she saw the ice tumble and scatter across the carpet and heard *"Jesus!"*

And she smiled, because she was worried about his Diet Coke, and here was a man to save her, finally, but it was too late, and . . .

And then it was over for Kelly White.

Which wasn't even the name she had been born with.

. . . 40 seconds

And on an upswing, Jack Eisley's hand slapped flesh. The guard's hand. The guard named Vincent.

"Buddy, buddy, what the hell . . ."

Jack reached out and clamped on Vincent's forearm. . . . Vincent, be it his first or last name, it didn't matter, but he clung to the man like he was never going to let go.

. . . 41 seconds

Brian Burke forgot the ice bucket, forgot the Diet Coke, held the woman in his hands, looked at her beautiful face . . . beautiful, except for the blood trickling from her nose and ears.

. . . 42 seconds

If I've only one life, let me live it as a blonde!

—CLAIROL ADVERTISEMENT

2:50 a.m.
Sheraton Lobby

For the last time, Kowalski reassured the desk clerk that he was fine. "It's just a sprain. Feeling a little tipsy. You know how it is." All the while, he was scanning the elevator car to see where it stopped. He already had an idea of where that would be. Floor five. Diet Coke dork with the ice bucket.

You need to keep her within ten feet of you at all times, but do not allow her to get too close.

It was coming together for him: All night, she had been in the company of others. Made a point of it. Pick up one guy at the airport, ditch him for another. A new guy with a hotel room to himself. She needed someone close.

I don't want to die, but if I have to . . .

She gets alone, she dies.

Never mind how. Figure that shit out later.

She'd kicked him out of the elevator, made a suicide run back up the shaft.

But maybe it wasn't suicide. Maybe she was going for that Diet Coke dude on five. Hoping he'd still be there. Keep the company of another man. Stay alive another couple of hours.

"Sir, I'd feel a lot better if you sat down here and let me call someone to take a look at your wrist."

But that made no fucking sense. What kind of government-created disease, plague, or virus—and it had to be one of the above; otherwise, CI-6 wouldn't be having him traipse around Philadelphia with a severed head in a gym bag for shits and giggles—worked only when the victim was alone?

No wonder the handler wouldn't tell him anything. This kind of thing went beyond spurned ex-lover territory.

What was CI-6 messing around with now?

Kowalski ignored the desk clerk and walked over and punched the up button. He knew he'd probably find a dead body up on five, if she'd made it that far. Which, okay, was not a great situation. He'd rather have Kelly tell him more. But if need be, he could liberate her pretty head from the rest of her body, give her a little reunion with Ed in the Adidas gym bag, and search for answers elsewhere. His handler and CI-6 weren't the only people in the United States with access to a laboratory.

"Sir?"

Kowalski turned, smiled, and waved at the desk clerk with his bad wrist. It hurt like fuck; he'd really torn something in there.

But given the circumstances, it was simply the badass thing to do.

2:52 a.m.
Sheraton, Room 702

Jack was amazed at how easily the lies slipped out of his mouth. He knew Mr. Charles Lee Vincent—that was the guard's name; another mystery solved—wouldn't believe the crap about the Mary Kates and nanomachines and Ireland and San Diego. Jack still hardly believed it, and he'd almost had his brain explode inside his skull.

So he needed to tell Mr. Charles Lee Vincent something he'd believe. Something that would keep him around.

"Listen, I have an extreme anxiety disorder. You saw an example of it a few minutes ago."

Ah, you silver-tongued devil, you. Pile it on thicker.

"My psychotherapist told me that being alone for more than a few seconds could lead to stroke."

Charles Lee Vincent's brow furrowed. "Okay, sir. I hear you."

"You have to understand. You can't leave me alone. Not for a second."

"I understand. But *you* need to understand that I have a job to do. And that includes calling the police, so we can catch the guy who did this."

The police. A few hours ago, Jack would have thrown his arms around the idea, French-kissed it. But now he followed it through to its natural conclusion. Jack in an interrogation room. Jack being offered a cup of station house coffee. Jack saying, "Officer, I'd like to report a murder." Officer saying, "Whose?" Jack saying, "My own." Jack watching the detective leave the room, close the door. Jack counting ten seconds before his brain exploded like a piñata.

And even if he were able to keep detectives in the interrogation room with him, what could he say to them? He had no proof that Kelly White existed. Wherever she'd gone, or had been taken, her bag was along for the ride.

"Okay, buddy, we believe you. We'll be right back with that coffee," the cops saying.

The door of the interrogation room closing.

Ker-bloooie.

"Just take me downstairs," Jack pleaded. "Let me sit with the guy at the front desk, and you can do what you have to."

That was his only chance. And from there, find a place with a lot of people. A crowded bar. Wait—it was close to three in the morning. Bars were closed. So were coffee shops and malls and post offices and food courts. . . . Oh Christ. This was Philadelphia in the middle of the night. A town where they reportedly rolled up the sidewalks after 6:00 P.M.

"Okay, I can do that. Come on. Let's get down there. That son of bitch took my cell—wait. Give me a sec to use the room phone, okay?"

Jack nodded, but then he realized what he was doing. The nightstand with the phone was on the other side of the room. Oh fuck. Was that more than ten feet away?

2:53 a.m.

For the past hour, nothing in Charles Lee Vincent's world had made a goddamned bit of sense. From Tokyopop and backward comics to tough guys who liked to choke people to this guy now . . . following him across the room, sitting close to him. Extreme anxiety disorder? Yeah, *extreme anxiety* that your wife is going to find out you had a hot blond hooker up here in your room. Tough titty said the kitty. It wasn't Charlie's problem. This guy had the bad luck to be in the wrong room at the wrong time. That's all.

Charlie told the front desk what he knew, rattled off a quick description, told them to seal the front doors until he got down there. He'd get the police over here now, and they'd go room to room if they had to.

Until they found the guy who liked to choke the air out of people. Charlie hoped he'd be with one of his ex-brothers on the force when they found this guy. They'd let him alone in a room with the fucker for a few minutes. Let *him* see what oxygen deprivation feels like. He also asked the details of the occupant of this room. Yep, as he'd figured. Married. Married, and damn near sitting on top of him in the bed. Like, hello? Ever hear of personal space?

"Um, ready to go downstairs, Mr. Eisley? There are plenty of people down there to keep you company."

2:55 a.m.
Sheraton Elevators, Right Bank, South Side

Jack worked out a plan on the ride down. More or less. Once he got to the lobby, he'd play up the anxiety disorder, make someone sit with him. Then he'd map out a plan. All he needed was proof that Kelly White's crazy story was true. The fact that hotel security saw some big bastard in a suit jacket show up to abduct her wasn't enough. He needed proof.

Those files in San Diego, specifically. He had to catch a cab, hop a plane to San Diego, go to the Westin Horton Plaza, grab the files, then call the police, the FBI, CIA, Homeland Security, and anybody else who would listen.

Except that he would be dead by 8:00 A.M.

The poison.

The *luminous toxin*.

He was most likely the only guy in Philadelphia with *two* things racing around his bloodstream—Mary Kates and luminous toxin—with the potential to kill him. Unless you counted AIDS-ridden crack whores. But even those sorry fuckers didn't have a time limit of five hours.

Think, Jack, think.

Even if he were in a plane that was taking off at this very minute, there was little chance he could be in San Diego by 8:00 A.M. Local time, sure, but the poison in his blood didn't care about time zones. When it did whatever it was supposed to do, Jack would be dead.

And that's even if he managed to stay within ten feet of a person the entire trip.

What if he had to use the bathroom?

With all of this racing around his head, he hardly noticed the elevator doors open. Charles Lee Vincent led him by the arm across the lobby, telling the desk clerk, "He needs someone to stay with him at all times."

And then the desk clerk was saying something about the Philly PD being on their way. "Christ, what a night. There's some lady passed out up on five, bleeding from her nose."

And then Vincent was responding, saying that he was going back upstairs to start looking for this son of a bitch. "Seal the front doors.... Jesus, didn't I tell you to seal the front doors?"

"I've never locked down completely. Where are the keys?"

"In my office, top drawer, lockbox marked with a black X in Magic Marker. You'll see the master key on the left. Says 'master' on it. Hit the revolving door, then the two on the sides."

"You got it."

Jack realized what was going on.

"Wait! Don't leave me!"

"That's right. You've got to stay with him."

"I'm just going to your office."

"He's got . . ." Charles Lee Vincent started to explain, then decided against it. "Look, I'll lock up. Stay with him, okay?"

As Vincent walked away, Jack realized that locking the front doors meant he'd be trapped in here. And then the police would arrive, and then, sooner or later, he'd be locked in a room for questioning. They wouldn't buy the anxiety stuff. In fact, they'd probably gather around the two-way mirror, passing around bags of potato chips, waiting to see him pop.

And that would be the end of Jack.

2:56 a.m.
Sheraton Hotel, Fifth Floor

Diet Coke guy had Kelly's head in his arms, and he was surrounded by other guests who had popped out of their rooms to see what the screaming was about. He looked up at Kowalski. Disappointment washed over his face when he saw that Kowalski wasn't an EMT. That quickly turned to rage when he recognized him.

"Hey! What did you *do* to her?"

Kowalski knelt down to examine Kelly. She was still breathing, but unconscious. Blood had spurted from her nose, ears . . . and yeah, he could see a little rimmed around the bottoms of her eyes, too. Diet Coke guy had some of it on his hands and lips.

"What's your name?"

"Brian."

"Brian, did you give her mouth-to-mouth?"

"She wasn't breathing. I saved her. And I asked you, What did you *do* to her?"

Kowalski sighed. "Spare me."

Brian tried to shove Kowalski backward, and it would have been impressive, had he connected. But Kowalski caught him by the wrist, taking care not to touch any of the blood, then twisted. Kelly's head bobbed in the guy's lap as he jolted.

"Ow!"

"See this? My girlfriend here's got AIDS. She's maintaining, but she passes out like this all the time when her T-cell count gets low. Wash off all of the blood you can. Scrub hard. Rinse your mouth out, too. You'll also want to get tested."

Brian turned white. Good, let him be afraid. Might be the thing that saves his life.

Truth was, whatever Kelly White was carrying, he'd probably already picked it up with the mouth-to-mouth thing. That's what chivalry gets you these days.

Kelly's head was gingerly lowered to the hallway carpet. Brian stood up, trying not to touch anything else, himself especially, then backed up and elbowed the up button on the elevator.

"Go ahead, wash up. I've got it from here."

Kowalski looked around the hallway.

"Go back to your rooms, folks. She's going to be okay once she gets hooked up to an IV."

He had a decision to make: Take her now, or later? He wasn't sure Kelly had a chance of making it down to D.C., as planned, without medical attention. Her breathing was shallow, and that much blood from the head was never a good sign. With the multiple distress calls of the past few minutes, the Sheraton was going to be swarming with uniforms. It was going to be tough carrying her out of there, past all of that. And his most recent instructions from his handler covered bringing her in alive, not dead.

The only chance she had was to let the EMTs take over from here. Hook her up, get her breathing stabilized. He wasn't equipped for any of that.

Kowalski could come back for her later. From the hospital or the morgue, if it came to that. Either would be easier to breach than this hotel in the next ten minutes. City EMT response times varied; he remembered reading that Philly had arguably the worst in the nation. Tonight, he hoped to be proven wrong.

Zero a.m.

She wanted to cry. He'd fought hard to force his air into lungs she couldn't feel. His lips mashed against hers, and she couldn't feel those, either. Maybe she was already crying. She wouldn't have been able to feel the drops on her cheeks.

She couldn't feel anything, but she could see and hear and think. That was the worst part.

She knew exactly what had happened.

Back in the lab, she'd overheard them speculating.

Partial engagement.

When the self-replicating supramolecular assemblies—oh, how the Operator hated the nickname Mary Kates, even from the beginning—were faced with a choice, they reset to zero. That's what must have happened to her. The doors of the elevator may have opened a full second, or a fraction of a millisecond, in time; that didn't matter to the Mary Kates. They reset to zero.

Leaving her brain-damaged in this oh-so-creative way.

This was not how she'd imagined it. She thought it would have been quick and efficient. And she hoped she'd live long enough for a bit of revenge.

Not to look up into the eyes of another man she'd doomed to the grave.

Her Diet Coke–loving savior.

Pressing his lips to hers, genuine concern in his blue eyes.

And then the other one showed up. The one the Operator sent.

"What's your name?"

"Brian."

"Brian, did you give her mouth-to-mouth?"

Yeah, this guy knew the score. But he wasn't a complete dick. Here, he was warning Brian—her savior had a name—to wash up, rinse out his mouth, like that would help. At least it was a gesture of humanity.

And then the Operator's man looked into her eyes, and somehow *sensed she was still in there, because he touched her chin with his index finger and spoke to her.*

"Now that wasn't very smart."

3:05 a.m.
Sheraton Lobby Eighteenth Street

The security guy, Charles Lee Vincent, had locked the front doors, much to the displeasure of a curly-haired guy in a tuxedo, who was missing his tie and had his cummerbund slung rakishly over his shoulder. Vincent didn't seem to give a shit. He pressed the master key into the desk clerk's hands and said, "Only for the cops and EMT guys. Got it?" He got it. And for the next nine minutes—Jack watched them tick by on the clock mounted above a shimmering koi pool in the middle of the lobby—they stayed locked. The curly-haired guy threatened all kinds of violence, both physical and legal. The desk clerk didn't seem to give a shit, either.

Now the cops had finally arrived. Showtime. Red and blue lights danced across the walls of the lobby. If the lobby lights had been dimmed, it would have looked like Disco Night at the Sheraton.

Jack got ready. All he needed was a cab to be outside those doors. This was a hotel. And sure, it was three o'clock in the morning, but cabs flocked to hotels like iron fillings to a magnet, right? Once he was in a cab, he could get to the airport. There were a lot of people in airports, no matter what time of day. He could feign an illness, get a security escort. Hang with that person the whole time. Buy a flight to D.C. He could use the home-equity credit card. They'd always kept that for emergencies, and Theresa hadn't closed out the account yet. If this didn't qualify for emergency, he didn't know what would.

In D.C., he'd go to the FBI. The CIA. Homeland Security. Whoever. Someone who would listen to his story, then dispatch somebody to the Westin Horton Plaza in San Diego and verify everything.

Somebody in the government had to be around at this time of the morning.

All he had to do was get into a cab, and he would have a chance to breathe again, and think this through a bit more. But D.C. still seemed like the right move.

There. A flash of dark yellow and black in a checkerboard pattern.

Go, go, go.

Slip past the bustle. Pray no one paid him any mind. Quick glance at Charles Lee Vincent: busy with an EMT chick. Laughing about something, probably a dumb joke to break the tension. Yeah, laugh it up. You're not the ones whose brains could explode at any given moment. Out the door, from the air-conditioned cool into the damp summer night. The cab, dead ahead.

Jack reached around to pat his butt cheek; his wallet was still there.

Funny if he didn't have that, huh? He could go back and tell Charles Lee Vincent all about it: You're never going to believe what I forgot up in my room. Har har har . . .

The cab rocketed away.

Fuck almighty. Was there even a passenger in the backseat? No, not that Jack could tell. Did he get a sudden call? Or had someone called ahead and said, "Hey, let's screw with Jack Eisley's life a little more"?

Jack found himself standing alone on the sidewalk as the seconds ticked away.

He scanned the sidewalk to his right, along the side of the hotel and up the length of Rittenhouse Square: no one. Then to his left. There. A couple, walking away from him, arms intertwined.

Go back inside, or race forward?

Forward.

Jack jogged, then power-walked, then tried to feign a normal pace. It didn't work. The taller one of the two, a woman, looked behind nervously. Jack blew air through his mouth, then offered a sheepish grin. The woman turned back and hurried the pace a bit. That grin wasn't fooling anybody. Jack now saw that her companion, the shorter one, curly brunette hair, was also female. Both were young. They must be walking home together after a night out clubbing, he figured, or whatever it is young women do in Philadelphia late on a Thursday night.

Ten feet. How far was ten feet?

So damned tough to judge. How long was a car? About ten feet? Did he need to keep a car length's pace behind these girls?

His head throbbed.

The women looked at each other; one whispered and the other nodded. The curly-haired girl appeared to be rooting around in her purse for something. *Christ, they think I'm a mugger.* Then again, why wouldn't they think that?

Down the street, rushing toward them beneath the mercury vapor lights, was salvation: another cab.

The taller nudged her companion to the right, shot her hand high in the air. High beams flashed and the cab swerved to the left, increasing speed. Jack ran forward, almost pushing the women aside. The cab must have thought he was going to race right into its path, because it braked hard.

The throbbing in his head worsened.

Fingers hooked under the door handle. It was greasy.

"Hey! Fucking asshole!"

"Medical emergency," Jack muttered, and yanked open the door.

"Sir, those girls hailed me first."

"I don't care. Just drive."

Jack slid across the seat and slammed the door shut. Then he autolocked the back door. The taller girl, whose eye shadow was eerily dark, and lipstick unearthly white, pounded on the window, shouted, "Asshole!"

The cabbie turned around and regarded him carefully. "Wait. I know you. You're the guy who puked in my cab before."

"Could you please just drive? I have plenty of money."

"You're not feeling sick again, are you?"

Another pound, one that shook the cab. "Motherfucker!"

And a tug at the door.

"I didn't puke in your cab. We pulled over, remember?"

Jack saw that the curly-haired girl was walking around the back of the cab, headed for the other door. He reached across and locked that door, too.

"God, you're a dick. This is no way to treat women."

"Fifty bucks just to drive away. *Now.*"

Angry slapping on the other door now. One slapper, one pounder—these girls made quite a team. Pretty soon, the tall one would peel back the roof of the cab and reach down for Jack, opening her jaws wide, endless rows of teeth . . .

"Just fucking go. It's life-and-death."

The cabbie shifted his vehicle to drive and gave a short burst of horn. Both girls jumped back, a bit startled. The cab lurched forward, the engine coughed, and then the driver continued up Eighteenth Street.

"Okay, Life and Death. Where do you want to go?"

"The airport."

"Again?"

"Fuck the flat rate. Charge me whatever you want. I need to get to the airport."

"Well, here's the sad thing. I'm not going anywhere near the airport. I'm off duty."

"What do you mean? You just picked me up."

"You notice the meter's off? I thought I was going to pick up those two ladies back there. Odds are, they were headed somewhere in Center City. I thought I'd make a last buck before punching out."

"I need to get to the airport as fast as I can."

"I would, but I got an errand to run. There's a package that needs to make it to a friend of mine at Fourth and Spring Garden. That's not on the way to the airport."

"I'm desperate."

"I can see that. You've had a night, haven't you?"

"Please. I just need a ride to the airport."

"Tell you what. Indulge me for a few minutes, and I think we can work something out."

Jack rested back into the seat. Whatever. He'd been indulging people all evening. Why not a cabdriver?

"Only a few minutes?"

"Not even. Say, you're not a Mormon or anything, are you?"

3:15 a.m.
Little Pete's

It was too soon for another breakfast. Worse yet, he was alone this time. Ed's head was tucked away behind the front desk of the Sheraton. Least Ed had company—plenty of cops and rescue workers and hotel staff—buzzing around him. Not Kowalski. He was totally and utterly alone, sitting at a table recently wiped down by a stocky Slavic woman with at least three hairs growing out of a mole on her chin. Good smile, though. So there's her.

Kowalski spun his cell phone on the tabletop and stopped it with a single index finger. It landed on the number one. He held it there; the phone speed-dialed.

This is Katie. Leave a message and I'll get back to you as soon as I can.

No jokes, no cutesy voice. That was Katie. Businesslike in every way except the important ones.

It had been months now, but he hadn't called to cancel the voice-mail service from her local phone provider. She had no other relatives—her half-brother was out of the picture—so there was nobody else to cancel it for her. Kowalski kept it going just to hear her voice. Seventeen words. That's all he had left. Every week, he called the access number to erase all of the hang-up calls. He was the only one who called her phone number anymore. Sometimes, he'd hang on the line, and he'd hear his own sigh. He hadn't known he sighed till then. He'd always thought he had better control than that.

The phone on the tabletop vibrated. It looked like a hovercraft, gliding over a sea of Formica.

Kowalski answered it.

His handler.

"How close are you? I have someone coming in to meet you in a little over an hour."

"You should run out to the Seven-Eleven, get a Yoo-hoo and a couple doughnuts for your guest. It's going to be awhile. Our girl's out of the picture for a bit."

Kowalski expected a quick rejoinder; that was his handler's style. Their conversations were like cutthroat racquetball. Bat one right at her head, she'd return the serve and there'd be a hard little explosion in your nuts.

This time, though, nothing.

"You're there, right?"

"Define 'out of the picture.'"

"Taken to the hospital. Something was wrong with her—she was bleeding from her nose and mouth. But still breathing."

Kowalski might have been imagining things—it was late—but he thought he heard his handler gasp. He tried to assure her.

"Give me a few hours, I'll recover her, dead or alive, and bring the matching set down to you. Okay?"

"That's not what I had in mind. Hold, please."

Kowalski held. Holding, no big deal. That was his thing. Hang out, endure the boredom, tempered by the thought that soon, oh so soon, the fun would start. The brief hot burst of joy: the weight of his finger on a trigger, the quick flash of a man's brains exploding out of an artfully executed shot. Nobody had picked up on the pattern yet, which partially delighted him, partially depressed him. If they were to take X rays of all of the skulls of the wise guys he'd killed over the past months, and laid them all on top of one another, they'd see that the entry holes formed a particular letter of the alphabet. Even the occasional *Sesame Street* viewer would see it. What starts with the letter *K*?

Katie.

Kowalski.

She used to joke about keeping her maiden name. Katie Kowalski? Sounded like a cheerleader. He'd call her "Special K," and make faces at her and short bus jokes, and she'd slap him—kind of hard, come to think of it—and . . .

"Your services are no longer required."

"Really."

"Good night."

"Wait . . . you're serious? Come on. I can still deliver what you want."

"No, you can't."

So true on so many levels.

And that was the end of their relationship.

3:30 a.m.
On the Way to Spring Garden Street

All the way up Eighteenth, speeding past construction sites and office towers and a giant cathedral and more construction sites and an underground expressway and row homes and then a left onto Spring Garden. Jack remembered the name of the street from the foldout map of Philly he'd purchased at O'Hare. Center City's northernmost boundary was Spring Garden Street. It sounded so pleasant on the map. But it didn't look like spring up here, and there certainly weren't any gardens. As the street numbers ticked down, everything looked increasingly industrial, as if civic leaders had simply thrown up their hands and said, "Well, it's not Center City anymore, build whatever the hell you want."

Eventually, the cab made its way to Third Street, hung a left, then turned into a shadowy alley. Jack didn't see a bar or a store or anything.

"What is this?"

"Best Sybian club in town, my friend."

"Best what?"

"Hang tight. Let me run this package upstairs; then I'll be back and I can take you down to the airport."

Alarm bells.

"No. Let me go with you."

The cabdriver hooked an arm around his seat and looked at Jack. "Best what, huh."

"I won't say a word. Let me go up with you."

"If it were up to me, that'd be fine. But it's a private club. I can't take you up there."

Of all of the random cabs he could have jumped into, Jack had to pick the one with a guy who doubled as a deliveryman for a Sybian club. Whatever the hell that was. *Sybia*. One of the former Soviet republics, maybe? The driver didn't have a Russian accent.

Was this a Russian mob joint? The driver turned off the ignition, and what little air-conditioning had been circulating in the car stopped.

"Crack open your door for air. I'll be back in a sec and—"

"No! Please!"

Jack opened his door and scrambled out of the backseat.

"Come on, chief. Don't make this weird."

"I'll pay you."

"It's not about the money. The people in this club wouldn't appreciate it. They wouldn't even like me talking about it, for Christ's sake."

"Name your price."

Jack meant it. There was enough on the home-equity card to cover whatever this guy had in mind. All for a ride to the airport. He took out his wallet from his back pocket to make sure the driver knew he was serious. There wasn't much cash left, but they could go to an ATM. A drive-thru. It'd have to be a drive-thru. Get a cash advance from his equity card.

The driver waited. He was considering it, obviously, but wanted Jack to throw out the first bid.

His wallet open, Jack looked down and saw her. Behind the laminate: a photo of his girl, Callie, playing inside a giant wooden airplane at their favorite playground. The smile on her face reassured him: Yes, this was all worth it. You want your daughter to grow up knowing a father, don't you?

Jack threw out a price.

The driver recoiled as if he'd tasted something rotten, so Jack threw out another one. This didn't offend the driver as much. But it took a third one to seal the deal.

3:31 a.m.
Little Pete's

Kowalski found everything he needed at Little Pete's. He'd asked to use the bathroom, knowing it had to be in the back, near the lockers and storage closet.

Changing your appearance doesn't require Lon Chaney–style theatrics. No hooks and wires, pinning your nose upward. At a distance, people recognize you by identifying characteristics like hair, physique, gait, clothing, and accessories. Facial recognition is secondary, at best. Want make sure someone doesn't recognize you? Simply change as many identifying characteristics as you can.

Kowalski raided the employee lockers—helping himself to brown-tinted sunglasses, a plaid jeff cap, a white short-sleeve button-down shirt, a beige windbreaker—then slipped into the bathroom. He had to be careful not to antagonize his wrist. He'd sprained it badly when Kelly had kicked him out of the elevator car.

He pushed his hair down on his forehead and thought about the limp he'd use. No, no limp. A smaller step. A mincing step. He left the Dolce & Gabbana on, since no other pants fit. The shirt worked, though, as did the glasses and cap. He looked older and slightly goofier. Outside the bathroom, Kowalski stuffed his black T-shirt in the back of the locker, then transferred the contents of his coat into the windbreaker.

When he left Little Pete's, no one seemed to notice.

A minute later, someone would ask, "Hey, is that guy in the dark jacket still in the bathroom?"

But by the time this did happen, Kowalski was already back at the Sheraton's front door, slowly walking backward, as if he were directing some rescue team into the building. A flash of his Homeland Security badge—the one with the embossed foil with the holographic flying eagles—got him into the employee lounge, where Kowalski was told to wait until Charles Lee Vincent got back; he'd want to liaise. Yeah. Okay. Whatever. Kowalski grabbed a server's jacket, slipped out of the lounge, and used the hotel staff elevator to make his way to the seventh floor. Along the way, he picked up a rolling luggage rack made of shining gold chrome. Rolled it back to 702, mostly using his good wrist. He hoped nobody had taken the bags yet.

In all of the fun and games, he'd forgotten all about them.

Philly PD was still in the room, so he rolled past and broke into another room a few doors down, using a passkey he'd found in the server's jacket. They had cleared the floor, so there wasn't a risk of running into a sleepy business traveler. Kowalski took off the jacket, walked back in with his Homeland Security badge. He could see it in the cops' eyes: Oh, Jesus, one of these assholes. They directed him to the lieutenant on the scene, who asked, "Can I help you?"

"Not really."

"If you need anything, ask. You check in downstairs?"

Kowalski didn't reply. He strolled around the room, looking bored, spied the luggage—Kelly White's bag, Jack Eisley's bag—already sealed in plastic and resting by the front door. Kowalski waited for his moment, then calmly picked up both bags and carried them to the other room. Jacket back on. Found an oversized piece of luggage, cleared out the contents. Ripped away the plastic evidence bags, then shoved the material inside somebody's trousers. Kelly's bag and Jack's bag went into the oversized piece of luggage, which was hunter green. Dropped it on the rack, escorted it outside and to the elevator bank. A member of Philly PD glanced up, didn't say a word. Even if they saw the evidence bags were missing, they'd assume someone else had carried them downstairs. This was an assault case, not murder. Not yet anyway.

Kowalski found an empty room down on five—hey, stick with what you know, right?—hauled the two bags from the larger one, put them on one of the double beds. He fished around in them, using his good hand.

Nothing terribly exciting in Kelly's, aside from a bottle of contact lens solution, Imodium wrapped in tinfoil, and a tube marked Tylenol, which was actually full of Antabuse. Did our girl have herself a little drinking problem? A random assortment of clothes and a surprising number of those little white plastic things that stores use to attach price tags to clothes. They were snipped in half and littered the bottom of her bag. Kelly White had done either a lot of buying or a lot of shoplifting.

He picked up a bra and held it to his nose. He didn't realize what he was doing until he'd already inhaled.

He had done the same thing when the police had brought him Katie's bag, the one they recovered at the Rittenhouse Square hotel where she had temporarily holed up with her bank robber brother. He had wanted to breathe in every last molecule of her that he could.

He had spent a lot of time with that bag.

Kowalski returned Kelly White's bra to her bag, feeling vaguely guilty. If she was dead, was she somehow looking at him now? Was Katie?

But it wasn't Kelly's bag he was interested in. It was Jack's. If he had a prayer of finding out what CI-6 wanted with Kelly White—no chance of his handler telling him—then he needed to find her companion: Jack.

He'd never left a mission incomplete before.

His handler's behavior was troubling.

Had they found out about his extracurricular activities with the Philadelphia branch of the Cosa Nostra?

And where they preparing to punish him for it?

The answers could be his only defense.

3:32 a.m.
The Hot Spot, Near Third and Spring Garden

It was a surprisingly small room—almost a vestibule, in fact—whose main feature was a bunch of curtained doorways that presumably led to other rooms. Could have been the second floor of a warehouse, except for the small bar, the vinyl-covered stools, and the dark red velvet curtains hanging from the ceiling. The scent of burning candles—plain wax, not scented—hung in the air. Before Jack had a chance to ask about the place, his driver had already disappeared through one of the doorways.

Thankfully, the place was small and full of people. This *was* 3:30 in the morning on a school night, right? Yet it looked like the lunchroom at a suburban corporate park. Suits galore. Hair still neatly parted, or combed forward and razor-cut.

Jack walked to the bar, which was cushioned with black leather and no bigger than the kind you find in somebody's finished basement. There was no menu, and he didn't see any beer taps. Or glasses. Or bottles.

A girl approached. She had black lipstick, nose piercings, and perfectly trimmed bangs that ran a disturbingly parallel line with her eyebrows. She cocked an eyebrow, which ruined the effect.

"Hi," Jack said, not knowing what to say next. Maybe this place had lost its liquor license and the drinks were kept somewhere else.

He looked down at the girl's chest and realized her torso had been strapped into a black lace corset. Her breasts were large and fat, and threatened to spill out over the top. Especially the right one. The father in Jack wanted to reach out and tuck it back into place, maybe straighten out her bangs while he was at it.

And by then, he knew what this place was, and why there was no booze at the bar.

He was about to laugh or panic, or maybe a little of both. But mostly laugh. Because he had lucked into the best-possible place for a man in his predicament, as unusual as it might be.

When you absolutely, positively, can't risk being alone? Visit an after-hours whorehouse in downtown Philly. It's the right choice, no matter how you look at it.

He needed to tip that cabdriver *huge*.

Morals aside—and let's face it, Theresa couldn't say a damn thing about his morals, not if what he'd suspected about her post-separation activities was true—this was what he needed. Somewhere he could think for a few minutes, or even an hour. He'd ask for a girl, pay her whatever she wanted, then ask her to sit with him for a while. She could stay dressed. She didn't have to say a word. Why hadn't Kelly thought of this?

The girl with the corset and bangs cleared her throat. Cocked that eyebrow again.

"I'd like some company," Jack said.

Some of the other guys turned to look at him. Had he said something wrong? Was there a code word?

The girl held out her hand.

Again, Jack was confused. Did she want to hold his hand? Or was she looking for payment in advance? Payment, most likely. He unbuttoned his back pocket and took out his wallet. Asked how much.

Wordlessly, the girl in the corset took the wallet from his hands and squeezed it into one of the tiny cubbyholes, which were in a row, built right into the wall. His wallet went in deep, then disappeared. Someone on the other side of the wall had taken it.

Maybe the wallet thing was a security issue; they'd hold on to it until business was done, so the working girls wouldn't be tempted to steal a little extra. Of course, the person behind the wall could be the one doing the stealing.

"Ready?" a voice behind him asked.

Jack turned around and saw his high school girlfriend, who was wearing a white tuxedo shirt, black slacks, and black boots. It wasn't his girlfriend, of course, but the resemblance was freaky. Same thin lips, long chestnut hair. She took him by the hand and led him through one of the curtained doorways and down a hallway to another room. He had seen enough movies to know what to expect: a Spartan bed, a nightstand, maybe a cheap piece of art on a wall.

But that wasn't what he got.

Inside the room was a short wooden table, and on top of that was a machine that looked like a saddle. Sticking out of the top of the saddle was a rubber nub a few inches tall. The saddle was electric. A cord ran down the side to an extension cord, which was taped along the floor.

The question had barely formed in his mind before the girl gently pushed him back against the wall and held both of his hands.

"Left or right?"

"What is that thing?" Jack asked.

"You'll see," she said. "Left or right?" After seeing the dumbstruck look on his face, she clarified: "Left- or right-handed?"

"Right."

The girl gently guided Jack's left hand to his heart, as if he were about to make the pledge of allegiance. Something clicked, and he felt cold steel against his wrist. Then another click, and a tightness around his bicep. His left arm was immobilized against his body and he was fastened to the wall.

The girl took a step back and smiled. "I've been waiting for you all day."

3:50 a.m.
Sheraton, Room 501

Jack Eisley's bag didn't yield dick, except for the fact that Jack was a boxer briefs kind of guy. And these days, who wasn't? There was also a piece of Sheraton stationery with "MK WHP SD" scribbled on it. Which could mean anything. Mr. Kent Whupped South Dakota. Make Whipped Sundae. Make White House President Sign Decree. Kowalski folded and pocketed it anyway.

No wallet or ID. Guy must have it with him. But the luggage tag bore the surname Eisley and a Gurnee, Illinois, address.

Okay, that waste of time was over. Next: Try another disguise, and play buddy-buddy with the man you nearly choked to death a short time ago. Mr. Vincent. He'd know where the cops were keeping Jack Eisley. A flash of his trusty Homeland Security badge, and he'd be in the room with him alone, piecing together the night's events. He could tell him what Kelly White was doing, flying around the country and generally causing trouble for married men and university professors alike.

Of course, Kowalski realized, he was making a big assumption.

Eisley might not still be alive.

That seemed to be the pattern for Kelly White's other male companions.

4:05 a.m.
Sybian Lounge, the Hot Spot

"Can I ask your name?"

"Call me Angela," she said, unbuttoning her tuxedo shirt to reveal a plain white bra beneath. The shirt was heavily wrinkled in places, and one of the cuffs looked like it had a splotch of tomato sauce on it. "What's yours?"

"Jack. So Angela isn't your real name?"

The girl looked scandalized. "My real name? Sorry. I don't do that. True names are powerful totems. Revealing my true name, without knowing yours, would lead to an imbalance of power. Do you want me to unbuckle your belt for you? Or can you do it with one hand?"

"I didn't realize you were going to fasten me to a wall; otherwise, I might have taken care of that ahead of time. Look, can we talk for a minute?"

Angela took another two steps backward and kicked off her boots, peeled off her black socks. The black slacks slid down her legs and bunched up on the floor. She stepped out of them. The floor was concrete. It looked cold to Jack.

"You come all the way here. At this time of night. In this kind of place . . . to talk? Oh, Jack, my man. You could have saved yourself a lot of money and gone to Silk City Diner down the street. There's always some interesting conversation there."

Her panties were purple but, like her bra, very basic. No satin, no thongs. Just functional, everyday underwear. The kind Jack's wife wore, except on their anniversary or for weddings.

"I need a moment to think," Jack said.

"And I want to get off," Angela said. "Very badly." She reached up and grabbed a remote that was hanging by a wire from the ceiling. She pressed a button. The plastic nub hummed to life, and even though Jack had never seen anything like it before, its design and purpose were suddenly clear. "Don't you?"

Jack didn't answer, because as soon as he figured out the saddle, another fact hit him cold. The saddle was across the room. Easily more than ten feet away.

And Angela was getting ready to mount it.

"No!" Jack yelled. "Wait!" He pushed his weight against his arm restraint; it was fiercely strong.

Angela took the remote in her hands and thumbed the button. The humming stopped. She looked wary. Afraid, even. *Fuck.* He couldn't afford to have her run out of the room. That would be his death sentence. The owners would come back and find a brain-dead white guy bolted to the wall. Explain *that* one.

Explain it to Donovan Platt.

Or Callie, someday.

Okay, Jack, calm down. *Callllm* down. Ask her for her help with something. Anything.

Then it came to him. His pants.

"I need help with this," he said, holding his belt buckle in his free hand.

"I can't touch you.... You know that, right? One of your buddies on the force explained this to you, I hope."

"Sure." *Force?*

"People can have all kinds of ideas. Like me being a hooker, or something. I don't play that way."

Angela walked up to him and unbuckled his belt. She smelled like she'd been in an Italian kitchen all night. There was perfume there, too, something warm and flowery and lush, but beneath that was the scent of garlic and tomatoes and even cigarette smoke.

She was careful not to touch his skin, only leather and buckle and fabric. And then his pants dropped to the floor.

Think, Jack, think....

"What if you moved that closer to me? That saddle thing?"

"The Sybian?"

Lightbulb. All of a sudden, the driver's reference to a "Sybian club" made sense. Clue phone, for Mr. Jack. Line one.

Angela regarded him carefully now. Suspicion was in full bloom. "This isn't your first time here, is it? Because I specifically requested that—"

"No, no . . . I'm just slow this late at night."

She looked at the Sybian, then back at Jack, who was still pinned to the wall with metal clamps and brackets.

"You seem like a nice guy. But I've had trouble before. In fact, I was the stone-cold bitch who insisted that they move that thing back a good ten feet, away from the wall. I'm all for the mutual masturbation, up until the point where you catch a hot load in the face."

What was Jack supposed to say next? That he was nearsighted? The words *mutual masturbation* echoed in his skull. The situation was finally starting to make sense. This wasn't a whorehouse or a strip joint. This was some kind of swingers club where nobody touched. Angela here wasn't an employee. *She was a member.* Right off work, most likely, from her waitressing gig. Some Italian restaurant. Serving manicotti and ravioli and meatballs and aching to finish her shift so she could sit in a room and hop on an electrically powered dildo-equipped saddle while some strange guy with his pants around his ankles yanked one off. Maybe she'd repeat the process a few times. Was this how the club got around a tilted male/female ratio? Men were good for one pop, maybe two. But women could be repeat customers.

"So I'm going to go over there, okay?" She took a tentative step backward.

"What if I didn't"—Jack searched for the phrase—"do anything? Just watched, I mean."

That suggestion, apparently, was as bad as not knowing how to identify the garden-variety Sybian.

"And I'm supposed to what, just watch you staring at me while I come?"

"Then unlock me. I'll be good."

"Until you decide to rape me. Uh-uh. No thanks." She patted his wrist. "Look, I've had a long night, and if it's okay with you, I want to hop on the machine and screw my brains out. If you don't want to jack off, whatever, at least humor me and pull your dick out. Or if you've changed your mind, I'll go get someone to escort you out of here. You tell me."

With a flick of her thumbs, her panties slid from her hips, then made their way down her legs. They stopped at her knees.

"So?"

"Thing is," Jack said. "I'm nearsighted."

4:10 a.m.
Security Office, the Sheraton

Kowalski found Just for Men hair dye in Room 508, along with a black leather jacket. Can you say *aging, overachieving fuckhead*? Probably out for a jog around Rittenhouse Square this early in the morning. Trying to outrun death. Good luck. Part of Kowalski wanted to stick around, say hi when he returned. Hey, guess what? All that running didn't mean dick! *Snap*.

The man's absence was all the better for Kowalski, of course. But still. The guy should be at home sleeping if he was worried about dying his hair blond. Less stress in your life.

A pair of black jeans from another room, along with a pair of reading glasses from still another—Kowalski nabbed 'em right from the nightstand in that case, with their sleeping owner two feet away—he was finally ready to say hello to Charles Lee Vincent.

Who didn't recognize him at all.

"So this is a DHS matter, huh?"

Kowalski smiled nervously, adjusted his glasses with his good hand. Kept his right tucked in the jacket pocket. His wrist was throbbing, and he didn't want it to give him away.

"If this is the guy we're looking for, then yes. He assaulted you?"

"He got lucky. If it hadn't been so late . . ."

"Of course. But don't feel bad. This man I'm after is well trained. Got deep with Mossad, did some mercenary work in Afghanistan."

"Still, I say he got lucky."

"You feeling okay, Mr. Vincent?"

"I'm fine. But I'm standing here thinking, you look so goddamned familiar. You sure we haven't met up somewhere else?"

"Pretty sure," Kowalski said. "Unless you used to be on the force here, because I was out in San Diego. Possible we met at a convention or something." That sounded vague enough to be true, and wide open enough to send Mr. Vincent here searching his memory bank in the wrong part of the building.

"Yeah, maybe that was it."

Kowalski asked about Jack Eisley, the guy in the room with the blonde. Vincent didn't know much: He had his driver's license and credit-card info on file, so Kowalski was welcome to that. Then Vincent explained how he'd escorted the guy down here, because Eisley claimed to have panic attacks if he was left alone, which seemed like grade-A bullshit to him, but whatever. Not good business to upset a Sheraton customer, so he'd humored him. Brought the guy down to the lobby, had a colleague baby-sit him. Next thing, though, the guy bolted. Probably worried that his wife would find out about the blonde in his room. Like that would do any good. Sooner or later, the cops were going to want him.

"And like I said, we've got his stuff on file right here."

"What do you have in the way of cameras out front?"

Vincent's eyes lighted up. "I'm ahead of you."

After switching over to the backup recorder, Vincent pulled the current digital tape and popped it in the playback machine, then used a large plastic knob to rewind back to 3:00 A.M., right around when the cops arrived, he explained. The more he moved the knob to the right, the faster the tape rewound. A few minutes went by, Vincent eased up on the knob, and then yeah, sure enough, Jack Eisley had left the building.

"Looks like he was headed south on Eighteenth Street," Vincent said. "Could be anywhere by now."

Kowalski kept watching the screen. Not much was happening.

"Waiting to see if he'll double back? Don't know what good it will do you. I saw that scumbag you're looking for a lot more than Eisley. We rode up in the elevator together. I'd be able to spot him in a second."

"You would, huh?" Kowalski said. "Wait—there."

A yellow blur on the screen. A cab, racing up Eighteenth Street. Kowalski twitched the knob slightly to the left and rewound the tape a few seconds. The cab sailed past again, and Kowalski returned the knob to dead center. The cab was frozen in the middle of the street.

"You can't see who's in there," Vincent said. You can barely see the driver's hands."

"But I can see the medallion on the hood. What button can I use to bring up the focus on this?"

"You're not going to be able to read those numbers."

Kowalski ignored him, punched more buttons. "You know how the blonde is doing?"

"I heard she was being taken to Pennsylvania Hospital, but it doesn't look good. Fucker probably pulled the same thing on her. Squeezed the air right out of her lungs, deprived her of oxygen too long. You should have seen it up there on five. Unless you already have."

"I have," Kowalski said, still working on the focus.

"Then you saw the blood on the carpet. How hard do you have

to choke somebody before they start spurting blood? I mean, fuck. That's hard. You say this guy was with Mossad?"

"They know no mercy. Hey, you got a pen and paper? I got those numbers."

"Holy shit. You did? This something they teach you at Homeland Security?"

Not really. Prior to 9/11 and the creation of DHS (and CI-6), prior to active CIA status, prior to the military, prior to University of Houston, Kowalski was an AV geek for a short while. Manned the control booth for a handful of basketball games, screwing around with the studio gear for a couple of weeks, but that was it. Brother Harry begged him to come back, but he needed to move on. With high school activities, Kowalski was like a locust. He wanted to try it all, master none. No baggage, even in high school. If he were to head back to his high school reunion—and oh, how watching that John Cusack movie made him long to do just that—he wouldn't be surprised to find that everybody sorta remembered him but nobody knew him.

"We learn a little of everything, brother," Kowalski said, locking eyes with Vincent. "Look, I'm going to run this down. If I catch this bird, I'll bring him back for the Philly boys."

As he said this, he pressed the button that would erase the five minutes of digital tape on which the cab appeared.

4:22 a.m.
Philadelphia International Airport

Within three minutes of his plane landing at Gate A22, the Operator was walking through the ridiculously oversized international-arrivals hall, with its images depicting Philadelphia as America's birthplace. Cute.

His seatmate on the plane hadn't been so lucky. He was a pale

Scot with some kind of strange rash on his hands. His eyebrows were so faint, you could hardly distinguish them from the pasty flesh of his forehead. It wasn't that he talked so much as that he scratched . . . and scratched and scratched, for most of the flight down from Toronto. Must have caught some kind of deal over from Edinburgh. The Operator didn't do connecting flights. If there wasn't an available flight between the two points he wanted to travel, then he simply chartered a plane. Which he probably should have done in this case. Sitting next to Mr. Itchy for the one-and-a-half-hour flight . . . maddening. Then there was that problem of changing his destination from D.C. to Philly at virtually the last minute. So yeah, he was in a bad mood. And maybe he had acted a little harshly when he decided to take it out on the Scot by pulling a stewardess aside and showing her his Department of Defense badge and telling her about the Scot sitting next to him, who, he said, was talking about all of the Pakis he was going to blow up on his trip to America with nail bombs and . . . and that was all it took. It would be a long while before the itchy Scot and his rucksack would see the beautiful patriotic artwork inside the international-arrivals hall. If ever.

Escalator to hallway and directly to a cab outside. No bag to claim; whatever the Operator couldn't carry with him at any given moment, he bought.

Interestingly enough, the cab had a Paki driver. "My friend the Scot would have loved you," the Operator said.

"Sir?"

"Don't mind me. I often get lost in my own fictions. Pennsylvania Hospital, please."

He wondered about her. What two weeks of running would have done to her face, her body. He'd been used to seeing her every day in the lab. Would she look the same to him? He remembered a certain college girlfriend who'd dumped him; he'd been able to score revenge sex six months later, but it wasn't the same. She looked different. Even tasted different. It was quite unsatisfying.

So would it be the same with her? With "Kelly White," as she'd been calling herself?

See there. Even the name was different. That alone would have taken its toll on her features.

His contact within CI-6 had said she'd been "incapacitated." The Operator hoped that she wasn't too far gone to be brought back. They had unfinished business, the two of them. Maybe they could go to a secret prison in Thailand. Where it would be just the two of them, once again. Even for a few hours.

Zero a.m.
Pennsylvania Hospital

She was awake but not awake. In this world but not of it. She could feel the sensations of movement, of hands, of needle sticks. She'd been this way since collapsing onto the carpet of the hotel hallway, and since then she had not been alone. If she had, the Mary Kates would have finished their job. She would be dead.

I should have thought of this days ago, she thought, and imagined herself laughing. And that was all she could do, because she was still paralyzed.

Which was going to make it difficult to get out of this one.

Oh, she was cracking herself up here tonight. This morning, tonight. Whenever. Wherever.

She stared at the insides of her eyelids and saw fields of stars and pulsars rushing past her. She wished she could open her eyes at least. See where she was. It was a hospital; she could tell that much. She could hear the beeping and gushing of oxygen tanks and faraway voices on an intercom. She could smell the harsh disinfectant. But it would have been nice to know which hospital.

She had been born on Holles Street, the National Maternity Hospital in Dublin. Was there any kind of symmetry with this hospital? Maybe this was America's National Maternity Hospital. National to National. Dublin to Philadelphia. The last of the great emigrations.

Because soon enough, she would be left alone in a room in this hospital, and she would die.

What gave her comfort in these final minutes—and she was sure that it was just a matter of minutes—was how much she'd accomplished in these past two weeks.

How gravely she'd wounded the Operator.

He'd never be able to recover from this.

And she would never have to look at his face, that mask of balding banality, those piercing black eyes like a manhole cover on a sewer of insecurity and depravity.

She never wanted to see that face again.

She preferred the dark.

4:30 a.m.
Sybian Lounge

Angela seemed to be considering Jack's proposal, as ludicrous as it was. My contact lenses, he'd explained. They dried up a couple of hours ago; I had to take them out.

"You know, I'm not like most women," she told him. "I like to look. But then again, I've always been a tomboy, so maybe there's that. Some circuits crossed in my head, you know?" Jack said he knew what she was talking about. He didn't.

Finally, she agreed to move the table closer, but she warned him: "If you spurt all over me, I'll beat the hell out of you." Jack said he could agree to that.

But the few seconds it took her to move the table closer were excruciating.

First the ticking away of the ten seconds, which Jack counted off too fast, and he hit ten and nothing happened and he thought he'd be fine and was relieved to think that maybe the effect had worn off or he hadn't been infected as badly as he'd thought. . . .

And then the first nauseating twist, deep in his brain.

Do not scream.

Then belt straps, wrapped around his skull and tightening, like someone had slid a steel rod through the buckle and was rotating, squeezing the leather against his hair and scalp and skull.

Scream and it's over.

And the icy hot needle sticks in his brain, with inflatable black balloons rapidly expanding . . .

Scream and she'll run, and the Mary Kates will finish you off. . . .

Then, Angela's palms were warm against his cheeks. "Hey," she said. "Are you okay?"

Jack was incoherently grateful, and he mumbled something about being tired. She gave him an uneasy smile in return. "You ready?" she asked politely. Of course he was ready. He'd do anything for her now. She'd come back to him; she had saved him from the abyss. He wasn't thinking of Theresa. Or his daughter, Callie. He was thinking only of the woman who was standing in front of him, wanting to watch him masturbate. How easy the slide into debauchery.

The Sybian hummed to life, and Angela mounted it.

"Take it out," she ordered.

She was shaved down to her skin, not a single strand of hair in sight. Jack'd been lying, of course. His contact lenses were in and his eyesight was perfect. And he could vividly see the buzzing fat rubber tip press up against the lips of her vagina. Her fingers worked the area for a few seconds, presumably trying to tease out her clitoris. Angela looked up at him.

"Dick?" she asked, nodding to his crotch.

Jack fumbled a moment, and though he could have sworn he felt nothing but white-hot fear from the hips down, as if his legs had completely melted away into the white noise—and buzzing—of the room, he was faintly relieved to find he had a modest erection.

He took his cock out of his pants.

Angela moaned in delight and thrust her hips against the Sybian. Her straining leg muscles made it look as if she could use her heels and knees to snap the saddle in half.

"Rub it," she said, eyes shut.

Jack was only slightly dismayed to find himself doing what he was told, and his body responding. . . .

Angela bucked as if he were touching her.

"Down to the head."

The door kicked open behind her.

Someone said, "Step aside, sweetie. We've got to ask this man a few questions."

Jack, with his dick in his hand, looked past Angela and saw two men standing in the doorway. A dark, curly-haired man in a suit, and an Aryan Nations poster boy, also in a suit, which was considerably more wrinkled. Aryan Man was more muscular, but the other guy looked harder, somehow. Leaner.

"We didn't see your FOP card in your wallet," said the curly-haired man.

"You're not on the job, are you, Mr. Eisley?" said his partner.

"We know you're not, by the way. We ran your license. You're not a cop."

The buzzing stopped. Angela quietly dismounted. Brushed strands of hair away from her forehead.

"I came here with someone," Jack said, trying to find his dick. Where was it? Oh God, oh God. Let's get it away. Quickly. "The cabdriver. He's still here, delivering something."

"What's his name, then?"

"You like being married, Mr. Eisley?" asked the curly-haired man. "What's she doing right now, your wife, back in Gurnee, Illinois? Think she knows you're here?"

Angela, meanwhile, seemed to float backward, gathering up her clothes from the concrete floor. Mostly, she looked disappointed, like she'd had a long day at the office and had been looking forward to that first ice-cold beer, and, wouldn't you know it, the damn tap was busted again. As she moved away, the two guys in the suits loomed closer.

"Want us to give her a call for you?" Aryan Man asked.

"I just want to leave."

"Gotta head back to your newspaper convention, right? Is that why you're here, newsman? Or you planning on writing about this place?"

Looking back, Jack couldn't have come up with a way to make this night any worse. His plans for Philadelphia had been so simple: meet Donovan Platt and try to avoid castration. And everything had gone so gloriously wrong, in ways he couldn't have imagined. Of course, Jack had always suffered from a lack of imagination.

Like this now. The curly-haired guy, holding up the cell phone. "Let's give her a call now, whaddya think?"

Jack hadn't figured on that at all.

Zero a.m.
The Dublin Inside Her Head

But the face, his face, that's all she could see now. *With nowhere to retreat but within her own mind, she kept coming back to him. It had been easier to avoid his face in the past two weeks, with the flurry of activity: booking flights, changing clothes, figuring out how she was going to use the bathroom . . . all in the presence of other people. Other men. That was the worst part of it, probably. The lack of privacy at the most intimate level. It's what he'd had in mind all along. Even before their* falling-out. Before this series of disasters she had initiated, and he had upped the ante. Him. Him. Him. She suffocated on him. Choked on him. Vomited him. Bled him.

All she'd ever wanted was to be alone.

It was why she had left university early, moved out of her mum's house, replied to that advertisement in the Dublin Times: "The Celtic Tiger Is Roaring! Exciting New Opportunities in Scientific Research. Apply Now, Citywest Business Campus, Saggart, County Dublin." She'd sent her résumé, glossing over the fact that she hadn't exactly finished her master's and had opted instead to stock shelves in a Waterstone's branch while she figured out her next move. The bookstore gig didn't pay enough to leave home, but this could. And it was something that vaguely promised that her biology degree would be put to some use.

She had been stunned when she was summoned for an interview within two days. The Operator met her at the door personally; she was stunned again to learn he was an American. The interview was brief. He asked many questions about where she grew up and what she wanted to do and then gave her the tour, and made a big deal out of all the security protocols. She felt like she was on the set of some spy show, like Alias or Queen and Country. Iris scans. Thumb-pad sensors.

The Operator had told her a fake name at first, of course: Matt Silver. (Only later did he wink and confide in her: "You know, that's not my real name. I'm not supposed to tell anyone that. And don't tell anyone this, either: We're a secret wing of MI5. British intelligence. They're paying us handsomely for our scientific innovation.")

He had hired her on the spot.

He had asked her out to dinner the third day of her employ. Probably thought he was showing restraint.

Sea bass, he insisted. She told him she didn't like dark fish with bones, and, like, hello, she lived here. But he told her it was the best, and he wanted her to have the best. What was the point otherwise? She remembered opening the door of her new apartment—after an awkward fumbling at the door, during which they kissed, which was not what she had intended at all—and sitting down on her futon, the one piece of furniture she had been able to take from home, and staring at the dingy white wall for an hour or more. Wondering if she'd exchanged one prison for another. At least she'd had twenty-three years to learn the rules of the first one.

By the end of the first week, they were "dating." He expected her to work late hours. Help him with a special project, for which he'd received special funding.

And when he explained it, and his eyes lighted up, she did feel her heart swell for him. It was an amazing project:

Proximity.

No more missing children.

No more kidnapping.

No more hostages.

No more international manhunts.

A small voice in her head said, Yes, and no more privacy. But in the months they worked together, the concept of privacy seemed to fade anyway.

Besides, there was nothing like them.

The self-replicating supramolecular assemblies.

"Proximity."

Or as she called them, "the Mary Kates."

She saw the accounts, so much money being pumped into their small research facility, which consisted of half a dozen technicians, Matt, and herself. Before long, she was named associate research chief, and her own salary was insane, and Matt had even found a way to fudge her master's degree for her. (She'd had only a semester and a half left to go; she didn't feel like she'd cheated.) She sent money back to her mum, and the first words out of her dad's mouth: "She's turned whore."

Then she saw the files that the Operator had tucked away. Shadow files, right on the same hard drives they used every day.

He must have thought her dumb. He'd left a box open one day. She couldn't venture a guess as to the password, so the next morning she spread talcum powder on the keys. When the Operator entered the system, she had him paged to a different part of the facility. Then she checked the keys. Wasn't hard to tell which keys had been touched. A, S, E, V, N.

She thought about it for a few moments. Evans? Vanes?

Wait.

Her own name.

Vanessa.

And what she saw, once she made it to his shadow files, turned her stomach.

4:37 a.m.
South Eighteenth Street

After he retrieved his gym bag—almost forgot about you Ed, ol' pal—Kowalski waited outside for the cab. When it pulled up, he had to laugh. It was the same guy who'd taken him to the airport last night. The dark-skinned guy who was going on about the flat fee. He wondered if there was a flat fee to the place Jack Eisley had gone. Take you from any swank Center City hotel to the S-M perv-out dive of your choice.

This one, the Hot Spot, was a real screamer: mutual masturbation. Kowalski had strong-armed the cab company to divulge the name of the driver corresponding to the medallion number he'd plucked off the video. Another call revealed the man's cell number. A quick call to the driver, and one mild threat later, he had a name and an address. And yeah, his boy Jack was still there. Having a good time in a back room, the way the driver told it. "Bribed me just to get into the place," the driver said. "And I don't even know where the hell he is."

Next, Kowalski called his favorite freak, a glam-vampire dude named Sylvester, who lived up in the Bronx, to give him some background. Last thing he needed to do was walk into a place like this blind.

The Hot Spot was relatively tame, Sly said. Married guys, mostly, went there to whack off while they watched women straddle high-powered Sybians. Direct clitoral stimulation with double the horsepower of any Black & Decker device. Guys liked it. Gals *really* liked it. Moaning, talking, sweating, but no touching. Because that would be adultery.

Ho, ho, people did amuse him sometimes.

But why would Happy Jack go there? He meets some saucy blonde, gets nearly strangled to death, then goes to an after-hours knuckle-shuffle club?

Unless . . .

Unless he didn't want to be alone.

Knew something bad would happen if he did.

"Third and Spring Garden," Kowalski told the driver. "Is there a flat fee from here to there, by chance?"

Zero a.m.
The Dublin Inside Her Head (continued)

Oh, she planned ahead before confronting him. This wasn't a decision made lightly. First, she created a new identity, courtesy of a girl she knew from childhood who'd died of brain cancer. Kelly Dolores White. Armed with a birth date, it wasn't difficult for Vanessa to build a new identity out of Kelly's ashes, starting with a driver's license. She had to take the dreaded test again, but so be it. She passed. Unlike the first time, when she'd failed and then had to wait nearly a year for another chance. Next came credit cards, and, being dead for nearly seventeen years, Kelly Dolores White had perfect credit. Together, those were used for a passport, the gold standard in identification. If Vanessa needed to vanish, she'd simply become Kelly White.

Meanwhile, she couldn't help herself. She became distant. But how could you pretend to love someone you were about to destroy?

The Operator knew something was coming—a boom about to be lowered. He called. And called. And called. And stopped by, unannounced. Then called again later, to make sure everything was okay.

She told him she just needed a little space.

"Space," he said.

"That's it. Just space."

"To see other people."

"No. Not at all."

"Space," he repeated.

Hurriedly, a package was prepared: USB key, documents, samples of Proximity in vials. She packaged one set and mailed it anonymously to MI5 headquarters—the Thames House in London. Another she packed in her travel bag, the one she carried with her everywhere. The one with Kelly Dolores White's license, credit cards, and passport.

When she could stand no more, she set a dinner date with him at La Stampa. The same restaurant as their first date. She insisted he order the sea bass.

And when the pinot noir was poured, she told him, "You're not going to finish this project."

All he could do was stare at her.

She continued: "What we've been working on and what you've told me are two different things. I thought I was helping you build a tool that would save lives. You're creating a weapon that can kill thousands with the push of a button. You're accountable to no one. I've checked the financials, Matt. We're not a quiet MI5 research facility. We're rogue. You plan to create this thing, then sell it to the highest bidder. You even have someone inside the American government willing to help you. Well, I'm going to stop you. Both of you."

"Really," he said.

"MI5 has all of the evidence they need, Matt. You're finished."

"Interesting," he said.

The pinot noir sat in their glasses, undisturbed.

"So are you *finished*?" he asked.

Vanessa nodded warily. What was he doing? Just staring like that?

Matt, the Operator—both fictitious names; Christ knows what handle he'd been born with—slapped something on the table. A thick envelope. Vanessa recognized the handwriting.

The envelope full of evidence she'd mailed to MI5. Postmarked but not delivered. Retrieved from the mailbox. How had he known?

"And I know about the virus you uploaded," he said.

An hour before dinner, with a disc she'd purchased on the black market—a superlethal data corrupter. She'd inserted it into every drive in the lab, then executed the program. She thought she'd killed the Mary Kates.

He reached out across the table and grabbed her hand. "Let me tell you about needing a little space."

She didn't see it until the last second. The thick needle in his right hand. He stabbed her in the meaty part of her right forearm and thumbed the plunger home.

"Space," he said. "The final frontier."

"Women like you don't deserve space. So I've fixed that. A matter of a simple command I inserted into the program. Before you fried it. And you know what? You're going to be very sorry you did that. Because I've prepared something very special for you."

"What have you done?" she asked, but deep inside, she knew exactly what he had done. He'd tried to get her to play guinea pig for months now, but she'd resisted. He'd wormed his way into her life easily enough without them. Imagine what he would be like with the Mary Kates inside her.

She was about to find out.

"Unless you have someone within ten feet of you at all times," he said, "*you'll die.*"

He enjoyed a long drink of pinot noir, nearly draining the glass.

"Looks like you're going to be a guinea pig after all. With special emphasis on the word pig.*"*

He took the napkin from his lap, slid back in his chair, stood, folded the napkin, and rested it on the empty plate in front of him. They had ordered, but the food hadn't arrived yet.

"Good luck, slut," he said. "I'll be looking forward to reading your autopsy report."

4:38 a.m.
Sybian Lounge

The dial tone, then ten digits, punched rapid-fire. The cell phone pressed to his ear. Ring tone. "Tell her, 'Hi, honey, it's me.'"

Ring tone. Ring tone. Ring tone.

"Okay, you've proved your point, stop it...."

"Hello?" Theresa's voice sounded weird. Maybe it was dry from sleeping with her mouth open.

The cell phone was shoved into the side of his head. His ear started to throb.

Tell her, the curly-haired man pantomimed.

"Hi, honey," Jack said. "It's me."

"What? Who is this?"

The curly-haired guy took the phone away and put it to his own face. "Hey there, Mrs. Eisley. How are you doing this morning? Hope I didn't wake you. Look, I've been hanging out with your husband, Jack, and I have the most amazing thing to tell you."

"Don't do this," Jack whispered between gritted teeth.

Curly Head glanced in his direction, then rolled his eyes and started walking across the room. He put his palm up to Jack, as if to say, Quiet, boy. I'm talking to your wife.

The Aryan rotated the wing nuts, removed them from the metal clamps around Jack's wrist and elbow. "Hold still," he warned. Once he was free of the apparatus, Jack wriggled the fingers of his right hand. Pins and needles.

"Hey."

Jack looked up at the Aryan. The Aryan launched a jackhammer blow to his stomach. Jack folded in half, dropped to his knees.

The Aryan grabbed Jack by his shirt collar and started dragging him across the concrete floor.

At least he isn't leaving me alone in the room, Jack thought, and then he coughed, and he swore he tasted blood.

Zero a.m.
The Dublin Inside Her Head (continued)

The first few days she spent in and around Dublin, afraid to go anywhere else, afraid to go home, for fear of involving her family. So she went to the pub, then to the bedroom of an ex-boyfriend from college; she figured she could hole up with him for a week, try to contact someone at MI5. But he was just interested in one-time-only revenge sex; he had a new girlfriend now. "And now that I've had you again," he said, "I remember you were always rubbish in the sack."

He said this to her at a party; she ended up with the host of the party, his best friend, a pimply guy named J.J. She knew he had always lusted for her. They didn't sleep together. A few stragglers who didn't want to drive home crashed on J.J.'s living room floor, and Vanessa and J.J. joined them. He kissed her for a while. Felt her tits. Tried to feel her below, but she kept his focus on her tits.

The next morning, J.J.'s cell started buzzing while they were all still *crashed out on the floor. J.J., feeling full of himself for finally having bedded the elusive Vanessa Reardon. Vanessa, meanwhile, worrying herself into a sickened state. What was she going to do next? She couldn't stay with this guy forever. And she had to go to the bathroom very, very badly. And not just pee, either. But the bathroom was more than ten feet away, off the living room, in the corner of the flat.*

J.J. closed his cell. His face was ashen.

"It's Ken," he whispered.

Her ex.

"What?" Vanessa asked.

"Ken's dead. Donna found him in the bathroom. He bled to death."

J.J. lost it. He put his hands to his face and wept. Vanessa didn't understand. Ken? Dead? The prick was only twenty-four years old. Couldn't have been drugs. Ken was as straight-edge as they come. She'd been with him the previous evening, and . . .

Wait.

No. That couldn't be right. The Mary Kates couldn't transfer that way. They had to be injected directly. For them to transfer through saliva meant that they had to replicate at an unprecedented—and unstoppable—rate.

Unless the Operator had changed the program.

Fuck. That was what he'd done. The mad bastard.

That's when she first appreciated the depths to which the Operator had sunk. This wasn't about her. This was about every person she loved. Or lusted for. Or kissed.

During her reverie, J.J. had pulled himself out of bed and shuffled to the bathroom. She hadn't been paying attention. Why would she? People went to the bathroom all the time. For men, the morning piss was—

And then it occurred to her.

"J.J.," she called.

No answer. She stood up, legs full of pins and needles, and stumbled across the sleeping bodies toward the bathroom. No one else was awake yet. She heard running water on the other side of the door. She leaned against it. The bathroom wasn't that big. Certainly no more than ten feet sepa-

rating her and J.J., who was probably at the sink, slapping cold water on his face, trying to wash away the tears. *You needn't be embarrassed*, she wanted to tell him. *Especially not in front of me. The woman who killed your best friend.*

"J.J."

Nothing.

Then came the horrible realization, and she flung open the door, and saw J.J. on the cold tile floor, and all of the blood.

Everywhere.

4:39 a.m.
Vine Street Expressway/II-676 West

The Operator spent the duration of the cab ride fantasizing about her. He found himself glad she'd survived this long. She had always been resourceful, despite her facade of bookish helplessness. He'd known she would go the distance. He never would have guessed two weeks, though. Vanessa must have tapped into some truly deep wells of ingenuity.

The cell phone in his jacket hummed. He plucked it from his pocket, flipped it open. It was his contact in CI-6. The woman he'd met during their tour of his facility six months ago. Back when he was still flirting around with Homeland Security, showing them a few impressive gewgaws and whatnot.

The one who was handling the buyers.

What was that Pet Shop Boys song about brains and looks and making lots of money? Well, he had the perfect killing machines. She had the contacts. It stood to reason that lots of money would follow.

Thanks to Nancy. His little shop double agent. Pretending to track down this mysterious "Kelly White" on one side of her mouth, arranging a virtual auction with the other. Nancy, with the pouty lips. She was no Vanessa, but . . . hey, he couldn't fault poor Nancy for not being Irish. No one would believe that's why he'd set up operations there in the first place. He *loved* Irish women.

"I'm in Philadelphia," he told Nancy.

She mumbled something vaguely apologetic, which was unusual for her. But then again, she had failed him. He'd have to remind her of that when they met again, face-to-face. Now wasn't the time.

"Have you decided where you're going to be handling the business?"

"Tijuana," he said. "Some friends from college went during spring break one year. Kept raving about it. I've always wanted to check it out."

"And it happens to be conveniently located in Mexico."

"There's that, too. I'll call you when I'm settled. Right now, I'm about to pay my last respects to the slut, so I'm turning off my phone. I don't want anything to disturb our final moments together."

Not true. If Vanessa were alive, he'd be keeping her alive for as long as she amused him. No need to get Nancy jealous, though.

Zero a.m.
The Dublin Inside Her Head (last call)

*I*t was the sight of *J.J.*'s blood that pushed her over. Something snapped, permanently. What she saw, she was not able to unsee. She would never be the same. She hated the Operator for that.

And for the fact that even when presented with the sight of the bloodsoaked corpse of a man she'd been kissing just a few hours ago, the most pressing need on her mind was this: Use the bathroom. She didn't know if she'd have another chance. Maslow's hierarchy of needs. She'd learned about it in high school. Urge to eliminate waste versus respect for a human corpse? No contest. The urge would win.

She used the bathroom, her body contorting to avoid touching any part of J.J.'s body. She hated herself for it. But she hated the Operator worse for having put her through these indignities.

It was the scorched-earth policy from then on.

She'd do what she must to destroy him.

Vanessa mastered many skills in the next few weeks: Meeting married men, seducing them. Not that it took much. Half the time, they were ready to rape her in the bar. But she'd say, "No, not here." She'd have them take her to their flat or a hotel room. Preferably a hotel. Buy her room-service dinner. Invite her into bed.

The next morning, she'd call for a cab and insist the driver escort her to it; she'd claim her companion had been abusive. Nobody would question that. And the subject would be most likely happy to get rid of her, once she started crying and raving. Happy until about ten seconds after she left. The Mary Kates only needed a few hours to replicate and spread throughout a bloodstream enough to kill.

They usually didn't scream, which was good. And it didn't bother her too much after the second subject. These men were adulterers, after all.

By the fifth murder, she thought someone surely would have come after her. The trail of bodies was too long to ignore. Didn't anyone do a blood test? See something a little off in there? She had been hoping for a public outcry: SHOCKING MURDERS, MEN FOUND ACROSS THE COUNTRY, BRAINS EXPLODED IN THEIR SKULLS. Once the nation was horrified, and Anderson Cooper was talking about it on CNN, she planned on turning herself in to the New York Times.

But nothing.

Where the fuck were the reporters?

If these men were buried with the Mary Kates inside them, her tour of vengeance was for nothing.

She became increasingly desperate. Tired. Her body revolting against *irregular feedings and physical abuse. If she hadn't lost it already . . . well, her mind was overdue for a serious vacation.*

Then a day ago, she'd been on a plane from Houston to Philadelphia and overheard someone say, "Oh, you're a journalist?"

This was a man she had to meet.

Journalist Jack Eisley.

Her Jack, her savior, her last hope.

4:42 a.m.
Third and Spring Garden

Jack spat blood on the sidewalk and wondered why he wasn't already dead. Not that he hadn't tried like hell to avoid it. He'd screamed and begged and held on to the molding in the stairway, for Christ's sakes, but the Aryan Man was stronger, and the begging had only seemed to piss him off. He'd been unceremoniously tossed out in the street, with the warning that he never even think about this place again, let alone come back or write about it. Or they'd come for his wife and daughter.

Out on the street, which was utterly fucking completely deserted.

Which was why he wondered, Why no throbbing? Did the Mary Kates malfunction?

"Better move it, asshole."

"Assclown."

"Ass bag." Throaty laughter. Something rattling around a pair of lungs.

Jack turned around.

There were at least two of them, lurking in the shadows, about six feet behind him. Crack whores. You know you've sunk to a new low when you're being mocked by crack whores. But as long as they stayed put, he'd be okay. He'd have a chance to breathe and think and wipe the blood from his mouth and nose. . . . And look, it was all over his shirt, too. Maybe he was being too fussy. Maybe he should just join the crack whores, which would guarantee him some company for the next few hours, until the poison finished him off. At least his brain wouldn't explode, and there might even be some interesting conversation in it for him. See, life was full of amusing options.

Maybe if he offered them money, he could sit with them for a while.

But no. He couldn't even do that. His wallet was upstairs. For good. No way could he go back to retrieve it.

Which meant another plane trip was out.

Which meant he was stuck here, would most likely die here.

Unless he could hang on until—when, eight? Is that when the Philly branch of the FBI would open? Or were they nine-to-five boys?

"Ass pass."

"Ass *master.*"

Jack didn't even know where they were located. Near City Hall, maybe? He looked westward on Spring Garden and saw the blue spikes of the Liberty Place towers, and a few other random skyscrapers, but nothing resembling the yellow-eyed clock tower of Philadelphia City Hall. Funny to think that he assumed he'd have all the time in the world to go sight-seeing after his 8:00 A.M. appointment at the Sofitel. He did want to see the Liberty Bell, no matter what Kelly White had said about it.

"Assaholic."

"Hey, fuck you guys, okay?"

One of them threw a bottle at him. It popped and shattered on the sidewalk in front of his hands.

"*Ass.*"

"Give me a dollah, *ass man.*"

He looked up and down Spring Garden. No yellow cars. No

nothing. But across the street was a Plexiglas bus shelter with the number 43 in small white letters affixed to the top beam. Standing beneath the shelter was a woman in a tuxedo shirt and black pants, brunette hair tucked over her ear.

Holy fuck.

Angela, from the club.

His only hope now.

Much as Jack fancied himself an agnostic—he'd spent too many years forced into the pews of Catholic churches—he could not help but notice the grand design every once in awhile. He believed that there *was* a higher power at work, and if you knew how to look for the signs, there was a way out of every situation. He called it his Batman Theory of Religion. The caped crusader was forever telling Robin, "Every trap offers its own solution." If life was a trap, then it offered solutions, too. Even when the trap appeared to be closing fast, the light fading, the jaws tightening. Because there she was. Angela. Why else would she be there, standing on the corner, waiting for a bus, if that wasn't part of the grand design? She could have had a car parked behind the club. She could have had a friend picking her up. She could have called a cab. But no.

"Have a good morning, ladies," Jack said, standing up and dusting his palms off. They were raw from sliding across the cement.

Down Spring Garden, a bus was approaching. He could faintly read the digital board on the top of the bus. Route 43.

"*Ass*matic."

Jack bolted across the street, not appreciating how much his right leg hurt until he was halfway across. He didn't know if he was stiff or if he'd really hurt something when he hit the sidewalk.

When he hit the median, his head started throbbing.

Oh Christ. Not so soon.

He crossed the remainder of the street at a full run but slowed down as he approached the bus shelter. The last thing he wanted to do was spook Angela, have her bolt. The crack whores were probably having a great laugh over this one. Lookit the white man put on the brakes. He's going to trip himself.

Jack thought Angela had been focused on the approaching bus. She fished around in her pants pocket for her fare. But without looking at him, she said, "What do you think you're doing?"

"Catching the bus," he said, winded.

"This is so *fucked*."

The bus pulled up. The brakes were shot; a high-pitched whine cut through the predawn quiet. The engine was rattling so fiercely, it was a wonder the panels of the bus were still attached to the frame. There was a pneumatic hiss, like a snort, and the two panels of the doors shuddered open.

Angela stepped up into the bus, dropped something into the scratched-up fare box next to the driver, then moved all the way to the back of the bus. Jack stepped up and tried to scan the fare signs quickly. Confusing as hell. Transfers, zones, base fare . . . two dollars. Two dollars?

"One ride costs two dollars?"

"Two dollars," the driver said. He had a patches of a beard on his jowls, and his eyes were red-rimmed.

Jack reached to his back pocket, then remembered where his wallet was. No. No no no. Front left pocket, nothing. Front right . . . oh, thank Christ. A ten and a single. His change from the airport bar last night.

"Can you break a ten?"

The driver sighed. "Exact change only." He nodded his head in the general direction of the fare sign.

"Come on, buddy. Can't you sell me a one-day pass or something?"

The driver didn't answer, as if the question was beneath him. "On or off."

Jack slid the ten into the fare box, cursing. He now officially had one dollar to his name, no credit cards, and was stuck in a strange city where a strange woman had both poisoned him and infected him with killer nanomachines.... Oh, and where his only friend in the world was a waitress who worked in an Italian restaurant and frequented kinky clubs where off-duty cops paid to watch her mount a saddle with a dildo attached to it.

"Don't forget your transfer," the driver said, handing Jack a flimsy strip of off-white paper.

The bus pulled forward.

4:45 a.m.
The Hot Spot

Kowalski thanked the cabbie, slid him a ten, grabbed his gym bag from the seat—oh, the hilarity that would have ensued if he'd forgotten Ed's head in the back of the cab. He could imagine the headlines in the local tabloid. OOPS, FORGET SOMETHING? Or maybe HOW TO GET A HEAD IN THE TAXI BUSINESS. They lived for crap like this. Ed deserved better than a bad pun in a runny egg-and-coffee tabloid.

The brown plastic intercom at the side door asked him for a password. Sylvester, his Goth snitch, had given him one that should work: "eyeball skeleton." (Hey, he'd used worse.) Kowalski tried it. The door buzzed, then clicked open. Sylvester was a big pain in the ass, but he did come through most times. Kowalski had to kick him a bonus. Let the guy buy himself a pair of vampire-teeth implants.

Now the tricky part: scouring a secret sex club for one white guy who probably didn't want to be found.

But after ten seconds in the place, Kowalski saw only close-cropped haircut after haircut, and weekend muscles, and that bored Catholic schoolboy look; he knew he was home free.

This was a cop sex club.

"Hey, buddy," he said, wrapping his arm around the nearest thickneck he could find. He flashed his Homeland Security badge, saw the guy's eyes light up. Oh yeah. He could see the embossed foil with the holographic eagles.

Hot shit, right?

"I'm looking for a guy who probably stopped in here a short while ago."

"Oh, I know the guy," the cop said, trying to stifle a huge smile. "You want his wallet?"

4:52 a.m.
Pennsylvania Hospital

The security guard was giving him shit. Actually giving him shit. "This card says I'm a member of the Department of Defense," the Operator said. "I know you probably had limited educational opportunities. You were probably dealing in high school, am I right or am I right? But even *you* have to know, somewhere in your feeble-ass mind, that the words De-part-ment of De-fense means something important, right? And that with one fucking phone call, I could have you sitting in a welfare office by the end of the day? Now open up these fucking doors and give me access to a hospital computer or I'm going to make sure you receive extended lessons on how the government *really* works."

Yeah, he was laying it on thick. All the heavy-lidded, jaundiced-looking guy asked was, "What kind of ID is that?" Probably out of curiosity more than anything else.

The guard opened the doors, and the Operator gave him another once-over, thought about taking the poor guy's ID badge, snapping it right off his leather guard belt and everything, but he had shit to do.

Down the off-white corridor, which needed a paint job, stat.

Around the welcome desk kiosk. Moved the mouse, got the patient-search program up.

Probably looking for Jane Does, right? Unless she was using that stupid Kelly White alias up until the end.

Ah, she was. Nice, Vanessa. Real nice.

Room 803.

4:55 a.m.
Spring Garden Station, Market-Frankford Elevated

By the time Jack made his way to the back of the bus, counting seconds all along the way—he'd had enough headaches courtesy of the Mary Kates, thank you—his savior, Angela, was standing up and pulling the dirty white cord that ran along the tops of the windows. A dud bell sound. The blue light at the front of the bus read STOP REQUESTED.

"Can I talk to you for a minute?"

"No," Angela said, and brushed past him.

"Just one minute."

"Fucking hell," she said, and not to Jack. She grasped the steel rail near the back exit. The 43 bus pulled off to the side of Spring Garden Street, beneath an overpass. Everywhere Jack looked, there was sidewalk and concrete walls, splattered with years of pigeon shit. What was she doing getting off here?

The bus stopped. Another pneumatic hiss. A pause. Then the double doors wobbled to life, swung open. Angela stepped down fast, exited the bus.

It was Angela or the bus driver. No real choice at all, really. For all Jack knew, this was the end of the line.

He hardly had time to consider the fact that he'd spent ten dollars for a bus ride that lasted all of two blocks. Angela was entering a station of some kind, built into the support columns of the highway above. Even at this early hour, with the sun barely making itself known on the East Coast, Jack could feel and hear the vibe and hum and speeding cars above. He caught a sign: MARKET-FRANKFORD EL. Okay, El like in Chicago. Philly's own Loop.

The transfer came in handy. It gave him admission to the platform.

A hip slide through the turnstile. Jack saw a rack of brochures along the wall—schedules. Maybe there would be a map inside. Would it be too much to ask, O Higher Power, for there to be map that identified the local FBI headquarters on it? Was it a tourist attraction? Maybe this elevated train would take him close enough. He could tag along behind somebody, a member of the early-morning commuter rush, follow him or her to the building, then scoot off into the front doors, find a receptionist, and tell her, "I need help now."

But if there was a commuter rush, it was scheduled for a little later in the morning.

There were only two other people on the platform: Angela and an older guy in a striped shirt. One of those striped shirts that had gone out of vogue at least fifteen years ago: different-colored stripes in various quadrants. The guy's one shoulder was red; his lower left torso was blue. There was some yellow and orange in there, too. A guy Jack knew from college had had one of these shirts. It was stylish for about five or six weeks, as he recalled.

The striped guy stood on the edge of the platform, facing toward Center City. Angela was on the other side, the one for Frankford-bound trains.

Jack hurriedly made his way next to the striped guy. No need to panic Angela until he figured this out. He flipped open the schedule. No map, but it showed that the first elevated train of the morning, the very first, would arrive at about 5:07, a few minutes from now.

But no. Look. Angela edging even farther away. He couldn't let her wander too far away. He needed to be able to make up the distance within a few seconds, before the pain grew too great. What could he say to make her believe his story? Now he understood Kelly's sales pitch. The whole poisoning thing, designed to get him alone in a room. Ready to listen.

Thing was, he hadn't believed her. Not until it was far too late. What chance did he have of convincing Angela?

The sun, a red circle at the end of a fat cigar, came rising over the horizon. Out on the riverfront, the half-constructed frames of two tall buildings were bathed in light. The air was heating up considerably. The humidity coaxed beads of sweat on Jack's forehead.

What would he say to her?

He'd figure it out. The important thing was to move closer to her. Not freak her out, but get closer. A polite distance—little less than ten feet. The length of an SUV.

She saw him out of the corner of her eye and started moving farther away.

Jack didn't want to die here on this humid El platform.

Angela moved even farther away now.

What could he say to her?

Zero a.m.
Pennsylvania Hospital

Movement now, in the real world. Doctors trying to hook her to machines, trying to figure out why she wasn't responding. Sterile needles plunged into her flesh. Maybe they'd hook her up to a smart machine. A machine that would see the Mary Kates in her blood. Probably not, though.

Then her eyes, forced open by fingers. Cold fingers, rough skin. The brightness was an assault, but when her vision cleared, she saw his face.

The Operator, looming over her.

"Oh. You dyed your hair."

The last natural blondes will die out within 200 years, scientists believe. A study by experts in Germany suggests people with blonde hair are an endangered species and will become extinct by 2202.
—BBCNEWS.COM

5:05 a.m.
The Hot Spot

Kowalski sat in the mutual-masturbation club, waiting for Jack Eisley's wallet, and he thought about a Raymond Chandler line he'd read last December: "You know how it is with marriage. Any marriage. After a while, a guy like me, a common no-good guy like me, he wants to feel a leg. Some other leg. Maybe it's lousy, but that's the way it is."

At the time, he'd been holed up with Katie, his dead fiancée, in a bed-and-breakfast in Stockton, New Jersey, about ninety minutes south of New York City. It was a favorite of hers, but it was the first time they'd been there. It was the first time they'd slept in the same room, in fact, since they'd met in Houston a month earlier. Her brother was there to pull a payroll heist, some sports nutrition company fresh off a fund-raiser, and she was sitting in a place called the Saltgrass, sipping a Chivas Regal on ice. A beautiful lady drinking scotch in a Houston bar. And Kowalski had thought he'd seen it all.

Her brother, Patrick, was weird about her dating people, so they'd started seeing each other on the sly. Their weekend in

Stockton was their first real date: time alone to pick each other's brains a bit, and drink Chivas and strip out of their clothes on the pretext of body massages.

So Kowalski had been sitting back, thumbing through a copy of *The Lady in the Lake* that Katie'd packed, and he read that line aloud, and she said, "You feel some other leg, expect to draw back a bloody stump. And then you'll be next."

Kowalski completely agreed. From then on, it was understood that they were going to be together for the long haul.

This club? It was all about the other leg.

But hey, who was he to judge? He'd never ended up getting married. Never had the chance; never even assumed he was the kind of guy who would marry.

But he hated the thought that he would end up in a place like this, doing the five-finger knuckle-shuffle in front of some inner-city burnout whose daddy didn't hug her enough.

"Here you go."

Kowalski took the slender black wallet, flipped it open with one hand. Not much in here. Illinois driver's license, a gasoline credit card, a Capital One Visa card. There was a single photo in the laminate insert: a pretty blond-haired girl, maybe four or five. Kowalski had never been good about guessing children's ages. He slid it out of the insert. Stamped on the back: *Paul Photography*. Written in pen: "Callie."

They'd never gotten as far as baby names. It was too soon. She was barely two months along when she died. But *Callie*. That was a beautiful name. That might have made it to the short list.

If Katie hadn't been killed, they'd probably be working on the short list right about now.

Okay, Mr. K., Mr. South Philly Slayer. Enough of that.

Shut that shit down.

Find this Jack guy, make him spill, then prepare your next

move. His handler was going to force his hand sooner or later, and it was always better to be prepared.

"When did he leave?"

"Brett threw his ass out of here—when, Gary?"

"About twenty minutes ago. I'm telling you, you just missed him."

"Guy was an asshole. You should have seen the girl he got paired with. She looked like she couldn't wait to get rid of him."

Kowalski couldn't keep one close-cropped skull distinct from the next. Like it mattered, right?

Jack came here in a cab, left by himself. Let's assume he needs to stay near other people. Leaving with somebody doesn't seem likely; he was unceremoniously escorted from the premises. Couple of possibilities: caught another cab, hot-wired a car, carjacked somebody. Wait. Scratch those last two. Jack isn't up for any hard stuff. Anything else?

"Any public transportation nearby?" Kowalski asked.

"Frankford El's two blocks down the street."

"In fact," somebody else said—Gary? Gerry? Who the fuck knew?—"the first train of the morning is at the Spring Garden station right now."

Half of the room turned to look at him.

"Oh, fuck you guys. My brother-in-law's a SEPTA cop. He's always bitching about his hours. That's how I know."

Kowalski processed it. Cab or El. Only one easy way to find out. Scanned the crowd. Yeah, at least one of those neighborhood knuckle-busters had to own a hog.

"Okay, boys," he said, puffing out his chest and flipping open his Homeland Security badge with his right hand. The movement hurt; his wrist was getting worse. "How would one of you like to do the U.S. government a favor and make five grand in the process?"

5:07 a.m.
Spring Garden Station

Two bright lights, coming out of the tunnel and up the tracks toward the concrete platform. The El. For the first time all night, Jack felt like he was on familiar turf. He knew Chicago and its El system cold; how hard could Philadelphia's be to navigate? The train rumbled and hissed to a stop. The doors opened.

Eastbound Frankford train making all stops, an automated voice said.

First disappointing development: The El car was empty. The train was headed eastbound. Guess nobody went eastbound this time of the morning.

Second disappointing development: Angela made her way to the opposite end of the car. Which meant he had to follow her.

The doors closed behind him.

Okay, this can't be that tough. Wait until she sits, then sit two rows behind her. That had to be within ten feet, easy.

The train bucked forward. Jack almost lost his footing. He reached out and grabbed a steel pole, then made his way forward. He could feel a throb in his temples already. He was too far away.

The steel cars accelerated along the track, then dipped down below the eight lanes of I-95, hanging a soft left along the side of an old church—one that had probably been here before the highway cut along one corner of it, and the El alongside it—before settling in for a straight shot until the next station. According to the map, that would be Girard. Jack counted up the line. Quite a few stations, at least a dozen, before the end of the line. Hopefully, Angela was going to the end of the line. It would give him time to think.

He chose the double seat two rows behind Angela. She'd pressed herself up against the window and was busy looking out at the tops of the buildings speeding by.

The track made a sharp turn. The train jolted violently. Jack almost fell again.

He sat down. The blue striped fabric of the seat was stained in places, and worn to beads in others. It sagged in the middle, as if someone had removed a central support. The entire cushion was loosened from its moorings, too.

Philadelphia. Fucking shit town.

The train pulled into the next station. Girard. Several people were waiting on the opposite platform, headed back downtown. Nobody stepped into their car.

Here's the thing, Angela. I've got an experimental tracking device in my blood, and ...

Look, Angela, I know we got off to a bad start, but I have this weird mental condition where ...

Yeah. Mention a mental condition. See where that gets you.

Jack looked at his watch. It was ...

5:08 a.m.
Under the El

Kowalski thought it would be a simple matter of following the tracks, but that wasn't easy at first. They popped out of a tunnel from beneath the city and led into a station that was tucked between eight lanes of an interstate. Then they dipped down again, and it was tough separating the columns of the El from the support columns of I-95. Then he saw the church, and the tracks, and it all made sense. Kowalski turned off the engine of the chopper for a moment. Below the din of the early-morning highway traffic, he thought he could hear the rumble of the train.

First train of the morning, according to his new cop buddy. Gary? Gerry?

And a fat chopper between his legs, courtesy of his other cop buddy.

Philadelphia. Such a friendly town.

If this indeed were the first train of the morning, and his quarry were indeed on it, then all he had to do was overtake it, hop on board, then do a car-by-car search. Convince Jack to go along with him to Pennsylvania Hospital. He didn't think he'd have to resort to his break-your-finger routine. Telling Jack Eisley that his life could be spared would be enticement enough.

Jack didn't want to end up like Ed Hunter, after all.

No offense, Ed.

The bag was hooked to the side of the chopper, bouncing a bit with the bumps in the asphalt.

Hang in there, my friend. Soon we'll have some answers.

5:15 a.m.
Pennsylvania Hospital, Room 803

I can understand why you'd do something like that, Vanessa—you being on a mission of vengeance and all that. But I miss your red hair. So beautiful, especially after sex. It always had this airy, wild look to it."

Silence.

"Oh look. You did your eyebrows, too. Though they're not perfect. Still, I'm impressed. You must have convinced someone to go shopping in a drugstore with you. Where on earth did you find a man to do *that* with you? Oh, I tease you."

Silence.

"Did you dye everything? Let's see."

Silence.

"Interesting. See, I thought that kind of thing would give you away. Maybe you haven't been quite the slut as I'd imagined. Did you talk them into staying with you? I would have loved to have been a fly on the wall for that one. You never were much of a talker."

Silence.

"Thing is, I don't know if you can even hear me. You could be a piece of broccoli lying here in this bed. Broccoli with red pubic hair. Ah, that would be a shame."

Silence.

"We'll find out soon enough, though. See, Vanessa, they're bringing up a machine that will let me check out your brain waves. If they're stable enough, I'll bring you out. I'm not going to lie to you. It'll probably hurt. Might even make things worse. But we'll be able to talk for a little while at least."

Silence.

"If you can hear me, let me ask a favor in advance. Spare me the cursing and the threats. You and I already know that you'd like to see me die screaming and all that. I get it. I'd want me to die screaming, too, if I were you. But we can save ourselves a lot of useless drama if you tell me a few simple things. Like who, exactly, you told about our work."

Silence.

"So yeah, give that a little thought. Not like you have much else to do."

Silence.

"Ah, here comes the machine I was waiting for."

Silence.

Whispering now: "Brace yourself. This is going to be more painful than you can possibly imagine."

5:16 a.m.

She couldn't move a muscle, but she heard every word. This son of a bitch wasn't going to die screaming. He would be too busy choking on his own blood.

5:16 a.m.
Frankford El, Approaching Allegheny Station

The El train bucked again, then slowed down. Fucking train. Jack was amazed that more people didn't puke during their morning commutes in Philadelphia.

Jack was running out of stations.

Only a few left after this one. Tioga. Erie-Torresdale. Church. Margaret-Orthodox. Bridge-Pratt. That was it. And his car was still relatively empty. An old guy a few rows back. A young girl with a schoolbag behind him.

He'd wasted the last few minutes staring out the windows, his mind tumbling around like a dryer sheet. He was tired. So tired. The contact lenses in his eyes felt like they were dried and permanently affixed to his eyeballs. Yesterday, he'd gotten up early to pack and make last-minute arrangements: phone calls, E-mails. So that meant he'd been up how long now, with the hour time difference? Twenty-four hours straight?

Decision time. Soon, it was going to be too late for anything. Had to focus. Either approach Angela and beg... plead... beseech, whatever... her for a place to talk, maybe even a place to stay until he had a chance to call some government agency and tell them what had happened. Then have them call Donovan Platt. Explain why he'd be "a little late."

Otherwise, it was a matter of finding someone else on this speeding train, someone he could convince—of what?

Like that would work.

Jack moved up another row. He was sitting close enough behind Angela to smell the smoke in her hair. There was a thin sheen of sweat on the back of her neck.

She must have been able to feel him staring, because she turned around, her eyes sharpened.

"What the fuck is your problem?"

Jack leaned back in his seat. "I need your help."

She sighed, turned back around. "What happens at the club stays at the club, buddy. Or Jack. Or whatever your real name is."

"Look, this isn't easy to explain, and I swear, if I weren't in desperate need of help, I wouldn't be bothering you." He looked at the back of her head. She didn't move. Maybe she was listening. "Can I just explain it to you? I know it's probably not going to make much sense. Doesn't make sense to me. But if you'll give me the tiniest sliver of trust, you'd be saving my life. Literally." Her shoulder moved, and she shifted in her seat. But she didn't get up and leave. That was the important part. For the moment, she was listening. "Last night, I met this woman in a bar at the airport, and she infected me with a tracking device. . . ."

Angela turned around to look at him. Her eyes were squinted, and her mouth opened slightly, like she was mentally asking herself, *What?*

"Which means, to make a long story short, that I can't be alone, or I'll die."

Her lips tightened and her eyes narrowed even more. Then she lifted her right arm.

"I know this sounds nuts, but . . ."

She squeezed the button on the top of the canister.

The liquid nailed him right in his eyes. But he couldn't even feel that at first. It was the skin on his face. Like jungle fields suddenly introduced to the flash strike of napalm, Jack's cheeks, nose, and forehead blazed with raw fury. He recoiled, but he couldn't move anywhere. His back was already against the seat. So he slid to the side and collapsed to the floor, screaming, "You bitch! Son of a fucking . . . *you fucking maced me!*"

He was too busy yelling to truly hear, but Jack could have sworn she muttered, "Asshole."

The burning didn't give up. The more he cried out, the more he moved, the more it seemed to hurt.

Worst of all, he couldn't *see.*

Where was Angela? Was she still sitting there? Smirking at him as he writhed on the dirty floor of the elevated train?

Stand up, Jack. Stand up and reach out. Get your bearings. For fuck's sake, man, get up and figure out where the fuck you are and where other people are and move closer to them, or you're going to die.

"ANGELA!" he shouted.

His eyes now . . . oh, he could feel those burn in their sockets. His contacts lenses were probably acid-burned to a crisp, and the toxins were sinking into his eyeballs. The more tears he produced, the more the fiery poison of the Mace spread, and he could swear it was already in his nose and throat, and he was swallowing it. . . .

Move.

Move now.

Find people.

Stay alive.

Try to ignore the burning hell on your face.

Jack didn't exactly know it, but as he stumbled blindly down the length of the car, he brushed up against the old man seated toward the rear. The man, the last person in Philadelphia to still wear a fedora on a daily basis, looked up at Jack with a bemused expression on his face. Ah, kids these days. But what was the deal here? Why was this fella asking out a lady on a train at five o'clock in the morning? That wasn't the way to do it. He deserved a face full of that stuff, the way he saw it.

The girl with the schoolbag slid over in her seat, moving closer to the window.

Meanwhile, Angela, who had pressed herself against the door at the opposite end of the train, had her cell phone out and was connecting to 911. She had fingered herself in front of enough members of the Fifteenth District to guarantee a quick and passionate response. Once this train reached the end of the line, this fucker was in for it.

If he came back toward the end of this car, though, she was going to have to beat the shit out of him.

She was prepared.

She wasn't above taking out an eye.

Down the length of the car, Jack smacked up against the glass of the connecting door. He fumbled for the handle. He knew he was in the very first car. But maybe there were more people in the others cars. He could try to cope with the burning in his eyes and face. Sit down near a crowd. Ride this out. Ride this out to the end of the line. Hope his vision returned. Follow someone down. Follow someone near a cab.

The handle opened. The door flung open. Jack rushed past it. Tripped. Threw his arms out, grabbed hold of the thick, greasy chains.

He felt the screaming in his blood, the pounding in his head.

The train was coming to a stop again. The whine of the brakes scraped the inside of his skull. Door handle. There. Turn it. Open it open it open it.

Jack stumbled. There was nothing where a steel platform should have been. His foot plunged down, down down. . . .

5:20 a.m.

Kowalski made it up to the platform as the train doors started to close. He got hung up at the token booth. Two fucking dollars for a subway ride? The clerk, an obese man who probably needed to be forklifted into the booth, pointed him in the direction of a token machine across the station. Yeah. He had time for that. Kowalski slid the guy a ten, told him to keep the change, buy a Slim-Fast. Hopped the turnstile to save time.

The doors were closing.

He made it in.

Almost.

His left forearm was caught outside the doors.

The one holding the gym bag containing the head of Ed Hunter.

"Oh fuck me," Kowalski said.

"Frankford train making all stops. Next stop Church Street."

The train sped forward. If he didn't find a way to pull his hand, along with the bag, into the car, it would smack against the metal gate at the end of the platform. The one that would be upon him in, oh, a matter of seconds. Probably snap his forearm in half. Maybe not sever it completely. No matter what, it was going to hurt. But even worse, he'd lose Ed. He hadn't carried him all night just to leave him on the platform of an elevated train.

The train accelerated.

"Fuck *me*," Kowalski said again.

And he wasn't the kind of guy to say "Fuck me" lightly.

Kowalski threw the bag up in the air, aiming for the top of the train, toward the back. His other wrist cried out in agony. This might have been spur-of-the-moment rationalization, but Kowalski thought he recognized these cars. He'd ridden them in Korea once, years ago. For all he knew, Philadelphia might have bought them used from Korea, then refurbished them—or not.

Point was, the cooling and heating system at the top had a generous space right in the middle of the housing. Enough to catch a decapitated head in a gym bag like a softball in a leather glove.

Kowalski knew this because he had once been forced to ride on top of a Korean subway car. Years ago. Ah, the glory days.

Then again, he might have been rationalizing. He was no subway car expert. Maybe this was a completely different model.

At the last possible second, Kowalski pulled his left hand through the doors, feeling the rubber guards burn his skin. The gate whizzed by. Then he steadied himself and scanned the windows, looking for a bag tumbling down the side of the car and hitting the steel tracks. Awaiting an El train racing in the opposite direction to burst it open like a balloon full of gray cottage cheese.

5:21 a.m.

Jack grabbed a stretch of greasy chain with both hands and steadied himself before he could slip down onto the tracks. He didn't know what was worse: the roaring of the car on the tracks or the roaring in his head. Get inside. Get near someone. *Now*.

He found the handle, yanked down. The door opened and Jack threw himself inside.

Still blind, he felt his shoulder bump into something. Something soft.

"Hey!"

He threw out his hands, looking for one of the metal poles attached to the seats and roof of the car. Instead, he found something else soft. Two things, to be precise. Draped in cotton. Warm.

A shriek.

And then a punch, right to Jack's ribs.

The pain made him want to fold in half, but it wasn't as bad as it could have been. He was near people again. The Mary Kates were retreating from his brain. That was all that mattered. Let them punch and kick and spit at him. Let everyone abuse him. Let his eyes burn out of their sockets. It didn't matter. He was alive.

For the moment.

"What the fuck is wrong with you?" someone said.

But Jack couldn't tell where the voice was coming from. Right next to him, or farther down the length of the car?

"I need to sit down," Jack whispered, and flung out his hands again. Feeling out for someone, anyone, to sit next to.

But all he felt was empty air.

He tried opening his eyes, but it hurt too much. He felt vibrations on the floor beneath his feet. Was that the usual rumbling of the train car, or were people moving away from him? Running away from him?

"Someone help me, please," Jack said.

As the train decelerated, the throbbing in his head returned.

5:22 a.m.

"*Church Street. Frankford train making* all *stops.*"

Okay, so the bag didn't fall down. Least he didn't see it fall. That meant it was up on the roof of the car. Hang on, Ed, comin' to get ya. Kowalski opened the connecting door, put a foot on the greasy cables between the cars. A simple heave-ho would get him up there. Easier than Korea. That was a real bitch, come to think of it.

But something inside the next car caught his eye.

His man. Jack Eisley.

Eyes closed, and waving his arms around like an orchestra conductor on crack. About a dozen other passengers in the car were moving away like he had a force field of *nuts* surrounding him. Nobody liked sharing personal space with the insane.

What the hell was Jack doing?

Maybe the virus Kelly White had infected him with had driven him over the edge. Made him nuts. Forced him to attack random people on the Market-Frankford Line. Maybe soon he'd sprout fur and fangs and growl like a dog. Wouldn't surprise Kowalski in the least.

The side doors were closing again.

Okay, think about Jack later. Get the bag first. Jack isn't going anywhere.

Heave-ho . . .

The train started moving forward as Kowalski planted both feet on the top of the car. He crouched down, making himself less wind-resistant. Ah, there was Ed. Unfortunately, he hadn't landed in the little basket in the cooling/heating housing. He was smack in the middle of the top of the car, like a flattened plum on a hot silver skillet. And the bag was sliding, sliding, sliding to the back and left.

Kowalski dived for it.

The train accelerated, bucked to the right. A huge gray stone church loomed on the left side, as if the elevated tracks ran up to it, then suddenly lost their nerve and swerved away.

The bag slid away faster.

Kowalski's ribs smashed against metal. Mother of fuck. He draped his left arm—the good one, thank Christ—over the side, fingers outstretched. Fabric brushed against his fingertips. There. He stretched farther, which was a small bit of agony in itself. Nothing. FUCK. Kowalski stood up. Balanced himself. His palms were burned. The metal of the roof was already hot.

There.

Ready to slide over the edge.

Kowalski heaved himself out of the metal housing, braced both feet on the metal surface, like he was surfing, and bent himself in half.

His hand grabbed the handles.

Gotcha, Ed.

He stood up.

And on the approach to the next station, the train bucked violently, as it did every time on this stretch of track. Ever since the city had rebuilt the tracks in the 1990s, and purchased the surplus cars from Korea in 2000, the Frankford El trains never glided along as smoothly as they had when the El was built in 1922. Too many engineering errors. Not enough to cause a crash, but enough to cause a jolt at predictable points along the route.

And Mike Kowalski was thrown off the top of the car, hurling through the air, two stories above the hot pavement, and smashing through a large plate-glass window on the third story of an old shop long closed to the public.

He went through the glass upside down, still grasping the gym bag in his left hand.

Kowalski's body skidded across the ancient wooden floor like a puppet thrown to the ground by an angry toddler.

5:23 a.m.

The train bucked and Jack was thrown into a seat, on top of someone. Someone who smelled like wet cats. His hand grasped fabric, but two meaty hands pushed him back into the aisle. "What the hell was that?" someone shouted, and Jack thought he heard glass shatter, which confused him. Had the train crashed? Had he tripped an emergency brake or something?

No. It was slowing down for another station. The last station? Jack had no idea.

But no matter. Hands found him. By the collar of his suit coat, by his arm. Dozens of hands. Guiding him along. Helping him. At long last.

Helping him right out of the car, onto the platform.

"Get the fuck out," someone yelled.

Jack stumbled forward into the humid air, his knees scraped against the cement, and he screamed.

This was no way to die.

"*Watch the closing doors,*" an automated voice said.

5.25 a.m.

The plastic robot face was the first thing he saw. A blue robot, solid jaw, face bolted together with plastic bumps meant to look like rivets. To his right, a fleshy strongman was torn open at the torso by a spear of glass. Pink slime oozed out of the wound. Yet the expression on his molded-plastic face remained the same. Now that was stoicism at its finest. Inspirational, even.

Kowalski lay broken in a sea of dusty toys, stuff he remembered from his own childhood.

That must have been when this shop closed down, the 1970s. Kowalski squinted and saw a painted wooden sign stacked vertically in the corner. SNYDER'S TOYS.

Cute.

All around him, toys. Rock 'Em Sock 'Em Robots. Stretch Armstrong. Role models, dating back to the era of *The Six Million Dollar Man*. His main man, Steve Austin. The man Kowalski had wanted to be when he grew up. Even if it took a grisly M2-F2 rocket crash, and parts of his mangled body needed to be replaced with bionic ones. *We can rebuild you. We have the technology.*

Well, here was his crash. Thrown from a moving train. His skin cut to ribbons, his right leg broken in at least two places, his wrist snapped. And a gash in his scalp so bad, he could feel the blood oozing past his hair and down into the dusty wooden floor, soaking it. Come to think of it, the wetness on his face might not even be sweat.

Where were the bionic parts now?

Where was Oscar Goldman?

Oh, that's right. He'd dumped his Oscar last year for the sister of a bank robber.

Katie.

Enough of that already. Get the fuck up. Kowalski rolled over, threw out a hand. Grabbed the edge of a splintery floorboard. Pulled himself forward about six inches. Then he had to stop. Getting dizzy. The pain in his leg was unbelievable. Must have been how he'd landed on it. He pushed toys aside. Chrissy dolls. White marbles. Shattered, yet still hungry, plastic hippos. Kenner mini sewing machines. Wacky Packs. Micronauts. Milton Bradley board games, whose cardboard boxes had blown out. Remco McDonaldland characters. The stuff was everywhere. He must have knocked over a set of steel shelves when he came through the window. It felt like his body was pressed against shag carpeting, the kind his parents used to have in the living room. He crawled a bit farther and found himself eye-to-eye with Mayor McCheese. He used to have a Mayor McCheese doll. Normal body, big cheeseburger for a head. Never knew what happened to it. Maybe it had ended up here. Maybe he'd ended up wherever *it* had gone. Maybe he was dead. Maybe he had been hurled through the air and had landed in his childhood version of heaven: his parents living room, Christmas Day, 1977.

Stop it.

It took him ten minutes to reach the other side of the room, where the gym bag containing the head of Ed Hunter had landed.

Behind it was a shimmering play mirror, about as reflective as a sheet of aluminum foil. But Kowalski was able to see his face.

He saw it.

And he screamed.

His body shook, raging against itself.

He pounded the floor with his right fist, clawed at the wood with the damaged fingers of his left hand.

He had been so good about keeping everything together. Because he was a trained professional. Guy who didn't let anything in. But the truth was, he was the same kid who'd played with a Mayor McCheese doll, the kid who would grow up to meet a woman and fall in love and make a baby with her, and both of them were dead now because he hadn't been there to save them, and now look at him, covered in blood, flesh of his cheeks torn and mangled, pieces of his ear missing, but those eyes, oh yeah, those eyes were the same he'd had since Christmas morning, 1977, and they looked back at him and they knew.

They knew what it was like to be trapped inside a monster.

5:30 a.m.

Vanessa could move. Finally. The room came into focus. She wriggled her fingers, felt them scrape against fabric. Moved her elbows. Then her neck. Just a little. Her head felt like it weighed a thousand pounds. But she could move. A little.

The Operator was standing over her. "You *are* there, aren't you?"

Fuck you, Vanessa wanted to say, but she couldn't make her mouth move the way it should. She felt drool run down the corner of her mouth. The thought made her gag. She coughed, and coughed again, and the sudden movement racked her with pain.

"Calm down, you're doing too much. You need your rest." The Operator looked over at the open door. "Hang on a second." He disappeared from view. Were her wrists tied to the bed? She couldn't feel any restraints, but she also couldn't lift her arms. She heard the snick of a door closing shut. Then he reappeared. "We need a little privacy."

"F-f-f-f-f-. . ." Vanessa spat. Clawed at the mattress.

"Shh, blondie. You know, you're not much to look at right now, but I can't help but be seriously impressed with you lately. This whole scorched-earth campaign of yours. Very, very bold. And *clever*. I didn't realize the brilliance of your airport visits until a few days into the game. You've got everything you need. Always a restaurant open. Plenty of places to buy T-shirts. Crowded bathrooms. Sleep on the planes, find a willing stud, get a free hotel room for a night. I may have this wrong, but there are at least five men you did the horizontal mambo with in the past week or so. I have a list on my PDA. Hang on."

The more she flexed her fingers, the more movement she had. Focus on that, she told herself. The left one. Get it going. Get your hand and wrist working first. Then the forearm. Then find something sharp.

"Yeah, here we go. Donn Moore. Investment banker, looks like. Always insisted on that extra *n* in his first name. What, *Donny* not good enough for you? Douche bag. Okay, who else? Jimmy Calcagno, lawyer. Allan Ward, another lawyer, although not as sleazy as Jimmy, who apparently had some real scumball clients. Did you know that? A simple Nexis search turned that up. Meanwhile, Allan seemed more like the tweedy type. Corporate law. I bet he was real sick. It's always the quiet ones. Anyway, who else, who else? . . . Rob Ormsby. Oh, a screenwriter. Nice. And finally, Simon Smith, who owned a boutique Web-design company. How delightful."

Vanessa didn't want to hear the names. She didn't want to think about the men attached to those names. She wanted to move the fingers of her left hand, over and over again.

"But I don't think you're a slut, blondie. I knew what you were doing. You wanted to attract attention, didn't you?"

"Y-y-yessss," she said. Her own voice. It was coming back.

"Yesssssss you did, didn't you?" the Operator mocked. "Aww, who's a cute little man-killer? That's right. My wittle Wanessa Essa."

"F-f-f-f-f... uck..."

"You did quite enough of that, didn't you?"

The Operator reached out with his coat sleeve and wiped the drool from her lower lip. She pursed her lips. Then he grabbed her face and leaned in.

"Is that how you infected them? Fucking them? Sucking their cocks? A kiss would have done it, you know. You didn't have to go all the way. Especially since you never did some of that with *me*."

Was this what it was about? Back in Ireland: Matt Silver, the big bad Operator, gently guiding her head down to his crotch. Vanessa refusing. Halfheartedly kissing him on the neck, trying to placate him. Thinking that a few scented candles and an Enigma CD would make her swoon, convince her to blow him.

"You're a bit weak in the mouth now, aren't you? Bet you wouldn't put up too much of a fight. You want another shot at it?"

The Operator squeezed her cheeks, then let go. He moved out of her field of vision. She tried to follow him with her eyes, but nothing. Turned her head slightly to the right, and the room began spinning.

"Thing is, my little Irish slut," the Operator said, "I wanted you to go out and see other people."

Oh, bollocks on that. Jealousy was the Operator's fundamental emotion. Along with envy. It guided everything. In the boardroom *and* bedroom.

"It's true. Sure, there was a chance you'd wind up alone somewhere and—kablooie—no more Vanessa Reardon. But I knew you'd try to survive long enough to avenge yourself. And you'd come into contact with a *lot* of people. Course, I didn't know you'd be fucking and sucking your way to San Diego and back."

She could move her left hand now. Pump it into a weak fist. Then release. Pump. Then release.

"Remember how I said Proximity needed another human host to survive? To eat blood cells and other cellular waste? Um, yeah, well, *I lied*. They can survive in any fluid environment on Earth. They're dormant until they reach another human being. Then they replicate like jackrabbits. Upload the DNA sequence to our satellite, which feeds it to our computer."

Vanessa stopped pumping. What was he talking about now? That was the built-in security feature of the Mary Kates. They needed a human host for power. Piss 'em out into the toilet, they'd die after a few seconds. That way, they couldn't replicate unless they were in close prox—.

Oh.

Proximity.

He'd designed it this way all along.

The mad, mad bastard.

"Thanks to your trip around the country, you've infected over fourteen thousand people. God bless you, Vanessa. You've done the hard part for me."

The Operator came back into view. Showed her the liquid crystal display of his PDA. A number ticked up, two, three digits at a time.

"See what you started?"

Jackson was amused. "He seems to know you."

The blonde smiled wryly. "A lot of people know me."

—DAY KEENE

6:01—6:46 a.m.
Fifteenth District Headquarters, Northeast Philadelphia

An hour before shift change, Officer Jimmy MacAdams caught the call: disturbance on the Frankford El. Up until that point, it had been a slow night on the steady out squad. Most exciting call was an abandoned 1994 Dodge Daytona over on East Thompson Street in Bridesburg. Yet another cracked steering wheel column, ignition pulled out and hanging over the top, strip of white fabric tied around the works. He was sitting on it until Major Crimes had a chance to take possession, haul it in. In this neighborhood, probably somebody who was too lazy to call a cab. But you never knew until you dusted for prints. So there he sat.

Then the call came in.

"Transit police: We've got a howling blind man up on the El platform at Margaret-Orthodox."

Howling blind man.

Oh yeah, MacAdams thought. He should have seen this one coming.

MacAdams crossed Torresdale and raced up Margaret, cherries flashing, no sound. He was at the El station in sixty seconds. Guy looked ordinary enough, except for the face full of Mace. Transit cop said he'd been raving but that he'd calmed down in the meantime. Even better. MacAdams read him Miranda, put him in the back of the squad car. Apologized for the lack of air-conditioning. That and the laptop had been down since start of shift.

"I don't care about the air," the guy said quietly. "Whatever you do, don't leave me alone."

Looked like he'd had quite a night.

"I'm just taking you in, okay? You won't be alone."

He escorted the guy, who said he was a Mr. Jack Eisley, up to the Fifteenth District building at Harbison and Levick. Walked him up to Northeast Detectives HQ on the second floor, which was done in navy blue with gold bands.

Then the guy started raving again, which surprised MacAdams. He'd been docile the whole ride up. Now he was screaming about not being left alone, needed to speak to someone right away, or else many people would die—all of the usual psycho crap. MacAdams was glad to step clear of that shit.

"All you guys," he said, and went back downstairs. Only a half hour before he clocked out.

But something made him hang around. He put a few coins in the honor box, popped the lock, and took a Diet Coke from the squad fridge. Drank it and savored how cool the can felt against his hand. He'd been in a slow simmer all night. Listened to the usual banter in the squad room:

"You've got a cold."

"Come over here, give me a hug."

"You always have a cold."

"And yet I love skiing."

Beat as he was, MacAdams admitted it: He was curious. So he finished his Diet Coke, tossed the can, and popped back upstairs to see what was going on. Through the one-way glass, he saw the guy talking to Detective Sarkissian.

Howling Man was saying, "... tell you everything, but you have to promise one thing: You won't leave me alone. I don't care who you have in here with me. The chief of police, one of you guys, a secretary, anybody. Bring in a homeless guy."

"I'm right here," Sarkissian told him.

"I know this sounds crazy, but please believe me. You leave me alone in this room, you'll come back and find me dead."

"I don't want you to hurt yourself, Jack. I want you to tell me what happened."

"I want to, believe me. Maybe some of it will make sense to you. Maybe you'll be able to help me figure it out. Because the way things are looking, a lot of people are going to die today."

"Hey. Come on, now."

"That is not a threat."

"Calm down."

"I'm perfectly calm."

Sarkissian waited him out.

"Hey, could I have something for my eyes? A bottle of Visine or something? My contacts are shot to hell, but maybe I could see something if I wet them down."

"Tell me a little first, and I'll get somebody to get you Visine."

"Okay. But..."

"Start from the beginning."

"I don't even know..."

"You said this started nine hours ago? Try there."

"I was at a bar in the Philadelphia International Airport. That's where I met the blonde. The first thing she said to me was..."

He told his story. Some really weird fucking shit. MacAdams didn't follow all of it. Barely followed half of it, tell the truth. Apparently, the guy was afraid that if he was left alone, some killer satellite would send a death beam to particles in his blood—yeah, weird fucking shit, right?—which would make him die in ten seconds.

The detectives were split. Some of them wanted to let him

sweat it out for twenty seconds, prove that he was batshit. Others thought that was asking for trouble. What if he got so afraid, he seized, died right there in the interrogation room? Then it'd be a world full of shit for everybody.

But Sarkissian was good at this stuff. He chipped away at him from the side.

"Mr. Eisley, you've got a wife and daughter. Were you thinking of them when you attacked that woman on the Frankford El?"

"I didn't attack her," Howling Man replied. "I was trying to talk to her."

"Your wife and daughter know you're talking to another woman?"

"They wouldn't mind. Not if they knew what had happened to me."

"And what's that again?"

"I've told you. I'm infected with a tracking device that will kill me if I'm alone."

"Why don't you go home to your wife and daughter?"

"I can't do that. I wish I could."

Some key facts gathered with a few phone calls:

Eisley flies here last night, even though he seems to have no business in Philadelphia. He's a reporter at a weekly newspaper in Chicago.

At about 1:57 A.M., a hotel resident hears fighting in his room. A male and a female. Hotel security officer Charles Lee Vincent investigates.

As he approaches the room, he's knocked out by an unknown assailant. He remembers there being a woman in the room, but that's about it. Vincent later escorts Eisley down to the lobby.

A little after 3:00 A.M., Eisley disappears.

At the same time, outside the hotel, according to two tourists, Christin Dubay and Sarah French, some "flaming asshole" stole their cab.

At approximately 5:16 A.M., Eisley attacks Angela Marchione, a waitress at Dominick's Little Italy. She sprays him with Mace. He goes on a tear through the elevated car, passes through to an adjoining car, then exits at Margaret-Orthodox, where he is apprehended by SEPTA police.

Eisley has no ID, no wallet. Claims he lost it at a nightclub on Spring Garden.

Still, they have a photocopy of his forged driver's license from the check-in desk at the Sheraton. They find his address and phone number on-line. Call his house. No answer.

However this story was going to shake out, MacAdams thought, it was sure as shit going to be interesting.

MacAdams watched them go back in the room and work with Eisley a little more, try to get him talking about his wife, his kid—what he's doing in Philadelphia. But the guy was stubborn and more than a little crazy. Kept clamoring for the FBI or someone from Homeland Security, yet begged not to be left alone.

Finally, Sarkissian made the call:

Let's give him a little privacy.

6:48 a.m.

Once you come to terms with the idea that you're a monster, it's easier to function. Your physical self is more forgiving of abuse, willing to strain against its own humanity. Because there is no humanity under all of that flesh, after all. Which was how Kowalski was able to drag himself up from the floor and try to piece himself back into some semblance of a man. It's what monsters did.

He'd looked around at the debris of forgotten childhood.

The best operations, Kowalski'd reminded himself, supplied their own tools.

First, he'd found a needle and thread from a Kenner mini sewing machine kit. The gashes on his body could be covered with bandages and clothes. But his face? His face needed work. Sanitary? Hardly. But what was that to a monster?

The metal supports from the shelves? Leg brace, *Road Warrior*-style. Sort the broken bones out later. Long as they would support his weight.

A little water from the employee sink, he was even able to smooth down his clothes, get some of the shattered glass and dust and splinters and wrinkles out of them. Wash away the crusted blood from around the purple-and-pink-threaded sutures.

By the time he left the abandoned toy warehouse forty-five minutes later, the monster was reasonably human. He checked his image in a plate-glass window of another store. Pale, but no visible blood. People saw blood, they got upset. Otherwise, they could deal with anything. Even his stitched-up face and rusty leg brace.

A few questions of a passerby got him what he wanted: Yeah, strange guy, howling, taken away in cuffs.

His boy Jack.

Alive, at least up until the point he was arrested.

Nearest police district was the Fifteenth; he caught a cab up there, flashed the Homeland Security badge, just about damn near dazzled Detective Hugh Sarkissian with his embossed foil with the holographic flying eagles, which distracted him from the purple stitches and rusty leg brace. Kowalski told him that Jack Eisley was part of an investigation he was running. No, he wasn't a terrorist, just a freaked-out informant.

"Who's still alive, right?" Kowalski asked.

"Yeah," Sarkissian told him. "But we're ready to let him sweat it out a little."

Kowalski took a chance. "He begged you not to leave him alone, didn't he?"

Sarkissian's face went wide. "*Yeah*. What the fuck is that about, anyway?"

Kowalski rolled his eyes in a "You don't even want to know, buddy" kind of way, then gestured to the room. "You mind?"

Which got him in the door of the interrogation room at precisely 6:48 A.M.

Not a second too soon, from the look on Jack's face.

He was hurting.

6:49 a.m.

I thought I was going to die just then."

"You're fine. Name's Mike Kowalski, Department of Homeland Security, making America safer for domestic fucks to rape the citizenry instead of the foreign fucks, blah blah blah," he said. "But does it really matter? After the night you had, Jack?"

"Who are you?"

Jack studied the guy, who looked strangely familiar, despite the purple-and-pink sutures in his face—what, had they run out of adult stitches at the hospital?

Wait.

The guy.

The hotel room.

The guy who strangled the security guard.

"Oh no."

Kowalski limped over to the table and slid into a chair. He reached out and took Jack's hand in his. Kowalski was wearing white gloves, stretched to the point of bursting. And Jack looked at them fast, granted, but he would swear one of them had the McDonald's logo—the Golden Arches—right on the wrist.

Jack felt Kowalski grasp his middle finger. "This will hurt."

And then Kowalski twisted his finger in a way he didn't think was physically possible. Jack screamed, writhed in his seat. The pain seemed to rocket up his very bones.

Outside the two-way glass, Sarkissian was saying to MacAdams, "*Don't you wish?*"

"Oh, fucking tell me about it."

"Bet he doesn't even leave a mark."

"I was trailing your girlfriend, Kelly White," Kowalski said. "She infected you with something. I want you to describe it to me."

"Fuck! Ow, Christ, leggo of my—*Ah!*"

"No detail is too small. Tell me how it works. Why can't you be alone?"

Kowalski pulled Jack closer to him, causing his metal chair to scrape against linoleum, and at the same time, he eased up on the finger. "Whisper it in my ear," he said.

Now that Jack was up close and personal, he saw that one of Kowalski's stitches didn't quite do the trick. Dark blood pooled around a pink strand, started to bead up.

On the side of Kowalski's nose, there was a thin sliver of glass, wedged beneath a few layers of skin.

Maybe the guy *is* with Homeland Security, Jack thought.

And if not, they should hire him. Because he didn't seem to give one fuck about personal discomfort.

What was Jack going to do? Talk back to him?

So Jack talked.

Started telling him all about how he'd met Kelly, but Kowalski didn't want to hear any of that. Sped him along to later in the night, in the hotel room. Jack tried to remember as much as he could about the Mary Kates, what their creator called "Proximity." Tracking devices in your blood, linked up to a satellite. Only

Kelly's had a fatal error. Kowalski nodded. Probed for more detail. Asked about nanoassemblies. Is that what she'd said? *Nano*assemblies? My God, it was like he believed him. Maybe he already knew about these things.

"Something else, too," Jack said. "She gave me a toxin. No . . . a luminous toxin."

"Luminous toxin, huh."

"Yes! That's it! She told me I'd be dead in . . ." He looked at his watch. "Oh fuck. About ninety minutes from now."

"Sounds serious. But I'm sure we'll be able to get that taken care of."

Kowalski released his hold on Jack's finger, then used this same hand to scratch his chin. Somehow, the tip of his finger avoided the two long gashes there. "Hmm . . . let me try a little something." Kowalski stood up and picked up the gym bag he'd brought into the room. He placed the bag on Jack's lap. "Hold this for a minute."

"What is it?"

"Don't worry about it." Kowalski stood up and limped over to the door. The metal brace on his leg squeaked as he moved. He knocked twice.

"Wait—where are you going? Didn't you hear me? If I'm left alone, I could—"

"Yeah, yeah. Humor me. Oh, and whatever you do, don't let go of that bag."

"This doesn't smell right."

The door slammed shut behind Kowalski.

6:55 a.m.

One, two, buckle my shoe.
Three, four, shut the door.
Five, six, pick up sticks.
Seven, eight, lay them straight.
Nine, ten . . .
A big fat hen.

Kowalski gave it another few seconds, just to be sure.

He opened the door and found Jack white and sweating and writhing in his seat, but alive. The gym bag still lay in his lap. "What did you do?" he gasped. "How am I still alive?"

The tracking devices in Jack's body seemed to have sensed the ones in Ed's dead fat head inside the gym bag. The host didn't have to be alive. The devices merely had to be present, within ten feet. Just like Jack had said.

Useful bit of info, that.

And that was pretty much all he needed. Now all he had to do was take back the gym bag, leave his guy in here, tell his pal Sarkissian to let him sit for a minute, let him process a few things . . . Ah, no. Not smart. What if Kelly White was indeed dead? He could use a living witness. For the short term, anyway. Until he got CI-6's game plan figured out.

He admitted it. He'd never been pulled off an op before.

And it stung.

So okay, new plan: He'd take this guy, find Kelly White—if she was still among the living. Stick this guy in a closet, wish him well in the afterlife. Tell him to say hi to Mayor McCheese.

If Kelly White was already gone . . . then yeah, get to a safe house, lawyer up, and prepare for a shitstorm, because CI-6 might be deciding to part ways with one Michael Kowalski.

And he couldn't let that happen. Not until he'd avenged his sweet Katie at least.

"You ready, Jack?"

"For what? Didn't you hear me? I asked you a question."

"Yeah, I heard you. I wouldn't waste time if I were you, though. That luminous toxin's a nasty bastard. And according to your count, you've got less than two hours to live. We need to get you to a hospital."

It took only a few minutes, and another look at that embossed foil with the holographic eagles, to have Eisley remanded to his custody.

While faking his way through the bullshit paperwork, Kowalski noticed a pair of wanted posters on the wall. One showed a crooked ex-cop believed to be on the run with his almost brother-in-law. Small world. Kowalski wished he could tell the FBI the truth, save them a little worry. Say that the crooked ex-cop was buried under thousands of pounds of concrete in Camden, New Jersey. Kowalski should know. He was the one who'd dumped him down that drainage pipe.

His almost brother-in-law, however, was another matter altogether. Kowalski had wanted to leave him for dead, but he couldn't bring himself to do it. He had been a part of Katie. A half brother. But still a part of her. Most likely the only part left.

So maybe Kowalski wasn't a monster after all. A monster would have let the guy die.

7:32 a.m.
Pennsylvania Hospital, Room 803

A flash of the badge got Kowalski the room number of the Jane Doe who had rolled in during the middle of the night; the spiky-haired blonde at the front desk seemed impressed. Homeland Security. *Oooh, ahhhh, keeping America safe.* People really dug the holographic eagles. He led Jack up to the eighth floor. Jack, who kept checking his watch nervously. Guy thought he was headed up to a poison-control center to get treated for luminous toxin poisoning. Hilarious. Hadn't this guy ever watched *D.O.A.*? He liked Kelly White even more.

Kelly was in bed, hooked up to machines. Her back was arched. Her eyes were fluttering beneath her lids. But she wasn't alone.

A tall man with thinning hair was leaning over her, syringe in his hand. "Oh," he said. "You're here to save Vanessa, aren't you?"

"Actually," Kowalski said, "I'm here for the breakfast. The sausage patties are out of this world."

Vanessa, huh.

The man straightened up and smiled. "You caught me putting her down for the night. We're getting ready for a long weekend getaway. Just the two of us."

"Sounds nice," Kowalski said, edging closer to the bed. His leg brace squeaked. "Somewhere warm?"

"Scorching," he said.

They were two monsters, sizing each other up. Kowalski saw it in the guy's eyes, behind the mask of teddy bear features and wispy blond hair. The eyes . . . yeah, the eyes revealed all. He'd seen some nasty things. Caused them, too.

"Looks like you're traveling light," Kowalski said. "Maybe you'd want to borrow my bag."

"Seems full already."

"Not much in here, actually. Take a look." He dropped the gym bag on Kelly's bed, right between her legs.

The thin-haired man looked behind Kowalski. "Who's your friend?"

"We're getting married in April. I always wanted to be a spring bride. Go ahead. Look in the bag."

"Does he scratch in bed? Your face is an absolute horror."

"He's rough, but we're in love."

Thinny here wasn't going to look in the bag. Too smart a monster for that. No chance for a distraction.

Yet, there was.

Kelly's eyes snapped open. She whipped out her left hand, grasped the Operator's hand—the one holding the syringe—and forced it down and back. A violent needle jab to the abdomen, many, many inches below the belly button. The man's mouth made a perfect O shape.

"*Fucker!*" Kelly hissed.

Kowalski moved quickly. He slapped Thinny across his nose with an open palm. But Thinny didn't seem all that stunned. So Kowalski hit him again with a backslap. Harder this time.

The guy wrenched his hand out from under Kelly's, grabbed the heart monitor from the rack, and bashed it across Kowalski's face. Wires whipped behind it like dreadlocks. Kowalski staggered backward. He smashed into a table of steel instruments, which went flying everywhere. He could feel the blood gushing down the side of his face even before he hit the linoleum. His hands trembled uncontrollably. Oh *fuck*.

7:34 a.m.

Jack watched the violence in front of him with the detachment of someone watching a violent car crash. I'm not part of that. That's not me. That's there. I'm here. And I'm still alive.

I'm still alive.

Jack looked at his watch.

It's past 7:30 and I'm still alive.

Luminous toxin my ass.

She lied.

About everything?

7:34 a.m. and 10 seconds

Vanessa tried to find the syringe again so she could plunge it in deeper this time. Rip it across his belly. Drive it right back into his fookin' spine.

But he moved away too quickly. He said, "You have a loose mouth, don't you, Vanessa?"

The Operator put his palm to her right cheek. Then he pushed her head back into her pillow, pinning her there. Didn't take much strength at all. He probably could have held her in place with one finger.

"Fun's over."

He pulled the security cord behind her bed.

7:34 a.m. and 30 seconds

Kowalski was being dragged across the floor. He could hear his rusty leg brace scraping along the linoleum. The pink-and-purple sutures on his face were popping open. This monster was coming undone. He'd taken too hard a fall this morning. Left him weakened, vulnerable. The bigger monster was in charge. Why had he thought a simple slap could subdue him?

A security alarm was in full roar. Lights flashed in the hall.

The bigger monster was lifting him up now.

The bigger monster was smashing a fist into his face.

The bigger monster vanished when everything went black.

7:34 a.m. and 55 seconds

"You." The man with the thinning hair pointed to the hallway. "Out."

He followed Jack, who stumbled out into the hallway, and nearly tripped over Kowalski's bleeding and semiunconscious body. It was bedlam in the hall. Nurses backing away. Worried stares from people in wheelchairs. Two security officers jogging toward them.

The guy who'd decked Kowalski pulled a badge from inside his jacket, barked something about "Defense Department," and told one of the guards to stand in front of the door. "Do not allow anyone in this room for the next hour. *No one.* Matter of national security." He was going to call in backup, he said. *No one* gets in the room, understood?"

The guards nodded. Oh, they understood. No one.

Then the guy walked down the hallway, rounded a corner.

Uh-uh, Jack thought. That bastard wasn't walking out of here. Not after what he'd been through all night.

Jack needed some fucking answers.

7:36 a.m.

Down the corridor, the Operator snatched a hospital gown from a pile stacked on a metal table. Pressed the down button on the elevator. Held the gown to his lower belly. She'd really nailed him. He could feel the blood trickling down his crotch, pooling in the bottom of his boxer briefs.

But no matter. All he needed was a few stitches.

And by now, Proximity would have done its job, and Vanessa would be dead. He wished he could have watched it happen.

Filmed it, even.

"Wait!" someone called.

The Operator turned. It was the guy from the room, the one who'd come in with the hardman.

"Who are you?" the guy demanded. "And how do you know Kelly White?"

At first, back in the room, the Operator had pegged this guy as a nonentity. He'd presented no threat; he'd made no move whatsoever. His friend had been the one to worry about—though not really, as it turned out. Someone had already put that bastard through a meat grinder. Knocking him down turned out to be surprisingly easy.

This one, though. Who *was* he?

Then again, who the fuck cared? He had a gash to stitch, places to go, a weapon to sell. . . .

"Piss off," the Operator said.

"No," the man said, "I'm not going to *piss off*. You know all about the things in Kelly's blood, don't you? The Mary Kates?"

Oh, that name.

The Operator sighed, then heaved his knee up into the man's testicles.

He shouldn't have to be doing this, you know.

He should be out bringing nations to their knees. Not this nobody.

7:37 a.m.

Inside her room, Vanessa wondered about two things.

First: Why am I still alive? And second: What the fook is in this gym bag?

Then her door crashed open.

7:38 a.m.

There had been no time for threats. No time to dazzle two hospital rent-a-cops with nifty holographic eagles. Not with his face bleeding, his right wrist throbbing, and his right leg screaming.

So Kowalski had thrust his palm out to the closest guard's chest. It was a blow sharp enough to stun, but not enough to chip the bone of the breastplate, driving calcium daggers into the heart. The man jolted, lost control of his limbs. Probably thought he was having a heart attack. Which is what that blow was designed to do.

The other guard caught the flat of Kowalski's palm in his throat. Again, the blow hadn't been hard enough to kill; merely discourage. The man dropped to his knees, put his fingers to his throat, as if he could somehow fix what was wrong there.

Kowalski hobbled past them, threw open the door, limped like a sorry fuck over to the bed, damn near crashed into it. And then he fell. Those two moves had taken more energy than he realized. His body screamed, *Stop it. Stop it. Rest.*

When I'm dead.

Kowalski reached up and clutched sheets. Then a bed rail. Pulled himself up.

"Hi, there," he said, staggering to his feet. He looked down at Kelly, who had a strangely bemused expression on her face. Farther down the bed was the gym bag containing Ed's head.

In the exact place Ed had probably hoped he'd end up last night. *There you go, buddy. Mission accomplished.*

"I don't mean to be rude, but I've gotta go catch your boyfriend."

"No worries," Kelly said, her words grotesquely slurred. *Nuh wurrrree.*

But Kowalski understood. He looked at the table near the sink, saw what he needed. "Hope you two aren't close."

He uncapped a sterile syringe, then unzipped the bag. Looked for the right spot—part of the neck stump—and slammed it home. Drew back the plunger.

"I'm going to zip this back up, and I want you to promise me you won't look. And that you'll keep this bag right here. Trust me on this."

Kelly reached up. Her fingertips found his chin. She squinted her eyes, as if to say, Oooh, that looks like it hurts.

"You're sweet. But I'll be right back."

7:39 a.m.

Jack Eisley was in the exact position he thought he'd be this morning: on his knees, clutching his testicles, feeling the worst pain of his life.

But instead of kneeling before Donovan Platt, he was standing in front of some beefy, thin-haired jackass. Someone who could tell him what this whole thing was about. The Mary Kates. The fake poison. His eleven-hour nightmare.

And even though Jack considered himself a reasonably nonviolent man, someone who preferred an honest conversation to physical blows—despite the fact that he'd punched a pretty woman in the stomach earlier this morning—he'd come to a philosophical breaking point. Before him was not a man for conversation. He was a man, clearly, who preferred the language of pain.

So Jack made a fist and nailed him in the lower part of his stomach—right where Kelly had stabbed him.

Oh, how he howled.

Jack liked the sound so much, he punched him in the same place again. The man had protected the area with his hands; Jack's second blow landed on knuckles. Still, it had an appreciable effect. The man cried out, stumbled back, fell on his ass. Jack tried to stand up, but the pain in his balls was too intense, too crippling.

"Nice, Jack," said a voice behind him. Kowalski. "Score one for the home team."

Kowalski limped past him down the hall, toward the man with the thinning hair. He had one arm behind his back, syringe in hand, thumb stretched out and on the plunger. In the tube was a dark red fluid.

Jack almost felt sorry for the thin-haired man.

7:40 a.m. and 10 seconds

First, Kowalski threw a sloppy chop to the throat. Something the bastard could see coming from around the corner.

As expected, Thinny dropped, kicked, and swept Kowalski's leg out from under him. Then he was on top of him like a college sophomore.

And Kowalski plunged the needle into Thinny's neck.

Thumbed the plunger.

Confusion washed over the man's face. He'd felt the stick, but didn't know the source. He rolled back. Reached up. Felt the syringe. Widened his eyes.

Kowalski could have said one of a thousand things, but he figured the silence was worse.

Just a smile. A small, quiet smile.

And a look. A telepathic exchange, more accurately: You know what that is, don't you, big boy?

Thinny yanked the syringe out of his neck. A thin ribbon of blood spurted from his neck. Then he raised the syringe up and behind him. Bared his teeth. Prepared to put every once of his weight behind a blow that would drive the dirty needle into Kowalski's face, past skin and bone, deep into his brain cavity.

Kowalski anchored himself with his good arm and bad leg.

The needle plunged downward.

Thinny's descent was blocked by Kowalski's foot, thrown up at the last moment and stretched back to its limit. He could almost kiss his knee.

Then Kowalski performed the one-legged press of his lifetime.

Thinny was hurled backward.

Shattered the window behind him.

Toppled backward out of the jagged frame.

7:41 a.m. and 45 seconds

HA HA HA HAAAAAAAA.

Kowalski wanted nothing more than to lie still, catch his breath, give his muscles and bones a moment to adjust to the multiple shocks. Then he heard the laughter. The shrill, mocking laughter of a school bully who'd just made it through puberty but lapsed back every once in awhile. *HA HA HA HAAAAAAAA.* It was coming from outside. Beyond the shattered window.

Was Jackie Boy catching this? Kowalski rolled over and raised his head, and yeah, it looked like Jack heard it, too. He was still cradling his nuts protectively, but he, too, was looking up at the window.

Son of a . . .

He crawled to the window. No shattered glass on the tiled floor this side of it, thank God. Heard commotion behind him. Nurses, doctors, security, maybe even priests and nuns and lepers and angels and politicians gathering.

First, one hand up. The good hand. Of all his woes, would you believe his fucking right wrist killed him the worst. The little present from his sweet Kelly.

Up and to his feet. There you go, soldier. Go on, look down. Look down the side of the building from the eighth floor and see what you see.

Ah yes.

The thin-haired bastard, clinging to the sturdy metal frame of an air-conditioning unit two floors down.

He was staring right at Kowalski, sneering. He'd been waiting for him.

"*It's not going to be that easy,*" he yelled.

Two floors down. Kowalski verified the distance the best he could, but . . . yeah. It seemed about right.

"You know what you are?" Kowalski asked.

Confusion on Thinny's face. Then he winced. Maybe he was starting to realize. Maybe his head was starting to throb.

Kowalski hadn't injected him with one or two of the Mary Kates. The blood from Ed's head was positively *teeming* with them. There was no need for hours of gestation, replication. There were plenty in there to do their job.

"You're more than ten feet away."

And Kowalski was glad he was the only one looking out the window. Because nobody else needed to see what happened next.

The burst.

The bright red quadruple burst out of his mouth, nose, and eyes, splattering the side of the building like a blast from a hose.

His fingers, slipping away from the air conditioner.

His body dropping straight down into the historic graveyard below.

Down where they used to bury the ones they couldn't save in the hospital, back in the early days, the Colonial times, when people died of natural afflictions, not microscopic machines that traveled to your brain and exploded.

Kowalski looked until he'd had enough. No twitching. No surprise resurrections. He'd seen it happen before.

But no.

Nothing.

He turned around and slid down the wall. Used his good hand to reach into his pocket, looking for his Homeland Security badge. Hopefully, those holographic eagles would work their magic one last time. Christ in heaven, was there some explaining to do.

7:50 a.m.

Within minutes, Kowalski had it squared away best he could. The tricky part had been apologizing to the guards he'd assaulted and *then* getting them to agree to guard the doors to room 803 until reinforcements arrived. But they did, God love 'em. Their agreement was encouraged, no doubt, by the fact that Kowalski told them the dead man in the graveyard was an international terrorist. And that they'd probably receive medals and shit.

The guards kept the staff away, and the four of them had the room to themselves.

Kowalski, standing against the wall.

Kelly, in her bed.

Jack, slumped back in a leather and wood visitor's chair.

Ed's head, in its Adidas bag, placed in the corner, near the door. He was really starting to ripen.

"You okay, Jackie boy?" Kowalski asked.

"Never better," Jack said, then looked over at Kelly, who was tucked under covers, eyes closed. "Though I wish I'd known I hadn't actually been poisoned, oh, about eleven hours ago."

Kowalski smirked. "Luminous toxin, Jack? It's from *D.O.A.* The original. Not that shitty Meg Ryan remake."

"I saw it, but I've never heard of luminous fucking toxin."

"She pulled a *mind op* on you, bro. I checked her bag back at the hotel. She slipped you disulfiram. One pill, five hundred milligrams. Odorless, colorless, dissolves fast. Right in your beer. Made you dizzy, made you puke, but it was nothing lethal."

"Disul what?"

"Disulfiram, aka Antabuse. The stuff they give alcoholics. She probably boosted it from some guy's luggage. Am I right?"

Kelly smiled faintly. Her eyes were still closed.

"What about the other thing?" Jack asked. "The Mary Kates. They made up, too?"

"I'm afraid not."

"Wonderful."

"Look. Hang with me, we'll get this sorted out. I really do work for the government. A department you're not supposed to know about, but still. I'm going to order you and Kelly some blood transfusions. That doesn't work, we'll get you more. This is Pennsylvania Hospital. Oldest hospital in the country. We'll find a way to get you back to normal, even if they have to break out the leeches."

Not likely, in all honesty.

But you had to give people something to hang on to.

Eventually, he had to get Kelly White—or Vanessa, if that was her true name—out of here. Worst case, he'd fill a syringe full of the old blood from Ed Hunter's head. The stuff full of the Mary Kates. Loaded with his DNA. Long as Kelly kept that near her, she'd be fine. Could be worse. Some people had to cart around colostomy bags.

Next, he'd have to arrange some transport to move from here. Sort out CI-6's stake in all of this.

Which, speaking of . . .

Kowalski picked up the room line, used the prepaid calling card, dialed the last number he had for Nancy.

She answered.

"I've got what you want."

"What do you mean?"

"I told you I'd come through."

"Michael . . . oh no. Michael."

She was using his first name. She never did that.

"Something wrong?"

"What are you doing? This mission was over for you."

"I never fail. You know that."

"You did this time. Where are you? And is anyone else with you?"

"Like who?"

Kowalski heard a grunt behind him, but he ignored it. He needed to hear it from her. How far into this she was. If she was eating from both sides of the trough.

"Did you encounter any opposition?" his handler asked.

"And I said, Like *who*? Perhaps a certain thin-haired individual, Nancypants?"

Something pelted Kowalski's shoulder. A dark pink cup made of hard plastic, hospital-issue.

What the . . .

When he turned around, he saw it right away.

Jack and the gym bag were gone.

Four people, down to two now.

He looked at Kelly: her eyes open, her mouth agape, her finger pointing to the door, her face with that expression that said, I tried to tell you.

"Let me call you back," Kowalski said.

THE
APPOINTMENT

7:58 a.m.
Hotel Sofitel, Seventeenth and Sansom

It was a short cab ride across town to the hotel. Donovan Platt had selected a swank place, probably because of the intimidation factor. Doormen with neatly pressed uniforms. A front entrance tucked away from the main bustle of downtown Philadelphia. And know what? It worked. Jack felt cheap walking through the front doors. He'd done some reading about this hotel back at home. A favorite of visiting athletes and musicians. Billy Joel had spent some time here recently, according to one gossip column. Imagine that. *Billy Joel.* The guy who wrote the song Jack and Theresa danced to at their wedding: "To Make You Feel My Love." And now he was here to see her divorce lawyer. By God, they'd come full circle.

By the time Jack entered the restaurant in the back of the lobby, he even had two minutes to spare.

Platt was sitting at a table covered with ivory linen.

Along with Jack's wife, Theresa.

They were holding hands.

Jack felt a cold weight in the middle of his chest, one that slid down his lungs and into his stomach.

His worst fears confirmed.

He'd been faithful after the separation.

She hadn't.

Jack sat down. Put the Adidas bag next to him so that it touched the side of his foot at all times. Someone tried to move it, he'd feel it.

"Who's watching Callie?"

"My sister," Theresa said. She wasn't looking at him.

"For how long?"

"A few days."

"We should get down to it," Platt said.

"Down to what, Donovan?"

"This is not going to be easy for you to hear, Jack. But I want you to think for a moment about what's best for your daughter."

"Fuck you, *Donovan*." He turned to his wife. "Therese, what's going on?"

Theresa still wouldn't look at him.

"Jack, just hear us out."

Us.

In that moment—and in the glance they exchanged—it clicked into place. Jack had been too buried in his work, indeed. Too buried to see that Theresa's weekend trips to her mother in Toledo were actually trips to Philadelphia. Sure, she'd taken Callie along. And left her at her mother's place. And his mother-in-law had known, condoned it, probably encouraged it.

"How long have you been fucking my wife, Donovan?"

"Jack," Theresa said.

"You have a choice to make, Jack. You can listen to us and still retain some visiting rights with your daughter, or you can choose *not* to listen to us. There's no court in this land that wouldn't award full custody to Theresa. Especially not here in Philadelphia. Not with the judges *I* know."

The chill had reached Jack's stomach and it exploded. This was the moment he'd dreaded, hadn't dared think about: losing Callie.

He didn't think he needed to worry, tried to tell himself that Theresa wasn't that kind of woman, no matter how rotten their relationship had become—she wouldn't deny her daughter the right to see her father. Theresa's own parents were divorced. Swore her daughter wouldn't have to go through the same thing.

"My advice to you," Donovan was saying, "is that you listen to my proposal. Otherwise, you're going to find it awfully tough to see your daughter, once she's out here with us."

"In Philadelphia," Jack said.

"That's right. Bryn Mawr, to be specific. The schools are phenomenal."

Jack looked at his wife. "Philadelphia."

She finally locked eyes with him. "Even when you were home, Jack, you were never home. Don't pretend now."

"It's the best thing for Callie," Donovan said. "Get past your pride, your anger, and you'll see that. You'll know it. And I know you're too good a father to let your own feelings stand in the way of your daughter's future."

Philadelphia.

A waiter approached, but Platt shooed him away with an upraised palm. He reached down and to his left, removed a navy blue folder that was embossed with the name of his firm in gold leaf: PLATT GLACKIN & CLARK. He handed it to Jack, who took it, then placed it on top of his napkin. He opened it. Saw various forms and agreements, with his name and Callie's name. There were dollar figures, too, and he saw the words *travel allowance*, but Jack's eyes couldn't focus on any of it. Clipped to the pocket of the folder was a blue pen with gold trim, and gold letters that read PLATT GLACKIN & CLARK.

You were never home.

Don't pretend now.

Jack realized that Donovan was right. There was only one thing standing in the way of his daughter's future.

"It's a generous deal, Jack. If you look at the first page on the left—"

"First," Jack said, "I have a request."

"Shoot, Jack."

"I want to kiss my wife good-bye."

"I hardly think that's—"

"Shut up, *Donovan*." Jack stood up, moved around the table to Theresa.

"Don't do this," she said, staring forward.

Jack leaned down and pressed her lips against his anyway. She put her cold hands up to Jack's face to push him away, but he held on, probed his tongue into her mouth. She tasted like bitter coffee. He pushed her back into her chair and held her head in his hands and kissed her more.

"For Christ's sake . . ."

Jack broke their embrace.

"Good-bye, Theresa."

And then he picked up the Adidas bag and started to walk away.

"Son of a bitch, Eisley, you get back here. Don't do this to your daughter."

Jack turned around.

"You hold on to her now, Donovan," he said. "She's the kind of woman you don't want to leave alone."

ONE DAY LATER

5:17 p.m.
Fernwood Court, Gurnee, Illinois

Theresa's sister was surprised to see Jack. She thought Theresa would be coming back, not him. "It's not your weekend," she stammered. Looked like she knew, too.

"Call her and check," Jack suggested.

He was tired from the ride. No easy trick, getting back to Illinois. Airport screeners would have had an unpleasant surprise waiting for them when they checked the Adidas bag. Not that his discovery had been any less shocking. Thankfully, he'd been in a fast-food restroom when he looked. He was able to more or less stifle the scream.

So a plane was out.

A car rental, too—not with his wallet gone, including driver's license and credit cards.

So it was either a bus or a train. Train was faster. A little over a day. Jack called his editor at the paper, convinced him to wire the money for the ticket to Philadelphia. He'd explain later, he said but he had a hell of a story.

Not for the paper. He wouldn't dare put this in the paper.

But he was going to put it *on* paper. And in a safety-deposit box, duplicated ten times over, with copies to be sent to various daily newspapers, both here and in the U.K., in the event of his death. Along with physical evidence, of course: vials of blood from the head.

Jack didn't know if he'd ever see Michael Kowalski again. But he wanted to be prepared if he did.

Somehow, he thought Kowalski would appreciate that.

From upstairs, Jack heard the stamping of feet, then saw his girl come bounding down the stairs. "*Daddy!*"

She gave the best hugs: full-on anaconda squeezes that threatened to burst his heart. There was nothing else like them in the world.

"*I missed you.*"

He wished he could hug her forever. Have her with him forever. And wouldn't that solve everything.

Of course, that wasn't possible. So after kissing her head and putting her back down for her nap, and telling Theresa's sister that, yes, he was fine, and, no, he had no idea when Theresa was due home, but he could take it from here, thank you very much (thinking, you know exactly where your sister is—Donovan Platt's an old family friend, after all), Jack took the Adidas bag—and a plastic bag of stuff he'd picked up at a Home Depot—down into the basement to work on the head. Filled as many vials as he could stand. Tried not to look at the face.

When he was finished, he took the bag into the backyard and dug a shallow hole. Nudged the bag with his foot and started covering it with the loose, pungent soil.

Jack thought about the locket he was going to buy for Callie. A heart made sense. Something with a hollow glass insert.

Something he was going to have to make her promise to wear forever, no matter what.

Just like the vial he had strapped around his neck.

Who knows.

It might even bring them closer together.

TWO DAYS LATER

9:57 p.m.
Adler and Christian Streets, South Philly

Kowalski had his night-vision sights trained on a nice little head shot. Yeah, it'd be messy.

The guy whose head was covered by a professional assassin's sights *still* had absolutely no fucking idea. And he was eating another slice of white pizza—was this all this guy ate? No Orangina this time. Chubby had a Diet Coke. Like that was going to do any good.

It was nice to be back on-mission. Sure, he had a lot to sort out. But no reason he couldn't do that *and* wipe out every single member of the Philadelphia branch of the Cosa Nostra at the same time.

They'd stolen one of his potential futures. His future with Katie and their child.

So he was stealing theirs.

Down to the man.

Steady now.

Index finger on the trigger.

Set angle to maximize blood splatter.

And . . .

And Kowalski's battered leg—in a proper brace, finally—started humming.

It was a new phone. He'd ditched the old one in the hospital biohazard dump. This one was exactly like it. Another razor-thin model with an armband meant for athletes. Only one person had the number. Kowalski plugged in the jack, hooked the receiver and mike around his ear.

"Are you busy?"

"Not really," Kowalski said. "You?"

"I think I slept all day."

"Good."

Once he was sure she was stable, Kowalski had moved Kelly—whose real name, he confirmed, was Vanessa Reardon—to an off-the-books safe house. One even CI-6 didn't know about.

Oh, CI-6 had assured him that Nancy, his ex-handler, his ex-girlfriend, had been sanctioned for her little side deal with one Matthew Silver, aka the Operator, aka the Guy in the Cemetery with the Exploded Head. It was a serious matter, and Nancy would be dealt with in the most serious manner. CI-6's assistant secretary sifted salt in the wound by informing Kowalski that none of his assignments that Thursday night had been official. In fact, his orders had been given by the Operator, and filtered through Nancy.

No, no, the assistant secretary didn't blame him for that. No way Kowalski could have known. She'd used the right protocols. And he was just following orders, right?

Right. But still . . .

The assistant secretary's sudden and insatiable interest in the Mary Kates—"What do they do again? Self-replicating, huh? You don't say. . . ."—worried Kowalski. The same way you'd be worried about a fifteen-year-old with a sudden interest in assault rifles.

That shit had to be nipped in the bud.

Especially if what Vanessa had told him was true.

That at least fourteen thousand people—and counting—had

this stuff dormant in their blood. Waiting for a command from a satellite somewhere.

The assistant secretary didn't know about that yet.

Kowalski purposefully kept intel flowing as slowly as possible; he needed time to strategize. He didn't tell them about the proof in San Diego. He told them he'd bring Vanessa Reardon in when the conditions were right.

But they were growing impatient. Soon, they'd send someone after him.

And Vanessa.

"What are you doing right now?" she asked.

"Cleaning up a few things. You know, I wanted to ask you something."

Chubby, still in his rifle scope, was coming to the end of his Diet Coke. Kowalski could tell by the way he craned his neck back, trying to suck out every last drop of caffeine.

"Yeah?"

"You wanna have dinner out somewhere?"

"I think I can stand a public appearance. You have no idea what a leisurely shower can do for a woman."

"Wearing the necklace, of course."

"It'll never leave my person."

In the hospital, with Ed's head missing, Kowalski had been at a loss as to what to do about Vanessa. She still couldn't be alone. A transfusion would be useless. Even a single nanoassembly left behind could replicate a thousand more. And going down to the graveyard to collect some of Thinny's blood wasn't practical. Not with cops and rescue workers swarming the scene.

Instead, Kowalski had suggested infecting himself, then swapping vials of blood. To wear on necklaces, à la Angelina and Billy Bob. They'd both be covered.

"You'd do that?" she'd asked.

"Am I not a gentleman?" he'd joked.

He'd suggested pricking their fingers; she'd reached up and grabbed his face and kissed him—his mouth, his scars, his bruises—sealing the deal.

"So where are you taking me?" she asked now.

Wait.

Chubby was on the move. Look at him adjusting his crotch. Getting ready for a little exercise. About freakin' time, right? The sights followed him.

"I was thinking . . ."

Steady now. . . .

Index finger on the trigger . . .

". . . San Diego."

BLAM

BLAM

BLAM

Acknowledgments

The Blonde would not have been possible without Meredith, Parker, and Sarah. Nor without Allan "Sunshine" Guthrie, "Marquis" Marc Resnick, or David "Hale" Smith.

The author would also like to thank Ray Banks, Lou Boxer (pharmaceuticals), Ken Bruen, Angela Cheng Caplan, Bill Crider, Aldo Calcagno (locations), Michael Connelly, Paul Curci, Carol Edwards, Father Luke Elijah, Loren Feldman, Nancy French, Greg Gillespie, McKenna Jordan, Jon, Ruth and Jen Jordan, Deen Kogan, Christin Kuretich (wardrobe), Terrill Lee Lankford (possum wrangling), Joe Lansdale, Laura Lippman, Emily MacEntee, Donna Moore, Kevin Burton Smith, Mark Stanton, Shauyi Tai, David Thompson, Dave White, the good people at St. Martin's Minotaur, the *City Paper*; his friends and family, and fair-haired people everywhere.

REDHEAD

a novella by Duane Swierczynski

You thought blondes had more fun?
Wait until you meet the redhead.

A Note to the Reader:

This is a sequel to The Blonde, *which you will find conveniently included in the front of this paperback. You should definitely read that first.*

If you purchased this book and thought you'd knock out the story in the back first, let me give it to you straight: Turn back now. Seriously. There's a lot of weird stuff (The Mary Kates, CI-6, The Operator) you need to catch up on in the full-length novel before you tackle this one. And there's even a spoiler in the first line.

So turn back now. Thank you for your cooperation.

(This story is for Terrill Lankford. He'll know why.)

—D.S.

"That's pretty deep for a redhead."
——U.S. Marshal Matt Dillon

"I'm a pretty deep redhead."
——Kitty Russell

The word spread early—they had Kowalski in custody, and The Blonde was dead.

Kowalski was flying in on an AH-64 Apache 2, due to arrive any moment.

The Blonde's headless body was currently under the knife at a small medical facility south of San Diego, not far from the border. The guys in the lab coats didn't want to hang around Mexico any longer than they had to. Cartels, and all. Things were bad. Decapitations were the order of the day. They didn't want to get caught up in that shit.

Nobody was too worried about The Blonde anyway.

They wanted Kowalski.

He was the one with the intel.

They prepared the secret prison facility like parents preparing the house for their five-year-old's birthday party—the first with friends from preschool. The landing pad was hosed down as well as the interrogation room. One staffer was surprised to find some blood and bone fragments still congealed in one corner of the room. He could have sworn he'd cleaned this place out good a few days ago.

Lights were checked, and in some cases, replaced. It was important to have the right amount of buzzing and flickering. Chairs were positioned just so. A new meat hook was hung suggestively from a metal eye towards the back of the room.

The government has secret prisons all over the country, tucked away in little corners. This secret facility was halfway between Scranton and Wilkes-Barre, Pennsylvania. Neighbors—the closest ones living a mile away—thought it was a place where they pulped books. That was intended to explain the screaming. Machines are high-pitched and loud, they'd explain, if asked, which was never.

The Apache landed at 4:46 a.m. Kowalski was rushed down the ramp, still in his street clothes, except for the hood. He'd been checked for weapons, of course. Outwardly, he was clean.

They whipped off the hood to give him a hit of sunshine right before pushing his head down and running him through the musty steel hallway that led to the inner chambers of the facility.

They walked him around a lot to confuse him.

They stripped him naked, even removing the metal brace around his broken leg. They saved the vial of blood around his neck for last. It took them a while to realize what it was. Even better: it was early generation, from a month ago. Well worth studying.

A guard reached out, enclosed the vial in his meaty paw, then snapped it off Kowalski's neck.

Now he needed *them*. Otherwise, he was fucked. If they wanted to kill him, all they would have to do is lock him in a room and wait ten seconds. Without anybody within a ten-foot radius of Kowalski, the nanites would travel to his brain and explode. There. Nothing easier.

For now, though, two guards stayed with him. They could kill him later. They needed information.

It was time for final security checks. They force-fed him something to make him vomit.

He did.

They repeated the process, and then checked his mouth and ass.

They hosed him off, sat him in a metal chair.

They'd opted not to put him on the hook. It was better to build up to something like that.

"Hey," Kowalski asked. "Is my brother-in-law around?" It was the first thing he'd said since being apprehended in Mexico.

They said nothing.

Others watched him wait, via fiber optic cameras.

Kowalski waited.

Sometime later the door opened. A guy Kowalski supposed was the interrogator stepped in. The guards stepped out.

The interrogator didn't look like much. But those were the guys you really had to worry about.

He didn't offer his name. He looked kind of bored.

"To be honest," the interrogator said, "I just want to get to the part where I hang you on the hook back there and start cutting away little pieces of you. Starting with your anal cavity."

"You guys are really fond of my ass."

"Shall we begin?"

Kowalski said, "I'll tell you everything."

"Crap," the interrogator said.

"And then," Kowalski said, looking up at the ceiling, "all of you will die. One at a time."

The interrogator perked up. "Oh yeah?"

"Every last one of you."

Huge smile from the interrogator. "Sure, sweet cheeks. Listen, let's get the story going. I'll call bullshit and then we'll have some fun."

"I outthought you bastards every step of the way." Kowalski stared at a corner of the ceiling.

The people watching him were impressed. He seemed to know exactly where the cameras were hidden.

"And yet," the interrogator said, "you're here."

He stood up and reached inside a pouch on his pants. He took out a small, thin blade with a black handle. It had a cardboard cover over the blade, which the interrogator removed. Apparently, it had been sanitized for Kowalski's protection.

"Here with me."

"We went to L.A. first," Kowalski said.

The interrogator sighed, then settled in to listen to the story.

"Let's go to L.A.," he told the blonde, whose real name was Vanessa. She'd come a long way in the past few weeks. She was napping less. Recovering most of her memory. Still, her mood remained the same: sad. Verging on black depression. Not surprising, considering that she'd almost died and, before that, spent a few weeks acting like a serial killer. Most people acting like that either ended up dead or in a padded room.

"I thought you said San Diego," she said. "Where I stashed the key."

"C'mon, L.A.'s fun. I'll take you to Musso & Frank for a steak. Then we'll drive down to San Diego."

"I don't eat red meat."

They decided to go to L.A. anyway. Kowalski was just about finished with his Philadelphia business—there wasn't much left of the original crime family who'd butchered his fiancée, except for a couple of low-level numbers men who really weren't worth the trouble. Already the Russians and the Poles were moving in to fill the void. They could have it, Kowalski thought. He could care less if he ever saw Philadelphia again. Maybe if terrorists nuked it he'd stop back, just to piss on the burning ashes.

It was time to stop thinking local, and start thinking global.

As in:

Global Apocalypse.

Vanessa told him as much as she could about Proximity. She relied on memory; the hardcore data was on a USB key in San Diego. But what she knew was frightening enough. Those little Mary Kate fuckers replicated like trailer trash: fast and furious and without much thought. And if The Operator—the dead headless bastard—was to be believed, the Mary Kates were currently busy inhabiting the bloodstreams of much of the population of North America. It had been a few months since their adventures in downtown Philadelphia. A lot of time for the Mary Kates to go forth and prosper.

Meanwhile, Kowalski's employers, CI-6, were slowly putting the pieces together, like a toddler with a plastic Tupperware shape toy. They weren't entirely stupid. Just big and awkward, like any government agency.

Kowalski didn't think he had much free time left with Vanessa. They were going to come looking for them, hard. Maybe within the week. He could tell by the way he was treated when he called in to ask about new assignments. A new chill had set in. Something was going on.

L.A. was the smartest move he could come up with.

She went along with it.

They rented a car and hit a mall in Neshaminy, a suburb just north of Philadelphia. They bought what they needed—small suitcases, clothes, some crime novels for Kowalski, some toiletries for Vanessa.

Kowalski flicked the paper shopping bag with a finger. "What's that?"

"Me skin wasn't meant for California sun," Vanessa said. Her Irish accent was back in full bloom. She'd been faking deadpan Midwestern American during her trips from airport to airport across the country. No reason to now.

"Your skin is just fine," Kowalski said.

Vanessa flicked the side of his plastic bag. "What's that?"

"I'm in a Ross Macdonald mood."

"Can't get enough of the Oirish, can you."

It was meant to be funny. Neither of them laughed.

They took the PA turnpike east, crossed over to the NJ turnpike, then flew out of Newark.

Yeah, I know."

"You know what?" Kowalski asked.

"I was there in Newark. I saw you. I was the guy who alerted the team in L.A."

"Bullshit." Kowalski shifted in his seat. The metal seat was cold against his balls and ass. He knew why they'd stripped him naked. It makes you feel that much more vulnerable. Not Kowalski—he really didn't give a shit. It was just uncomfortable, and that pissed him off.

"No, seriously," the interrogator said. "This probably isn't professional of me, but I was there, three rows away. You were trying to read a paperback copy of *The Way Some People Die*, but you kept looking at your blonde friend. She looked distracted. Maybe even a little sad."

"Did she, now?"

"Don't take it hard. I'm good at what I do. As you're about to learn."

"Well, your L.A. team sucked."

The interrogator smirked. "Yeah. They did suck, didn't they?"

Kowalski spotted them just a few yards out of the gate at LAX. He didn't tell Vanessa, because he didn't want to worry her. Not until it was necessary.

As it turned out, it never was.

Out of the rental place, Kowalski avoided the freeways and found La Cienega and rode it all the way up, right through the hoods. He lost them near Inglewood. Kowalski hoped they weren't fresh CI-6 recruits. They were fond of plucking them right from colleges, filling their head with junk, patting their fannies, and nudging them out into the field. If they didn't have a few ounces of street sense, they would be eaten alive. Not that this was Kowalski's problem.

"This is L.A.?" Vanessa asked. "Jaysus, it's just another slum. With palm trees."

"They're dying out, actually," he said. "Some kind of fungal disease. Pretty soon it'll be just slum."

"Maybe the Mary Kates got to them already."

Kowalski watched her as he drove. She touched the vial on her necklace. It matched his, which he also wore around his neck. Hers with his blood, his with hers. The vials kept them both alive.

Forty minutes later they made it to the safe house.

It was the sweetest safe house imaginable—a one-bedroom apartment up in the Hollywood Hills. The place belonged to a screenwriter friend of Kowalski's, a guy he used to pal around with at places like Boardner's during the early 1990s. For a few hardcore weeks there, Kowalski and his buddy had tried to kill as many brain cells and bang as many aspiring actresses as possible. Now Lee Michaels was up in Vancouver shooting his first big-budget movie—a radical update of a hyperviolent 1980s TV show called *The Eviscerator*. Kowalski kept in touch with Lee over the years, buying him a rib eye and a couple of lagers whenever he found himself in L.A. In exchange, that bought him access to Lee's pad on occasion.

Lee's pad was completely unknown to CI-6.

Lee's pad was also famous.

Or famous enough, if you liked Robert Altman's version of *The Long Goodbye*. Lee's pad was where Eliot Gould, playing Philip Marlowe, lived. Upstairs, they filmed parts of Kenneth Branagh's *Dead Again*.

Vanessa had never seen either film, so the fame was lost on her. So was the apartment.

She didn't even look out the window.

Even Kowalski had to admit the view was pretty spectacular:

rolling hills of green and brown dotted with model-sized multimillion-dollar homes. In the distance, you could watch the glimmering lights of downtown. If you had to be in L.A., this is where you wanted to be.

Didn't Vanessa even want to look?

"I'm going to have a shower," she said.

Kowalski decided to have a beer.

The shower was off the bedroom. As usual, Vanessa took a long time. Kowalski idly wondered what she did in there. But he had a pretty good idea. He was halfway through his third Sierra Nevada when she stepped into the kitchen, towel around her torso.

"How about that wine?" she said, smiling as if she meant it.

Kowalski looked at her bare legs, then the towel, then her body beneath the towel, then her face, then her hair.

It was red.

Jesus fuck, she had dyed it red.

"What?" she asked, defensively. "I was tired of looking like me."

Katie had been a redhead.

Katie was his dead pregnant fiancée, who was waiting to give birth sometime in the afterlife, whenever Kowalski could arrange to be there.

"Huh," he said, then took another slug of beer.

And that's when people started showing up to kill them.

"You have to admit, the second team was pretty good," the interrogator said.

"Yeah," Kowalski said. "They were pretty good."

They were:
  Ms. Montgomery, a.k.a. "Ana Esthesia."
Mr. Brown, a.k.a. "The Surgeon."
Mrs. McCue, a.k.a. "Bonesaw."

Their skills complemented each other, which was part of the reason for their silly nicknames.

But they were also a surgical strike team, specializing in accidental and bizarre sanctions. If you want someone to die and have nobody think twice about it, you call in these kinds of people.

So, yeah. Surgical strike team, surgical nicknames. CI-6 had a fondness for the literal.

Bonesaw dug her name. Then again, she was a pain freak.

The Surgeon hardly ever spoke, so it was difficult to ascertain what he thought of his nickname, or if it even occurred to him that he should have an opinion. He did Sudoku. He answered most queries with "Yep."

Ana Esthesia had a mental defect; she claimed to be able to rid herself of any kind of pain by inflicting the equal and opposite pain on others. Shoot her in the leg, and she'd immediately recover after shooting *you* in the leg. CI-6 experts could find no physiological basis for this claim; they thought she was nuts. She considered it a superpower. They tagged her "Ana Esthesia" as a joke. She called them names—*asshat, fucktard*—so she'd feel better. Sticks and stones, and all that.

She went in first.

There were only two ways into Lee Michaels's apartment: up a caged elevator within a high tower that gave the complex its name, or up a winding set of concrete stairs. The elevator clacked and hummed so loudly it might as well have been an announcement: *Hello there—coming up to kill you!* So Ana opted for the concrete stairs.

She jumped a white partition meant to give the apartment's patio a little privacy. She crouched down then inched her away around to the glass-paneled door, which opened out.

She didn't carry weapons. She liked to use what she could find.

She found something on the patio: a little metal table, with a glass ashtray and a couple of Corona Extra bottle caps littering the top.

She cleared off the crap, hurled the table through the glass.

She stepped in directly behind it.

Kowalski was too distracted by Vanessa's new hair color to fully comprehend why the glass patio door had suddenly exploded and a surly-looking teenager had come charging through it.

The teenager pushed Vanessa to the floor. Vanessa's towel unraveled. The sight distracted Kowalski for another fraction of a second. In the time they'd been living together, he'd never seen her naked before.

The teenager charged and smashed her forehead into Kowalski's. His eyes teared up, and he staggered back into the kitchen. It was difficult to keep his balance; his leg was still in a light brace. The Sierra Nevada slipped out of his hand, shattered on the floor.

The teenager was grinning.

Through blurred vision he could see her face a little better, and okay, maybe she wasn't quite a teenager. She had young features, though—small mouth, upturned nose. And her dark hair had an ice-blue streak running down the front, which is some kind of silly shit teenagers do to worry their parents.

She reached out and slapped Kowalski's face, as if to get his attention.

Then she followed up with a short, shockingly hard punch to his mouth, which loosened two of his teeth.

Kowalski slapped out at her, like he was trying to kill a fly. It was suddenly very hard to see. There were three teenagers standing in front of him. He was swallowing his own blood. Blood and pale ale: not a recommended combination.

Goddamnit, what had just happened?

The three teenagers wound up for another punch. Kowalski

snapped off something cheap and dirty at the middle teenager. Her lip split.

Her eyes fluttered, and her lips quivered, as if she were going to cry. Jesus, he'd just punched a little girl in the fucking face.

Then she lashed out and nailed him in the mouth again. That one did the trick. Kowalski felt two teeth roll back onto his tongue. He had big teeth.

The teenager's face changed. Tears went bye-bye; now she was beaming like it was Christmas morning.

"Hah!" she shouted.

What the fuck was wrong with her? Kowalski thought, trying to catch his own teeth before he swallowed them.

And how did they know about this place?

How did you know about the place?"

"You led us there," the interrogator said.

"So I didn't lose the first team in Inglewood?"

"No, you did. They were even shot at by a couple of gangbangers. Which made for an amusing getaway interlude. People are still giving them shit about it."

"So how did you find us?"

The interrogator paused, then smiled. "You really don't know, do you? Ana must have hit you harder than I thought."

Kowalski looked down at the table. His vision still wasn't right. His perfect 20/20 vision went away the moment that blue-streaked teenager headbutted him. The bitch.

Cunt," Vanessa said, then smashed the teenager in the head with a steel tea kettle.

The girl fell to her hands and knees, scream-cried. She sounded like a tea kettle. Kowalski followed through with a boot stomp on her back, smashing her into the jagged remnants of the Sierra Nevada.

Kowalski looked up to Vanessa, who had three sets of breasts and six nipples.

God his vision was fucked.

Think about that later. Kowalski turned and spat blood into the sink. A tooth landed on porcelain. Another tumbled down the drain.

"Shit," he said. He'd lost some upper teeth before, never one on the bottom row. It had been a point of pride with him. A small point, but still. Mother*fucker*. He picked up the remaining tooth, closed it in his right fist.

The teenager on the floor was sobbing violently now, her lungs pumping hard, her fingers shaking, her eyes squeezed shut, and a blood-line of drool connecting her lower lip to the floor.

"Hey," Vanessa said, crouching down. "Come on now. Stop it." She reached to touch the girl's leg.

"Wait," Kowalski said. "She's . . ."

Too late.

The teenager nailed Vanessa in the tits with her boot, sending her backwards across the kitchen. She crashed into the table, one end of which flipped up and hit her in the back of the head.

It would have been funny if it hadn't looked so painful.

The teenager sprung to her feet, never mind that the act of pushing her palms against the bottle shards cut them deeper. She still was an absolute mess, all drool and blood and tears, but she looked deliriously happy.

Vanessa moaned and struggled to catch her breath. Her fingers clawed at the linoleum as if there were some kind of painkiller hidden beneath.

"You're sensitive there, I can feel it," the girl said, then saw a corkscrew on the kitchen counter. Kowalski had bought it at Vons along with the pinot noir. The teenager considered it quickly; decided it would do.

She reached out for it.

Kowalski wrapped his right arm around her neck and squeezed. This was Kowalski's signature move. He likened himself to the trash monster from *Star Wars*: once he had you locked in, there was little you could use outside the power of the motherfucking Force to free yourself.

Unfortunately, the teenager was quick. She already had the corkscrew in her hand.

The Motherfucking Force vs. $3.99 corkscrew from Vons over on Sunset.

She sliced his cheek. Kowalski tilted his head back, squeezed harder. She whipped around, caught him on a love handle. The sharp point tore his flesh. Fuck, she was a squirmy thing.

He continued squeezing.

By the time the teenager was unconscious, Kowalski had puncture wounds and gashes in his leg, back, face, and forearm. As well as his right love handle.

He let her drop to the kitchen floor, then sat down to collect his thoughts and take stock of his injuries. Which were fairly numerous, for what was essentially twenty seconds of wild slashing violence. He ran his tongue around his mouth, feeling if anything else was loose.

Across the room, Vanessa pushed herself up on her arms.

"I fooking wish you carried a gun," she said.

"I wish I carried dental insurance," Kowalski said. He opened his right fist and looked down at his bloodied tooth.

Vanessa reached out and found the towel. Kowalski realized that the free show was over, and he hadn't any time to fully appreciate it.

Who was he kidding. He wouldn't have allowed himself to, anyway.

"You okay?" he asked.

"I won't be bringing the girls out to play anytime soon." She rewrapped the towel around her torso.

"We have to get to San Diego. Now."

"Figured that."

They were silent as they quickly gathered their things.

Haven't figured it out yet, have you?" The interrogator was loving this. Possibly as much as the idea of using his little knife. What was that anyway? Something he took from the kitchen at home? Something his wife ordered at a Pampered Chef party?

"Yeah," Kowalski said. "I figured it out. The first team pushed us to a specific car rental place. You had someone there waiting. You tagged the Taurus with a homing device."

The interrogator shook his head, made a *tsk-tsk* sound. "And she said you were the smartest operative she ever worked with."

He didn't have to say who. "She" was enough to wedge the blade under his armor.

"Then again," the interrogator continued, "she's no longer with us."

Kowalski said nothing.

"In answer to your theory: No, we did not bug the Taurus. We had something else."

Kowalski said nothing.

And then it came to him. Oh, of fucking course. How stupid can one man be? Maybe he *had* been knocked in the brains one too many times.

He'd known it had happened. He just didn't know it had happened so early.

"The Surgeon certainly thought the device came in handy."

The Surgeon watched the targets take the stairs down from the apartment. They faded in and out of view. That was okay. He also had them on his handheld tracker. Two pulsing red dots, making their way slowly across a grid. No way of losing them.

So he was more or less relaxing, smoking a Pall Mall, something he had a hard time doing practically anywhere in L.A. In this empty apartment, though, it was okay. Maybe a rental agent would detect a faint hint of smoke, but by then, he'd be long gone.

He only expected to be here a few more minutes, actually.

Maybe just sixty seconds.

A quick phone call (fuck the Internet; The Surgeon was old school) had revealed that Lee Michaels owned the third garage on the left. The garages were positively Stone Age: just a box of concrete wedged into a muddy hill with corrugated steel doors. It was enough to accommodate most midsized vehicles. Like a Ford Taurus.

Even the most primitive of garages, however, have a door handle.

The trap was so easy to set. Just put The Stuff in your right-hand pocket, grab a stack of supermarket circulars, walk up to the apartment gate, give 'em a circular, then on the way back quickly put on some gloves and coat The Stuff on the handle.

The Stuff was great. Mr. Brown loved working with it every chance he got.

The Stuff killed on contact with skin. Not right away, but within fifteen to twenty minutes. Knocked you unconscious. For good.

The Stuff was completely untraceable. Not even the CIA knew about The Stuff. Not *this* Stuff.

So Mr. Brown staked out an apartment across the way and smoked while he waited. He also tore open a packet of mint pastilles, and he scooped a handful into his mouth between cigarettes. It fought the nicotine breath. Women were so picky about that.

Maybe after this he'd go down to Sunset and try to get himself a date.

The great thing about the garages was that they were so narrow. Only one person could squeeze in at a time. The thing to do was worm your way into the driver's seat, back the car out, then have your passenger lower the garage door for you before hopping in.

That meant two people touching the garage door handle. The driver. And the passenger.

Oh, and here they were, heading to the garage, thinking they were about to make a clean getaway.

Yep.

The Surgeon was mildly surprised that Ms. Montgomery had failed to take them out herself. She was usually good. He hoped she wasn't dead.

But then again, it was nice to strut his Stuff, too.

Kowalski reached for the garage door.

"Wait," Vanessa said.

"Nobody's hiding in the garage," he said. "I rigged it. If this had been opened in the last few hours, I would have known."

"Rigged it with what? A piece of tape up in the corner?"

Kowalski didn't say anything, because that was precisely how he'd rigged it. A piece of tape, up in the corner. It was still there.

"I'll open it quick," he said. "We jump if there's an explosion."

Vanessa looked at him. "Bollocks." She reached down, grabbed the handle, and yanked the door upward. It rattled as it moved along the rusty tracks and settled into place above her head.

No explosions.

No gunfire.

No nothing.

Kowalski gave her a *See?* look.

"Well, go on then," she said.

"One down," mumbled the Surgeon. He helped himself to more mint pastilles.

But there was a problem now. The girl was good as dead, but the male target—this Kowalski—was squeezing himself in alongside the car, making his way to the driver's seat. Which meant he wouldn't touch the garage door handle at all.

It was a good thing he'd prepared a secondary device.

This was even more ingenious. It was a strip of clear tape, running across the length of the garage, about six inches away from the outside of the door.

The tape was pressure-sensitive. Step on it—hell, stomp on it, hard as you can—and nothing. Just an ordinary piece of electrician's tape. But roll the approximate weight of an automobile over the tape, and watch out.

Ka-Boomsville.

You can do all the forensic analysis you want, and all you'd find is a blown back tire that somehow, incredibly, sparked the gas tank, resulting in catastrophic combustion. That would be your best guess, anyhow. The tape would have long burned up into nothingness. You'd have nothing to analyze.

The Surgeon watched the male target start the car. Popped a mint.

Then he hit the remote control that activated the tape.

K owalski started the car. He didn't like this feeling. Jittery. Nerves on edge. Things moving too fast. Being forced out of his safe house—the safest place he knew—in less than an hour. Compromised. This wasn't like CI-6. They weren't usually this sharp. He thought he'd have more time to prepare. A week would have been nice.

Worst of all, he still had beers left up in Lee's place. God, that pissed him off.

Kowalski reached for the gear shift. His hand missed. On the second try, he found it.

There was a fluttering in his stomach. He was almost *never* sick to his stomach.

Kowalski sighed, then turned off the ignition. Stepped out of the car, feeling the blood rush out of his head. Squeezed himself alongside the Taurus.

"I need you to drive," he said.

He threw the keys to the redhead.

She caught them, no problem. "I don't know how to drive in America."

"We'll be on the 5 the whole time. Just stick to a lane. You'll be fine."

"To be perfectly frank, I don't know how to drive. Like, at all."

"Piece of cake. Just stay between the white lines."

This was a lie, and Vanessa looked like she knew it. But there wasn't much choice. The nausea was full on now, and the dizzy feeling refused to go away, no matter how much Kowalski controlled his breathing. It was going to take some effort to stay conscious in the passenger seat, let alone the driver's seat.

Vanessa slid alongside the car, hopped behind the wheel, and turned the ignition. Kowalski stepped back. *If she makes it out of the garage in one piece, I'll consider it a good omen.*

She put the Taurus in reverse and backed out of the garage.

The Surgeon braced himself.

He had a vision of the blast taking his target's head off, bouncing it against the window here, leaving a smudge of burned flesh and a smear of blood.

Yep.

Vanessa managed to avoid running over Kowalski. She pulled up alongside him, hammered the brake. The Taurus rocked on its suspension.

"Getting in then?" she asked.

What the fuck?!

He saw it. The car ran over the tape. *Right over the tape.*

His devices had never failed before.

Never.

It was a good thing he'd brought along a tertiary device.

Kowalski had just snapped his seat belt—hey, she admitted she didn't know how to drive—when this tubby, balding guy came stumbling out of the doorway, gun in hand. Running towards them. Aiming for them.

"Go," Kowalski said. "Go now."

Tubby fired once. The windshield cracked. Vanessa screamed.

"Gas pedal," Kowalski said. "Gun it."

She gunned it. The car shot backwards ten feet before she pushed the brake with both feet. The Taurus rocked. Tubby aimed again.

Kowalski plucked the cigarette lighter from the dash.

Tubby fired.

The shot went high.

Vanessa pushed the accelerator. The engine screamed.

"Put it in drive," Kowalski said, then opened his door and winged the cigarette lighter at Tubby's head. It nailed him in the mouth. Which was okay, but Kowalski had been aiming for his eyes. Tubby's lips trembled, like he was fighting a sneeze. Kowalski reached down, grabbed the gear shift, said, "Brake, now!" and Vanessa did, and then he slid it into drive, and was about to tell her, "Gas!" but she was already there, slamming it.

The Taurus rocketed forward, smashed into Tubby.

"Go!" Kowalski said.

Tubby was airborne.

The Taurus raced down the hill.

The Surgeon tried one last time to shoot the girl in the face, but by this time he was tumbling through the air. He squeezed the trigger, but the bullet went wild.

Way wild.

Right into the ground.

Right into a strip of clear electrical tape, running parallel to the front of the third garage.

Walk on it, stomp on it... nothing. You need something with the mass of a motor vehicle to set it off, when charged properly.

Of course, charged or not, there's something else that will set it off.

A speeding bullet.

Yeah, that'd do it nicely.

So before The Surgeon was even able to crash into the ground, the explosion blew him back and upwards into the air, flipping him head over heels at least twice before he crashed through the very window he'd been looking through a minute ago.

And in that way, one little bit of the Surgeon's vision came true. For a fraction of a section, burnt flesh was smeared against the glass, along with a little bit of blood.

Then the glass shattered, and through it came the Surgeon.

"That guy just blew up," Vanessa said.

"Drive," Kowalski said.

"Why did he blow up?"

"Just drive."

"Michael."

"What?"

"*Why did that guy blow up?*"

"Drive!"

"Jaysus." She sighed.

"Now a left," Kowalski said.

The blast woke Ana.

Her eyes fluttered open, and quickly she realized she

was drowning in a sea of pain. Delicious pain. Pain she could use. Just as soon as she stood up.

Oh.

She couldn't.

One of the two fucktards, either the cripple with the missing teeth or the naked bitch, had smashed in one of her kneecaps. Perhaps the most sensitive part of the human anatomy, aside from the sexual organs or the eyes. Physical trauma applied to the kneecap was immediately crippling, engulfing the pain centers of the brain to the point of overload.

Thus, a source of overwhelming power.

Ana wouldn't need to walk. She could crawl on her elbows and one remaining knee and smite those who had done this to her. Smite them with their own *pain*.

She sat up.

Or tried to, at least.

But her arms were pinned above her. Handcuffed around the base of a toilet.

No no no no.

This meant that the pain would have to stay within her, with no chance of release. And that was unacceptable. Because there was one thing Ana could not handle for long, and that was *pain*. Especially pain of this magnitude.

Ana screamed and cried and begged for release.

Any kind of release.

Oh how it HURT!

Kowalski had to take a piss. But he'd be damned if he let the interrogator know that.

He considered just letting it go, right here, right onto the concrete floor, the body-temperature liquid splattering the interrogator's shoes.

"Tell me," Kowalski, "how you found her."

"She came to us," the interrogator said.

"What, she had your address?"

"Hang on, now. We're off track here. I'm supposed to be asking *you* questions. You know the deal. You don't answer, I slice pieces off you and put them over there." He pointed to a metal bucket, which had been placed in the corner. "You continue to be stubborn, I get to feed you those pieces."

"I'm answering your questions."

"I know. You suck."

The interrogator played with the paper cover of his little Pampered Chef knife.

"Well, go on. San Diego."

"San Diego," Kowalski repeated.

"San Diego."

"SAN DIEGO!" Kowalski shouted.

The whole drive down to San Diego, they had no idea. No idea that a third assassin had wiped the garage door handle clean, disabled the explosive tape. Just to fuck with The Surgeon. (Arrogant prick.)

No idea she was tracking them now, with a handheld device, courtesy of CI-6.

She was called many things. Assassin. Killer. Psycho.

But what she really got off on was her CI-6 nickname:

Bonesaw.

It just sounded painful. And she liked that.

Her specialty was the odd, seemingly random killings you hear about on the news every once in a while. Those freaky *serial killings*. Sure, there was media attention. Once in a while, even a movie option. That was the point. Cops and reporters went hunting for a lone madman. They never thought it was the government.

Bonesaw liked that, too.

Oh, she had a real girly name once—Monica McCue. Ugh. Poke the back of her throat, make her gag. She never felt like a *Monica McCue*. Since she was a little girl, she'd always felt like a . . . well, a bone saw.

It was rare they let her do her thing. Which was why she took it upon herself to push The Surgeon out of the way.

She wanted to show them what she could do. She had a whole bunch of new ideas. Sitting around last night, she jotted something like forty-two of them down in her notebook.

Ways to kill people.

That morning Bonesaw got up, stepped into the brilliant California sunshine, and narrowed it down to a half dozen ideas. She sipped some iced coffee, bit her lip hard thinking about those ideas. A little blood got in the coffee. Gave it a little salty kick. She liked that. And that decided it for her.

She'd bring a box of syringes with her. She'd have to stuff the box with cotton, because she didn't want them rattling around in her backpack. The cotton would come in handy anyway.

"They're not going to stop, are they?"

Kowalski looked at her. The multiple of hers. He definitely had a concussion. Even turning his eyes made him want to vomit. So he turned his whole head. Watched the trees and buildings and clouds and vehicles whiz by the driver's side window. That made him even more nauseous.

"They sent two," he said, "so there's probably a third on the way. It's never just two. Either one is enough, or they order double backups."

"I mean after."

"After what?"

"After we go public."

"Depends on what you have in San Diego."

Vanessa had told him that before she quit the lab in Dublin, she'd dumped as much as she could into a USB key. She was fairly sure she saw Excel files. Which probably meant financial transactions. If they could financially tie the Proximity nanovirus to CI-6, the fuckers would sink under the weight. Nobody could survive scrutiny like that, no matter how secret or buried.

You try bankrolling something that winds up infecting most of North America—and, like, can kill on demand via satellite. See how far your career goes then. It's not exactly something you can hide on your résumé.

Kowalski had held off on rushing to San Diego. Bolting there right away would have raised eyebrows, he thought.

Now it didn't seem like it fucking mattered.

But he hadn't lied. CI-6 was predictable. They wouldn't have just sent two killers. What was strange, however, was that they usually tried to make it look like an accident. The first one—random home invasion. He got it. But this second killer just charged at them with a gun. I mean, where the hell was the finesse in that?

Maybe the third killer would be just as obvious.

He hoped.

"I just keep going south on 5?"

"Wake me up when you see signs for Solana Beach."

"If I don't get us into a massive collision."

"Wake me up if that happens, too."

"Now it's time for the interesting part," said the interrogator. "Come on, on your feet."

"What?" Kowalski asked.

"Pain time. Remember? The bucket? Little pieces of you on the menu?"

"Hey, I'm telling you everything."

The interrogator smiled. "I *know* you're not telling me everything. And I know you're not just going to sit here and piss away the only card you have left. Not this easy."

The word "piss" reminded Kowalski. He wouldn't be able to keep his bladder on clampdown too much longer. He needed to get this moving.

"So c'mon then," the interrogator said, pushing his chair back. "Let's get you on the hook the easy way, okay? You'll want to save your strength for the main event."

"You want to know what was on the USB key? I'll tell you. I'll even write it out for you."

The interrogator stood up, looked down at the tiny knife in his hand, then back up at Kowalski.

"You know, this isn't fucking fair. They told me you'd be impossible to break. Can't you just play along?"

"What can I say? One look at you, and I'm ready to spill everything."

Kowalski locked his eyes on one of the surveillance cameras. "The man who authorized the purchase of Proximity was a spook named David Murphy. First payment was sent July 12, bank routing number 4987B . . ."

"Oh you're no fun at all," the interrogator said.

Nobody tried to kill them outside the Westin Horton Plaza. Nobody flinched when they went to the front desk and asked for a package for "Mary Kate." Nobody tried to stab them in the elevator. Nobody was hiding in their closets or in the shower. Nobody even noticed when Kowalski filched an Apple iBook from a portly dude in a black T-shirt.

Once they were inside their room, Vanessa decided she needed another shower.

"Got to wash the boot print off my tits."

Kowalski couldn't argue with that. He wished he could wash the boot print off his skull, but it seemed to be permanently stamped there. Once he knew what was on this USB, maybe he'd have the luxury of some real sleep in the near future.

"Anybody breaks in and tries to kill us," she said, "just knock on the door three times."

"Enjoy your shower."

Kowalski suspected she went in there just to be alone, and to cry. She showered a lot.

He used to do that, too. Right after Katie.

He fired up the computer and looked for Excel files. There was a lot of junk on this USB key. All he needed was a name he recognized. Come on, come on. Give me something to work with, baby.

Something pinched his neck.

"Ow," he said, and reached up to feel his neck. Or at least, he thought he did. But his hands remained frozen over the keyboard.

"Shhhh, now," said a voice at his ear.

Oh fuck.

Hello, third killer.

The shower water pummeling tile made for nice, soothing white noise in the background. The voice, which was female, was almost as soothing.

"I put a needle in your spinal cord. You're paralyzed from the neck down. I'm going to push it in a little further now, and that will freeze everything else. You *might* be able to blink. But that's iffy."

"Wait..."

She did.

He was lucky. He still could blink. That was something.

The woman set him up in a chair in the corner so he faced the rest of the room. He heard the ripping of tape. She was probably using some to keep the needle in his neck in place. As if he could someone how blink hard enough to make it wobble and fall out of his spinal cord.

She leaned over him as she worked. Her tits were in his face. She smelled faintly of rubbing alcohol.

She crouched down in front of him. "I've been asking myself, who would be the victim? I think it has to be the redhead. You're the one with the scarier background. She's only been killing for a short while."

How do you know about her? he wanted to ask.

Of course he couldn't.

She reached into a backpack which was by her feet. Kowalski hadn't know it was there. Shit, he hadn't even known she was there. Where didn't he check? The drapes? Fuck. He was better than this. It had to be the concussion.

Yeah, sure, blame the concussion.

Admit it. You've gotten sloppy, monster.

Otherwise, you wouldn't have received the concussion in the first place.

"Guy like you," she continued, "killer virus in your blood . . . It could make anyone snap."

She showed him a white cardboard box, raised her eyebrows. She was actually strikingly beautiful. Even when she opened the lid and showed him what was inside.

Many, many syringes.

"You freaked out, Kowalski. You thought you could save her. One vial of blood at a time. If you could take enough blood out of her veins, you could help her get rid of the virus. Isn't that right? You kept drawing more and more and more blood until she fell asleep. You stuck the full syringes on the wall over there, and you made the shape of a heart, because you know, during these past few months, you've fallen in love with her. And that's why you're trying to cure her. Because you love her, Kowalski. You love her don't you?"

Sloppy, sloppy monster.

"And then you're going to realize that your cure isn't going to work, because she's lost too much blood now, and she's gone. And the only thing left to do is sit here in this chair and slice your own throat with a shaving razor. You're a trained professional. You know exactly how deep to cut."

Inside the bathroom, the shower water turned off.

"Of course, that's after you cut off *her* head," she whispered.

Kowalski had heard stories about these types of CI-6 killers. Pain freaks loved to work with nervous systems, either numbing them to the point of paralysis or exposing them to agony so extreme that few human beings could process it. They were smart people. They had to be. But they were also fucking nuts.

He watched her position her back to the bathroom wall, syringe in her hand, ready to strike Vanessa the moment she emerged. She'd know exactly where to plunge the needle, too, to paralyze her instantly.

And then she'd start drawing blood.

The bathroom door opened. Steam flowed out of the doorway. Vanessa liked her showers hot.

The pain freak winked at Kowalski.

And then something white and round whipped around the corner and smashed the pain freak in the face.

Vanessa emerged, toilet seat in hand, and gave her another mad powerful whack.

The syringe tumbled out of the pain freak's hand and stuck itself in the carpet. She followed right behind it. As she fell, Kowalski could see that part of her face had been destroyed. He'd be the last man to see her look so good.

Vanessa was completely dry, wrapped in a towel. She hadn't even stepped into the shower. It had all been a ruse.

"Been curious about something," she said.

Kowalski blinked.

"You're a professional killer. Why don't you carry *any fooking guns?*"

There was nothing Kowalski could do, except blink twice.

Which he hoped sounded like, "Bite me."

It took a little while for Vanessa to figure it all out. She was all like, What the hell is wrong with you? Why aren't you moving?

Kowalski gestured with his eyes best he could. Look. Look at the back of my neck. See all that tape? No, no. Back. There. Finally Vanessa got the clue, looked behind his head. "Jaysus," she said. There was a little more one-sided back-and-forth, with Vanessa finally instituting a blink once for yes, twice for no system, and asking questions like, "Are you paralyzed?" and "Is that needle why you're paralyzed?" and finally, at long last, "Do you want me to pull the needle out?" FUCKING YES, Kowalski wanted to yell, I'd like you to pull the fucking needle out of my neck. Such a move could paralyze him permanently. But that would be fine. He could always blink until Vanessa realized he wanted to be mercy-killed.

"Don't move," she said, leaning over him, and then realized what she said.

She started laughing.

"Sorry."

There were a few harrowing moments there at the beginning, and Kowalski honestly thought he would be paralyzed for life. But sensation came back, and with it, a dull throbbing pain in pretty much every part of his body that featured nerve endings.

"Is she dead?" he asked, when he could.

"Not yet."

"Good. Grab that box of syringes."

"You left our three operatives alive," said the interrogator. "Why was that?"

"Three?"

"Yes. Three."

"What about the guy who blew up?" Kowalski asked.

"He made it, too. He'll probably have a surgery every couple of days until he dies, which may not be too far off in the future. And Ana's not happy about her kneecap. Nor, Bonesaw, about her face. But my point is, you didn't go back to finish the job. That's not the Kowalski we know. What's the deal?"

Kowalski thought about it. What did it matter if he told him? "Vanessa lost her taste for killing," he said.

"Oh really."

It was true. Vanessa Reardon may have flown across the United States, killing men for the sin of trying to pick her up, but somehow, she'd compartmentalized it. She hadn't been Vanessa Reardon then. She had been Kelly Dolores White, and she had been created by Matthew Silver, a man who'd tried to fuck, marry, and then finally, kill her. Kelly White was capable of murder because that was what she knew from birth.

But now, ever since Silver's brains had been splattered all over the side of Pennsylvania Hospital in downtown Philly, Kelly White had been fading away. Vanessa Reardon had been coming back. And she was more than a little horrified about what had happened while she'd been gone.

"So it bothered her to kill people," the interrogator said, "who had been sent to kill her."

"That's about the size of it."

"Then explain one thing."

"What's that?"

"The seventeen people she killed in Mexico."

Rosarito was the only place that made any sense. It was not too far over the border, and it was a familiar enough place for Kowalski. He'd spent seven months here in 1995, recuperating from injuries after a field op had gone to shit. It was a fine place to put your mind and body back together. He had rented a small house south of Rosarito proper, right on the beach, for pennies. There were very few ways in, so you could easily see enemies coming. There were enough tourists around, so you never stuck out.

Kowalski also had a box of plastic-wrapped weapons buried

near his old rental house. Right on the beach. Unless someone had dug it up since then.

Most importantly, Kowalski knew a good cheap Mexican dentist who might be able to put his remaining tooth back in his mouth.

He wasn't ready to give that up just yet.

They crossed the border at dusk. There were no problems, especially since they'd traded the car with the cracked windshield in for a less conspicuous vehicle. It was another beige Ford Taurus. Vanessa said she'd just gotten the hang of it, and it would worry her to change it up.

Just over the border she announced she was famished. Kowalski told her they'd be sitting down to real Mexican food in under thirty minutes, but she asked him for a dollar anyway and bought a bag of fried bread from a kid on the street. She regretted the purchase after taking a bite. She dumped the rest in a compartment between the driver and passenger seats.

Roads in Mexico were much more challenging than I-5 south. Painted lanes? Yeah. Sure. And then there were the potholes the size of kiddie swimming pools.

"Fooking hell," she said. "This is worse than L.A."

And it had been a while for Kowalski, so he was a little confused as to which road would take them down to Rosarito. Had they moved the roads since then?

Maybe it was his concussion. Or being paralyzed.

The darkness didn't help, either.

After a while it seemed like they were seeing the same gas stations and shuttered buildings and nonsensical road signs. Kowalski wanted to close his eyes. That wasn't going to happen. Not for a while, anyway.

Until he finally saw the sign for Fox Studios Baja.

James Cameron had built this massive tank down here for *Titanic*, and since then a bunch of movies involving large bodies of water had been shot here, too. Kowalski had been gone before they built the thing, but he visited enough times to know he was close.

"We're here," he said.

"Thank Christ," she said. "I'm starving."

"First we have to go to the beach."

"What?"

"You were the one complaining about my lack of *fooking* guns."

The little cluster of houses was still there. Only now there was a guard at top of the road leading down to the beach. Vanessa flirted with him best she could while Kowalski crept down to his old house, which was occupied, of course. He made his way to the spot on his hands and knees, and was grateful that nobody had decided to install a cement patio over the spot. The box was three feet down. The tops of his fingers were raw by the time they brushed against the dark green metal. There was no sound in the house. Just the sound of his own breathing and the waves crashing on the shore.

He thought about taking the whole box, but that might be tough to check in to a hotel. So he grabbed a few essentials.

A 9mm Luger.

A 9mm Beretta Brigadier, for Vanessa.

Boxes of ammo for both.

And finally, an M-79 40mm grenade launcher, along with some high-explosive rounds and shotguns rounds (20 ought buck). For those close-call getaways.

He stuffed the guns in his pants, ammo in his pockets, then reburied the box, slung the M-79 over his shoulder, and crab-walked out of there.

Vanessa left the road guard incredibly confused yet undeniably aroused.

"There's a hotel and restaurant up the road," Kowalski said. "Maybe ten minutes."

"You said something similar when we crossed the border."

Kowalski reached into his pants, pulled out the Beretta, handed it to her.

"Happy Birthday."

"Wow," she said.

"Just drive."

Ten minutes north was the Rosarito Baja Resort and Cocktail Lounge, with emphasis on the last part. The place made a half-hearted attempt at being touristy, but mostly attracted tourists who didn't give a shit about that kind of stuff. Tourists who wanted to eat cheap Mexican food and drink themselves stupid.

Kowalski left the M-79 in the trunk, but took the Luger. He told Vanessa to put the Beretta in her bag. He carried the laptop and USB with him, in the little carry bag he'd stolen along with the computer. He carried in his tooth, too.

They were ready for dinner.

The restaurant was mildly crowded. It was the late dinner, early drinking set. Outside the windows, and across an empty pool, Kowalski could see a giant patio covered by a tent. Beneath it, there was a large crowd of people square-dancing. Yeah, that's what it was. A crowd of Asian tourists, square-dancing. That, or his concussion was getting worse.

Their chicken enchiladas and empanadas and nachos and salsa and bottles of cold Dos Equis had just about arrived when the stranger sat down at the table with them.

She dressed like a tourist: white hoodie with stripes running down the arms, Corona over the right breast, jeans. Hair up with a clip.

Strangely enough, she was a redhead.

"She gave you some Proximity tech," Kowalski said. "Which is how you were able to track our movements so precisely."

"Precise *is* the word." He fished around in the pocket of his trousers and pulled out a small plastic unit with an LCD display.

He showed it to Kowalski. The display had a map of North America. There was a pulsating dot in the northeast corner of Pennsylvania. And another around San Diego.

"And see, I thought she came right for us."

"She had the blonde's DNA, from the lab back in Dublin. We gave her yours." He looked down at the device. "Funny how Vanessa's still registers, even though she's dead."

"Yeah. Funny. So how did she find you?"

"She didn't," the interrogator said. "She tried to make contact with your, um, ex-girlfriend after she'd been removed from her post. We intercepted the message. We made contact. We brought her in. She told us what we needed to know."

"And then you just let her come after us?"

"Well, not exactly. She kind of fucked us over on that. We wanted you alive. She went out there to punish you."

"Right."

"Which brings us to the point of our meeting, Michael. We need to know where she is now. And you were the last person to see her, according to the hotel staff—right before your little blonde friend went on her second killing spree."

"Listen—"

"Hang on now. Don't just blurt it all out. Think it over. Because the moment you tell us, and we verify, you're a dead man."

"Look, she's—"

"Shhh now. Shhhhh. Don't you want a little more life? Or the chance that we'll keep you alive until you tell us?" He played with the small knife in his hands.

Kowalski smiled. "You forgot what I told you."

"What's that?"

"You're the one who's going to die. Every fucking last one you."

"You killed my brother," the stranger said, then reached over and helped herself to a sip of Kowalski's beer.

Which was the only thing he'd planned on eating. His teeth were too messed up to chew a steak or even a taco, and he hated burritos. So it was pretty much beer—and later, when he found the right guy, some painkillers—on the menu. He'd ordered food so Vanessa wouldn't feel self-conscious.

"That's my beer," Kowalski said. "Who was your brother?"

"You knew him as Matthew Silver," she said. "He was lusting after this one for a while. He used to e-mail me about her." She turned to glare at Vanessa. "My brother made you sound like a real prude. Couldn't you have done the world a favor, spotted him a handjob?"

"Your brother was a whiny little bitch," Vanessa said.

"Look at us. We could be sisters."

"Died like one, too."

"Ladies, ladies," Kowalski said, pretending to play peacemaker, but actually reaching down into his trouser pocket for the Luger. He wrapped his hand around the grip.

The strange redhead, meanwhile put a black purse on the table and opened it.

Here we go.

Kowalski was ready to shoot her through his pants, if need be. A messy gut shot, but it would stop her.

But the stranger wasn't going for a weapon. Rather, a small plastic box with an LCD screen. There was a digital map of North America on it. And right at the top of Baja California, approximately right where they'd sat down to a hot Mexican meal and two cold beers, were two pulsing dots.

"I helped my brother create Proximity," she said. "It's something we'd joked about at Georgia Tech. It got real a year ago. I was his silent partner."

"Got a name, little sister?" Kowalski asked. This might be her. The financial link they'd been searching for.

She smiled. "Let's see. We've got a Silver. And it was Kelly White, wasn't it? So call me Ms. Black."

"I am *not* going to call you Ms. Black. That's ridiculous."

"Lucia, then."

Kowalski scanned his memory. *Lucia, Lucia, Lucia* . . . Was the name anywhere in those Excel files? Not that it mattered, really. They would subdue this one, make her talk. She would tell them everything they needed to know. He was rusty, but he still had some moves. He knew how to make it hurt.

"After I heard what happened," Lucia said, "I flew to my brother's lab. There was enough to piece together the story. As well as a tracking device."

She showed them the little plastic box again.

"How can we help you, Lucia?" Kowalski asked.

"I wanted to meet you in Los Angeles, but you were busy. I didn't know they'd try to send someone to kill you so quickly."

"We're here now. What do you want?"

"Not here. Some place quiet."

Some place quiet was an empty banquet room down a tiled hallway that featured a giant oil painting of a bull that had been stabbed with three lances. Kowalski kicked out the door stop. With a pneumatic hiss, the door closed behind him.

Kowalski gave Vanessa a look, and they both pulled their guns on Lucia.

He had no idea if Vanessa even knew how to use a gun. But the intimidation factor had to be a bonus.

They both aimed for her head.

"I'm unarmed," Lucia said.

"Of course you are," Kowalski said.

Lucia quickly pressed a series of buttons her little plastic box. "Mr. Kowalski, you're going to want to back up right about now." Lucia moved closer to Vanessa.

"Hey," Vanessa said. "Stop."

Something beeped.

"Or what? You'll shoot? You won't shoot me. Because if you do, you'll have no way of reversing what I've just done to you."

"What did you do?" Kowalski asked.

She turned and raised her eyebrows. "Mr. Kowalski, really, back up. At least ten feet."

And now maybe it was the concussion, or the sip of beer he'd had, or a delayed reaction the paralyzing needle prick from the gorgeous pain freak in San Diego . . . but Kowalski's head really started to throb badly. Worse with every beat of his pulse. Like there was something expanding in his brain, trying to push his eyes out of their sockets from within.

"Fuck," he said. He meant to step backward, but ended up tripping forward.

It got WORSE.

Holy fucking GOD.

Is this what they all went through, right before the Mary Kates ate their brains?

"Back, Mr. Kowalski. That's the other direction. Quickly now."

"*What did you do to me!?*" Vanessa screamed.

He was finally able to scoot backward, out of range. The pain seemed to diminish slightly. But he still wanted to throw up.

"I've reprogrammed your nanites. You're now a killer for real now, Vanessa Reardon. Anyone comes within ten feet of you, you'll trigger the Proximity in their bloodstream. You'll make their brains explode."

"You . . ."

Vanessa reached out, trying to touch Lucia's shoulder.

"Me?" asked Lucia. "Honey, I'm immune. I shut down the nanites in my blood before I flew out here. Injected myself with a nanite that eats Proximity. I could drink your blood right now and be perfectly fine."

Great, Kowalski thought. Like brother, like sister.

"Unfortunately for you," she continued, "most of the continent has been infected by now. Including, I'd guess, all of the people in this hotel."

Vanessa shuddered, dropped her Beretta. Kowalski doubted she even realized it. If it was possible for a human being to fold up inside herself and disappear, Vanessa was doing it now.

"You're a killer, Vanessa. And there's nothing you can do about it."

Kowalski picked up his Luger and aimed it at Lucia's chest.

Of course, there was no way he could pull the trigger.

"That's just sick," the interrogator said, then exhaled a short burst of air. "Wow."

"Isn't it, though?"

"I mean, Jesus. I'm a guy who makes his living carving out people's assholes with a knife. But even that strikes me as going too far. Even for revenge."

The interrogator played with his knife a little more, then seemed to have a bit of a revelation.

"Oh . . . I get it now. She didn't really mean to kill those seventeen people, did she? They were collateral damage."

"You could say that."

"Man, that is wicked *cold*. I have got to meet this Lucia chick."

"You'd make a nice couple. Anyway, can I finish? I really have to take a leak, and we're almost at the end."

The interrogator put his little knife on the table then spread his hands. "By all means."

Kowalski leaned forward to finish his story.

"By the time I stood up, Vanessa was gone. She ran out of the room. So did Lucia, cackling the whole way. My head was a wreck. It took a lot of effort to stand up. I made it out to the parking lot, but the car was already gone. Vanessa took it. I didn't have much to go on. She didn't know the roads down there. She could have gone anywhere.

"I hotwired a car and went looking anyway. My vision was shot, and it was night. But I kept driving.

"A couple of hours later I saw a body by the side of the road. It was an old woman. I pulled the car over and got out. It looked like her head had been run over with a truck tire. But I knew that wasn't what happened. I'd seen that kind of gushing head wound before. Vanessa had been here. She'd killed that woman because she got too close.

"An hour later, I found two more bodies. It was a little shore town that didn't even have a name. I can only imagine that Vanessa had pulled in there because it looked dark, and maybe had beach access. She probably thought she could go to the beach and be alone and try to figure this out.

"I drove into the town and got out, and there were bodies everywhere. This is probably where you found most of the victims. Must have been a party that let out . . . something. I don't know. A couple of kids were gibbering in Spanish about *pelirrojo, pelirrojo*. Redhead.

"I ask them what happened. They told me about a crazy woman with wild hair who kept telling them to stay back, stay back. Shouting at them. Waving her arms. Trying to run away. But still, people approached, wanting to help help her. They would only make it a few steps before dropping to their knees.

"'*Ella es la plaga!*' the kids shouted. She is the plague.

"I kept driving but didn't find her. It was almost morning. She could anywhere. So I went back to the hotel, hoping she'd make her way back eventually. Once she had a chance to calm down.

"And yeah, I know that was ridiculous. The last thing she'd want was to come near me.

"I hadn't even checked into the hotel. So I waited in the lobby, drinking Diet Coke to keep myself awake.

"A couple of hours later, after the sun came up, she had me paged. I picked up the hotel's house phone.

"She told me she was at a pay phone somewhere, not to bother looking for her. She told me she was tired of killing. Of being a monster. There was nowhere left to go, she said. I told her to calm down, that I'd help her. We'd figure it out, just like we did in Philadelphia. She told me I was sweet, but no. There was no way out. Not out of this.

"She thanked me for saving her.

"She thanked me for trying.

"She thanked me for the Beretta.

"And then I heard a gun crack. I dropped the phone. A while later, I called you guys to turn myself in."

The interrogator stood up and started clapping.

"Bravo," he said. "Bra-*fucking*-vo." He turned to a camera on the ceiling. "Did you get that on tape? I mean, cut it right now and submit it to the Academy. That is fucking Oscar-caliber material."

The interrogator walked around to Kowalski's side of the table, then leaned in close to his ear. "Two things, buddy boy. You said she dropped the gun in the banquet room. Hard to blow your brains out with a gun you don't have."

Then he grabbed Kowalski's chin and used his thumb to pull down his bottom lip, exposing his lower teeth.

"And you've got all your teeth. When did you have time to see a dentist?"

Kowalski twisted his head away.

The interrogator looked practically orgasmic. "It's pain time, Mikey boy."

The next minute was what Kowalski expected. The guards came back into the room, handcuffed him, then dragged him back to the gleaming meat hook. They lifted him up, looped the links of the handcuffs over the hook, then let him drop. The cuffs cut into his wrists. Meanwhile, the interrogator had retrieved his knife. The blade caught some of the fluorescent lights in the room. It glistened.

The interrogator approached. Kowalski was hanging high enough so that his nipples were at eye level with the interrogator.

"Let me ask once more for the record," he said.

"Sure," Kowalski said.

"Where's Lucia Black?"

"I don't know."

"*Yes!*"

The interrogator moved in with the knife. Predictably, he immediately started trying to spread Kowalski's legs. Going for the anal cavity. The interrogator gestured to the guards. "Grab a leg, each of you."

This was going to hurt.

Not the anal cavity.
    His mouth.

Specifically, pushing the tooth out of his gumline again.

It was going to really hurt.

The interrogator had been right. Kowalski had been spinning him a line of bullshit, ever since the stuff about the banquet room, after Lucia Black had announced she'd reprogrammed Proximity.

Sadly, that last part was true.

Vanessa had been turned into a walking, talking killing machine.

But what Kowalski hadn't mentioned was that he'd grabbed Lucia before she could run away.

Vanessa had bolted, yes. She had driven away and inadvertently killed seventeen people. Many of them American tourists. It was not pretty. Kowalski wasn't going to lie to himself.

He couldn't imagine the horrors taking place in her mind.

She was still shell-shocked over the adulterers she'd slaughtered.

But instead of searching for Vanessa, Kowalski had attacked the problem at the root. He took Lucia Black and applied his signature move: arm around her neck until she was unconscious.

She woke up an hour later, strapped to a dentist's chair.

A chair belonging to Kowalski's Mexican dentist friend, who was just gearing up for a long tequila-fueled night.

Kowalski told him not to worry. He'd take it from here.

First he kissed Lucia. Deeply.

He wanted to get those Proximity-eating nanites into his own system.

Then he settled in for some real work.

Lucia resisted for a while. But by the time Kowalski was finished with the drill, she was not only ready to deactivate the nanites in Vanessa's bloodstream and tell Kowalski how to reprogram Proximity from her handheld, but perfectly willing to reveal the formula for Coke as well as the eleven herbs and spices in Kentucky Fried Chicken.

She spilled *everything*.

Even how her brother used to finger her in secret when they were kids.

Kowalski thanked her, then smothered her with a wet towel. Figured that was doing her a favor. Later, he'd cut off her head, tell them it was her. Vanessa. Their mysterious blonde, now a redhead.

The real Vanessa *did* call the hotel near dawn, crying and ready to end it all, even though she didn't have a gun. Kowalski was glad she didn't remember the grenade launcher in the trunk of the Taurus.

After Kowalski assured her she was safe, and unable to kill anyone else, they met up again. They talked. They made plans. They used Lucia's handheld device to do a little reprogramming of their own. They figured out a way to end this, for good.

For good, at least for now.

Make them suffer a little in return.

They visited Kowalski's dentist again, who by this point had mostly sobered up.

"You want me to do *what?*" he asked.

He was intoxicated enough to do it anyway.

Kowalski finally worked the tooth free, then spat it out.

The interrogator smirked. "Come on now. I haven't even touched your face."

Kowalski smiled. Revealing the small trigger mechanism he'd had implanted in his gum. A tiny LED in the middle of the trigger pulsed red.

Blink blink
Blink blink

The trigger would tell Proximity to reprogram the nanites in his bloodstream.

But not to kill at ten feet. Kowalski and Vanessa had discussed that, and decided it wasn't enough. So they used Lucia's handheld device to reprogram the distance to, oh, say, quarter of a mile. In all directions.

I'm going to let myself be captured, Kowalski had told her. *And then, when I'm sure all of the rats are in one place, and I know what they know . . . they're dead. Every last one of them.*

The interrogator stared at Kowalski's mouth, dumbstruck, but at the last moment he seemed to get it. Not everything, of course. Just the idea that yes, Kowalski had indeed outthought them every step of the way. And yes, they were all about to die. Every last one of them.

Kowalski depressed the trigger with his tongue.

"Good-bye," he said.

The guards dropped first, followed by the interrogator. They were all screaming. Kowalski counted to nine in his mind, and then . . .

Yeah.

Twin sprays of red.

Then a third.

Kowalski swung his body back and forth until he had enough momentum to hurl himself up and slip the chain from the hook.

He landed on his feet.

First thing he did was walk to a corner and take the most satisfying leak of his life.

Then he checked out the rest of the facility.

There was one guy still alive. He represented the freaky 1 percent who remained uninfected by Proximity.

That was okay.

Kowalski gutted him with the interrogator's Pampered Chef knife. It really was pretty fucking sharp.

Everyone else was dead.

Fortunately, his brother-in-law wasn't among them. They must have shipped him off to a different secret prison facility. Or maybe he was already in the field. Wouldn't surprise him. CI-6 loved to rush things.

Kowalski kept a loose count as he walked through the facility. He was into the low fifties before he stopped. A lot of dead bodies. More than he thought he'd ever see.

And all of them redheads now.

The rest was routine. A burning of the last twelve hours of surveillance video. A gathering of research files. Some borrowed clothes. Weapons. Key cards. Water. Food. The interrogator's little knife.

Kowalski left the facility. He pushed the trigger in his gum, turning off the killer nanite effect. There was no need anymore.

It was still early morning in Pennsylvania mountain country. The air was bitter cold. Not even the sun was enough to warm you up. A rainstorm had passed through recently, so Kowalski's borrowed boots sunk into the chilly mud a bit with every step. It felt nice to stretch his muscles like this again. Too much time in planes, in cars, on rooftops. He liked that he had a walk ahead of him.

Kowalski walked and enjoyed the cool air and thought about Vanessa. Thought about how they parted ways.

For good.

I'm not like you, she'd told him. *I'm no monster. You can do this. I can't. I mean, I did for a while. But not anymore.*

I want my life back.

That's when Kowalski kissed her, deeply, giving her what he'd stolen from Lucia. A kiss from the monster Prince Charming.

You've got your life back, he said.

Don't try to find me, she said.

I won't, he said.

After a few hours of wandering he sat down by the side of a road and opened an oatmeal bar he'd taken from the snackroom.

Yes, even secret government prisons had snackrooms.

Kowalski enjoyed a brown sugar and cinnamon oatmeal bar. It was the first real food he'd eaten in a long while. But a chunk of oat got caught between a tooth and the trigger mechanism. He tried pushing it out with his tongue; nothing doing.

He thought about what he could do with the quarter-mile shield of death that surrounded him. He could find every secret CI-6 prison in the country. He could visit all of the front companies they had, scattered around the globe. He could stop into certain offices in the U.S. Capitol Building. He could kill them all with a flip of the switch. Death with a smile. They could throw everything in the world at him. The National Guard, even. Unless they had a sniper that could work with a quarter-mile accuracy, he was unstoppable.

And maybe he should. Because CI-6 wasn't going to stop. This facility was just an interrogation room; there were others in the organization who knew. They wouldn't give up a weapon like Proximity.

Maybe he should keep going until they were all dead.

Kowalski took another bite of the oatmeal bar. Another piece got stuck between his teeth. He pulled out the interrogator's Pampered Chef knife then used it to dislodge the chunks.

He could still feel it, though. So he kept using the knife, digging at his jaw. There were no mirrors out here in the country. He had to go by feel. The blade against his tender gums. Scraping. Don't mind me, he thought. *I'm just a man sitting in the middle of the Pennsylvania countryside doing a little dental surgery.* The brown sugar was gone; his mouth tasted of copper pennies now. But there was still oatmeal in there. So Kowalski kept working. Strangely, as the pain enlarged, his vision grew clearer. Maybe it was the film of tears in his eyes. There was no sound except the occasional chirping of a bird, and his own heavy breathing. It focused him on the task at hand.

Eventually he realized that his chin and stolen shirt were covered in blood.

But the trigger came out, and Kowalski stared at it for a few moments, feeling the cool morning air on his fevered face, before using a rock to smash it to pieces.

Yeah, I'm a monster, he thought.

But not that big of a monster.

He wondered where Vanessa was now.